THE REDEMPTION OF A ROGUE

THE DUKE'S BY-BLOWS BOOK 4

JESS MICHAELS

To Oscar Isaac and Marissa Tomei, for bringing the energy I needed for this book. For Mackenzie, for being the best editor ever.

And for Michael, for being my quarantine buddy and the greatest partner.

CHAPTER 1

1816

I t had all been a mistake from the beginning, but there was no
changing it now. At least that was what Imogen Huxley kept
telling herself as she stumbled down the long, dingy hallway of the
Cat's Companion. The brothel was in the very worst corner of
London and yet she'd seen many a very important man haunting its
not-so-hallowed halls. As many as in the finer establishments of
its ilk.

And Imogen had been to them all recently. Or at least it felt like
she had. Since her husband's death, since she realized that Warren had
left her with absolutely nothing to her name...

Well, what choice did she have but to seek a protector? By any
means and at any location necessary.

"You gonna stand in the way, luv, or go earn your keep?"

The sharp female voice startled her from her thoughts, and
Imogen pivoted. It was Maggie Monroe who stood there, hands on
her hips, dark eyes barely visible through her smoldering glare.
Imogen had met the woman once before, the first time she'd come

here. The time she'd sworn she'd never come back. Maggie was abjectly terrifying then and it was no different now.

"I-I was just about to go in," she said, pushing her back against the wall so Maggie could pass her in the narrow hall.

She did so, smacking Imogen with her shoulder as she moved. "You'd best forget you're a lady right quick," the woman snapped as she continued up the hall. "If these bastards wanted a lady, they would have stayed home."

Imogen bent her head. She'd been a lady her whole life, daughter of a second son, wife of a third son. It was a sheltered life, she knew that now more than ever. Until it wasn't. Until she'd been thrown out into the cold.

She took a long step toward the door she was meant to pass through. In that room was a man who wished to bed her. If she pleased him, he might take her as his mistress, he might pay for her to have a home and a little allowance. Lying on her back could save her.

"God, I hope he's at least a good lover," she murmured, trying not to think about the inexperienced fumblings of the man she'd been with last time she was here. She shuddered as she lifted her hand to open the door.

But before she could, there was a shout from behind it. A very drunken shout, indeed. "Where is that bitch?" the voice grunted, and there was a great crash. "I'll not be made to wait by some poxy whore."

She stepped back away from the door, her heart racing as she flattened to the wall as if she could disappear into it. In that moment, she wished it were true. That she could sprout wings and fly away.

There was a second bang from within the chamber, and she shook her head. "I will not do this," she whispered, clenching her hands into fists at her sides as she pivoted toward the front exit of the establishment. But up that hallway were a group of loud and very drunk men. They were watching her. Go that way and it was out of the frying pan and potentially into a very bad fire.

So she turned the other direction, toward where Maggie had gone a few moments earlier. There were a dozen exits to this place, she

THE REDEMPTION OF A ROGUE

knew that from the chatter of the other girls hired to work here on a more permanent basis. Plenty of modes of escape for client and light-skirt alike.

Now Imogen just had to find one of them and get out. Find some other means of getting protection. At least her best friend Aurora would be pleased. She hadn't wanted Imogen to come back after the last time.

Imogen pushed those thoughts aside and scurried up the hall before her intended client burst through the door and simply took what he wanted. She meandered through the halls, turning left, then right, lost in a maze of dark hallways and closed doors. Moans and cries came from behind them, some pleasurable and others that were...not.

Her stomach turned and she blinked to clear the tears in her eyes. She needed to be focused now.

There was a door ahead, one with a big rusty smokehouse lock that dangled open from the hinge. Those locks were often used to protect the outside doors, and Imogen gasped in relief as she pushed the door open. But what she found wasn't escape but a staircase that led to a little courtyard one floor below, closed in by the building's walls. It wasn't a pretty garden, though, but a dirty bricked-in place, smelling of piss and garbage and despair.

She moved forward to look down into the square, hoping to find some direct exit onto the street. There would be hacks there, waiting for the customers to leave. She had just enough blunt stuffed in her slipper to get home.

And then she'd have to work out what to do next.

Her fingers closed around the rusty metal railing, and she looked down into the abyss. To her surprise, there were people down there. Maggie, from the looks of it, and two men with her. They were talk-ing, not overly loudly, but the closed-in walls made the sound bounce back up toward Imogen.

"Wrap her up in the damned carpet!" Maggie was snarling, pointing toward something at her feet.

When she moved, Imogen gasped. A woman laid there on the dirty brick, unmoving, blonde hair fanned out around her, her body twisted at an unnatural angle.

Dead. Imogen realized in a horrible flush of a moment that she was dead.

"Shut your whore mouth, Maggie," one of the men said. "I'm a bloody earl—I don't work for you."

"You're an earl who just killed one of my best girls," Maggie snapped back. "I swear, Roddenbury, you can't keep doing this just because they don't please you. Now help Charlie. We can have her in the river before sunrise and that will end that."

Imogen's hand came up to cover her mouth as the full realization of what had happened dawned on her confused and horrified mind. Roddenbury...an earl...a friend of her late husband...had murdered one of Maggie's girls, and they were working to not only cover up that fact, but dispose of her body before anyone else knew.

Imogen's breath was coming sharper and harder as the truth of this matter washed over her. She needed to get out of here. Before they saw her. Before she joined that poor girl in the carpet. Bile lifted in her throat, and she swallowed hard to keep it down as she pivoted to go back into the bawdy house and find another escape route.

As she did so, she staggered and her fist hit the door with a clang that echoed through the courtyard as surely as the voices below had. She froze in horror and then looked back over her shoulder.

All three faces were turned up toward her from below. Maggie, Roddenbury and a huge hulk of a man she now recognized as the door guard.

"You there!" Maggie called up. "Stop!"

But Imogen didn't stop. She tore the heavy door open and ran.

Oscar Fitzhugh sat in his carriage in the alleyway behind the Cat's Companion, staring up at the imposing building. His hands clenched against his thighs as he struggled to rein in the emotions that threatened to overwhelm him. It was the same any time he came to this place. Anger. Grief. Bitterness.

But mostly guilt. He came here and guilt washed over him.

"You should have done bloody better," he muttered.

But doing better was why he was here, wasn't it? Why he came here once a month, every month. Why he circulated into the crowd and tried to determine facts that would somehow absolve him. Or at least facts that would avenge *her*.

With a sigh, he opened the carriage door and got out. His driver glanced down at him with concern, but Bentley had long ago stopped expressing his uneasiness with this endeavor out loud.

"Wait here," Oscar said.

"Yes, Mr. Fitzhugh," Bentley said softly, his gaze darting away with something suspiciously like pity.

Oscar's stomach clenched at the sight. No one fucking pitied him. Even when he was pitiable. He stepped forward, ready to make his way through the unlocked back door to the place. He'd been banned from the official entrance months ago. But this entrance allowed him to sneak in and blend in. Another faceless man in a sea of faceless men there to take their pleasure. Take advantage.

But before he could open the door, it flew out toward him. He stepped back, just barely missing being cracked in the face, and opened his arms to regain his balance. Which allowed the woman who had thrown the door wide and now raced from the darkened, smoky hall to collide directly into his chest.

Oscar closed his arms around her, a natural reaction to keep them both from depositing themselves on the dirty ground. The moment he did so, she began to thrash, tugging to escape him.

He was about to release her when she cried out, "No, please! Don't! They'll kill me! Don't!"

He froze at those words. How many months had he come here, searching for some proof that nefarious things were happening within these walls? Dark and desperate things, like murder.

And now this slender reed of a woman all but shouted that proof in his face. The extremely beautiful and terrified face now turned up toward his. His heart stuttered at the abject terror reflected in a remarkable pair of amber eyes. Almost like a cat's, they were so lovely.

"What is going on, miss?" he snapped out, perhaps more harshly than he intended thanks to the shock of her crashing into his chest, her wild words and her lovely eyes.

"Please!" she wailed, her voice catching now. "They're coming! They're right behind me. You must release me or I'll never get away."

He heard voices from behind the door, shouts within the walls of the building, and it kicked him from his shock. He grasped her arm and yanked her toward the carriage. She scrambled to escape as he hauled her up and slammed the door shut.

"Stop kicking me," he growled, tugging her even closer and speaking low against her ear. "I am trying to help you."

As he said the words, the door to the club opened and two large men burst out. Oscar leaned closer to the window, but didn't recognize either of them. Two of Maggie's ruffians, it seemed.

The woman froze in his arms, trembling as one of them shouted up to his driver, "Did you see a whore come out here?"

"Went that way," Bentley said from above, and the men took off toward the docks.

Oscar smiled. He only hired the best. And Bentley would get a nice bonus in his wages this week for that lie.

"Please let me go," the woman said, softly this time, and Oscar realized she was still in his arms, pressed with her back to his chest, her breath coming short and heavy.

He loosened his grip on her arms as he said, "Don't run."

She ignored him and lunged for the door. He sighed heavily and caught her wrist to pull her away from the door as gently as he could.

"*Please* don't run," he repeated. "I've no intention of hurting you. As I said, I want to help."

Her struggle ceased, though from the way her body slumped, he felt it was more out of exhaustion than any kind of trust. She slid to the carriage seat across from his and he released her. She stared at him, wary, like a bird being stalked by a cat, and rubbed her wrist. He didn't think he'd hurt her—he'd been trying very hard not to—but he wondered if she was trying to soothe herself with that touch.

"Why were those men chasing you?" he asked.

She didn't respond, but folded her arms and looked longingly toward the door he was blocking.

He arched a brow. "Did you steal something?"

"No!" she cried out, indignant as she glared at him. "No, sir!"

"Then why were you running?" he repeated, more slowly, more firmly.

She shook her head. "Won't you please let me out?" she asked. "The men are gone, at least for the moment. It will give me time to get a hack and go home."

"That isn't happening," he said. "They could return at any moment. You're clearly in danger, miss, and I am your best hope. Tell me what is going on."

She bent her head, and her breath came sharp and hard in the quiet of the carriage. Oscar could see she was fighting tears. Winning that fight, though he wasn't certain that would last long. Every graceful line of her body spoke of her deep fear. It wasn't an act, it wasn't a trick. In his line of work, he had long ago learned to spot those.

No, this was real.

"Please," he said softly.

Her gaze lifted to his, and for a moment their eyes locked. He could see her reading him, analyzing if he could relieve her distress, or if he was just another part of it. Then her eyes darted back to her lap and she whispered, "They...they killed a woman. I-I saw her body."

His gut clenched, and for a flash of a moment he thought he might cast up his accounts all over the carriage floor. But he drew a deep breath, calmed himself as he'd learned to do over the years, and opened the carriage door.

"Bentley, home," he ordered before he closed them in again.

She jerked to the edge of her seat. "No! Sir, please. You cannot take me. You must let me out. Please!"

He leaned forward, hating that his presence was as much a fear to this distressed woman as anything else she'd been through that night. But he also knew he couldn't let her go. Not under these conditions.

"Miss, you are in real trouble, and if I let you out of this carriage, you'll be in even worse. Let me take you somewhere safe and we can work this out."

"Work it out on my back, you mean?" she snapped, and through the fear he saw a spitfire nature that he would have liked but for the horrific circumstances. "You were here for a purpose, weren't you? And now you act like some hero come to save me? You are just as dangerous as those men after me for all I know. You're nothing but a stranger who forced me into a carriage."

He blinked. She had a point at that.

He leaned forward and extended a hand. "Mr. Oscar Fitzhugh at your service, miss. I'm the owner of Fitzhugh's Club. And while I agree that you have no reason yet to trust me, I do vow to you now that I won't hurt you. I will try to save your life if you let me."

CHAPTER 2

I mogen pushed herself into the farthest corner of the carriage and stared at the man across from her. His hand was still extended as if to greet her, but she didn't take it. She already knew the strength of that hand, for it had wrapped around her upper arm, her wrist, and kept her from escape. Touching him again felt...dangerous.

And yet she felt a bit less fear than she had when she'd first crashed into him and he had dragged her into his carriage. Then she'd been in a pure panic, certain she had thrown herself into perhaps a worse situation than she had left.

It was clear that wasn't true, though. And there was something about this man's voice that was almost...mesmerizing. Something rough and hard, but not unkind.

She looked across at him in the dimness of the carriage. He was cloaked in shadow, but she could still make out the fundamentals of his features. He had dark hair that was a touch too long, streaked with fine lines of gray, mussed like fingers had run through it recently. His own or someone else's. He had an angular face with a salt-and-pepper beard. Not in fashion, perhaps, but it suited him. It made him all the more handsome and somewhat mysterious, as well.

His low brow furrowed as he withdrew his hand at last and his dark eyes speared her in place. This was not a man to be trifled with, that was immediately clear. He was confident and intense. He likely stole the air and the attention of any space he entered. Including the tight carriage they currently both inhabited.

More to the point, he had to know the command he wielded. He very likely used it to his advantage.

"I-I know your name," she stammered as she fought to look and sound more composed than she felt. "Fitzhugh's Club. My...husband was a member."

His gaze flitted over her face, his lips thinned slightly. "You are married."

"I *was*," she whispered. "To Warren Huxley. Not that I expect you to recall him. Your club is quite popular. It rivals White's, or so I've heard."

There was a flicker over his face. Almost a smile, but not quite. The comparison pleased him, it seemed. Then he was serious again. "Huxley," he said. "Third son of the Earl of Briarstone. He died last year."

Her eyes widened. "You recall that in an instant? Without reference?"

He shrugged one shoulder. "I make it my business to know all my members. And so *you* are Mrs. Huxley."

"Imogen," she said, for it seemed almost obscene to go by her married name when this man had found her in the alleyway of a brothel. "My name is Imogen."

He nodded once and then looked toward the window again. "We are arriving at my home now. You'll come in and we can discuss this further."

She should have refused him. Should have asked him, once again, to simply allow her to go home. She wanted so desperately to pretend that what she'd experienced and seen tonight wasn't real.

But how could she?

Even if he let her go, the image of that body down on the filthy ground was seared in her mind. And now that the shock of what had happened was wearing off, the heartbreak of it became sharper. It sank past her defenses, the ones meant to protect her and keep her running despite the devastation, and her whole body shuddered at the memory.

"Mrs. Huxley," he said softly as the carriage stopped at last. He reached out as if he would touch her, and she almost wanted him to, just to know that he was real. That she was real. Just to have the comfort of physical contact, even from this stranger who felt dangerous but not sinister.

"I-I—" she stammered, uncertain what she wished to say next.

"Come inside," he repeated, firm but gentle as he yanked his hand back and offered no comfort.

She nodded as the carriage door opened. He stepped out first, saying something to his driver that she couldn't hear, and then he turned back. That same powerful hand extended out to help her and she caught it, clinging to him as she staggered down the little set of steps. He cupped her elbow, holding her steady as she swayed.

He was very tall. She hadn't fully marked it in that terrifying moment when she careened into him. But he was at least a head taller than she was. She looked up and up, into those dark eyes. They bore down into her, almost like he could see into her very soul. A terrifying thought, and she took a long step away and turned her face so she was no longer pinned by his regard.

"Lead the way, Mr. Fitzhugh."

If only her voice didn't shake. If only her entire being didn't shake.

He did as she requested in silence, leading her up a short staircase into the townhouse. The night had a damp chill to it that she hadn't fully noticed until she moved into the warm, bright foyer. A butler was there, speaking to Fitzhugh already. She blushed as he glanced over his master's shoulder at her. His gaze flitted over her from head to toe, then he looked away and nodded.

"It shall be done, sir," he said, and stepped away, leaving them alone again.

Fitzhugh motioned her to follow, and she staggered after him down a long hallway. They entered a parlor with a black leather settee and matching chairs. A bright fire burned in the tall fireplace, and she found herself moving toward it and lowering her suddenly frigid fingers before the flames.

"Brandy?" he asked.

She jolted and looked back at him. He had already poured her a glass and was holding it out. So she took it, for what else could she do?

"Give me a moment," he said softly. "Make yourself comfortable."

He left her then, and she sank into the settee before the fire. She noticed now it had gold plated fish as feet and absently wondered how much those must have cost him. *Comfortable*, he had said. Dear God, how could she be that? Now or perhaps ever again?

Her brain dragged her backward, to earlier in the night. To looking down over the rusty metal railing to see that woman's broken body. To the cruelty of her killers' words as they spoke about her. To the horrible moments when Imogen had been forced to run for her own life. With every heavy step, she had believed, utterly and completely, that she would die in a bawdy house and be thrown into the river like trash.

Her hand was wet. She glanced down and saw that she was shaking now. Brandy had sloshed onto her thumb and the top of her hand. She set it down on the table beside the settee and sank her head into her hands.

The collapse happened swiftly as all that had transpired that night washed over her, on a hideous repeat. She shook as hot tears streamed down her face, bitter bile rising to her throat. It was only the sound of another throat clearing that jolted her from the hysteria. She jerked her face toward the door and found Fitzhugh standing there.

He looked uncomfortable, and she rose to her feet as she wiped the tears from her cheeks. "My apologies. It's been a very long night," she whispered.

He shook his head. "It's understandable. I must ask you a question, though."

She swallowed, trying to gather herself. "What is it?"

"Do they know your name?"

Her brow wrinkled as she stared at him. "My—my name?"

"Yes." His frown deepened. "Did you give anyone at the Cat's Companion your real name?"

"I'd given it at a few other brothels in the past," she said. "So, yes, they…they know my name."

He bent his head, and she thought he swore beneath his breath. Then he sighed. "Then you cannot go home. You'll stay here."

Her mouth dropped open as she stared at him "What? No, please!"

He moved into the room toward her, and she should have backed away, but how could she when he held her in place with one pointed look? "Mrs. Huxley, you have been shocked by your experience and are in no shape to have a discussion with me about what you saw tonight. I can see that now. But I cannot let you go home because if you saw what you think you saw—and judging how those men chased you, I have to believe you did—then they will hunt you. If they know your name, it will be too easy for them to do that at your own home. I might as well have abandoned you in the alley if I'm just going to push you back into their arms."

She jerked a hand up to her mouth. "My—my servants—"

His expression softened a bit. "It credits you that you are concerned about them. I would wager you need not be. These people will likely not wish to raise a fuss. They'll stalk your home, but won't move unless they're certain they can get to you. But I will have someone sent to watch your house tonight. You, however, will not return there."

"You can't make me stay."

Something dark flared in his eyes, and he edged a fraction closer. "I don't think you want to test that. I'm telling you that you are in danger. And you endanger anyone else you come in contact with until we can resolve this. If you care about that, as it seems you do, you will *listen* to me and let me do what I can to protect you. We can discuss the rest of this in the morning and I'll get more details."

Her shoulders rolled forward. It would be considered wrong by most in her circles to stay the night in the house of a stranger. Especially a male stranger who possessed such…command. But then again, they would also certainly judge her for her decision to go to the brothel at all. They would judge her for all she'd lost and all she'd done to keep some sliver of her life.

What was one night? Especially if it kept her alive and her servants unharmed. "Very well," she whispered. "I won't argue."

"Excellent," he said, and motioned her toward him with a crook of his finger. "Let me show you to your room."

~

O scar wasn't exactly prepared for guests. He didn't invite people to his home. Only Louisa had ever stayed here, and that felt like a lifetime ago. Still, as he opened the door to the guest chamber, he had to give his servants credit. They had made the room presentable in hardly any time at all. It was a comfortable room with a bright fire burning in the hearth. Not fancy, perhaps, but serviceable.

He pivoted toward Mrs. Huxley, and his breath caught. To be fair, it had caught each and every time he'd looked at her since they came into the bright light of his home. He assumed it was the same for most men who cast their eyes upon her. She was, after all, exquisitely lovely. Even more striking than he had judged her to be in the alleyway or in the darkened carriage.

Dark hair, those stunning amber eyes, an expressive face that currently reflected all her fear and anxiety. Yes, she was…beautiful.

He cleared his throat and pushed those inappropriate thoughts away. "Will you need help with your gown?" he asked as he looked over the yellow dress she was wearing. It buttoned in the front, the neckline was far too low, and looked as though it had been altered to make it thus, but the fabric flowed over her soft curves perfectly.

"No," she whispered, and pink filled her cheeks as she looked away. "I-I picked this one so I could manage it myself in the…in the…"

She couldn't finish, and he nodded so she wouldn't have to because the subject of the brothel obviously made her uncomfortable. It made him wonder how a widow of a third son of an earl had come to such a dire place.

But that was a question for tomorrow.

"I understand," he said. "Please, try to rest. It will help, though I know it doesn't feel that way right now. If you need anything, please don't hesitate to ring. My staff is at your service, as am I."

He executed a little bow and turned away. He had almost reached the door to the chamber when she said, "Mr. Fitzhugh?"

He turned toward her shaking voice and found she had taken a long step toward him. Her cheeks were beyond pink now. Red flushed down her neck, over the curve of her breasts. He forced himself not to think about how much lower it might go.

"Yes?" he asked and heard the roughness to his tone. The strain.

"Thank you," she murmured.

He inclined his head and then left her. As he closed the door, he recognized his heart was beating fast. That wasn't something that happened all that often. After a lifetime, he had trained himself not to react to almost anything.

But then again, this woman…Imogen… *Mrs. Huxley* was attached in some way to the place where Louisa had also died. That was probably what drew him to her. She was a chance to ride to the rescue in a situation where before he hadn't been able. It made sense, really.

And it also meant he had to carefully and calmly work this problem out. Emotion would only hurt everyone involved. Best to tamp it down. For Mrs. Huxley's sake as much as his own.

CHAPTER 3

Imogen looked at herself in the mirror and let her breath out in a shaky sigh. She'd told herself over and again that it would be better in the morning, knowing it wasn't true. Dawn had come and she still felt like hell. Looked like it, too, but there was little else she could do to fix herself. She'd finger combed and pinned her hopeless hair, shaken out the dirty dress she'd never look at the same way again. The dark circles beneath her eyes from a lack of sleep and crying weren't something she could fix, nor was the pallor of her skin.

"As if the man cares about your appearance," she muttered as she smoothed the wrinkled gown once more and turned away from the mirror to cross to the door.

She drew a shaky breath and walked into the hall. It was a quiet house. Only the distant click of a clock filled the air rather than a bustling set of servants.

Of course Fitzhugh lived alone, so far as she could tell. She certainly could see no sign of a wife or children because there were no portraits hung to advertise them. No sounds of childish giggling or soft feminine whispers from behind chamber doors. She trailed down the stairs, marking the neatness of the house. There obviously *were* servants in his employ, even if they seemed invisible at present.

The butler was at the bottom of the stairs, and as she reached the bottom, he turned from whatever it was he was doing and inclined his head toward her. "Good morning, Mrs. Huxley. Was your chamber comfortable?"

Heat filled her cheeks at the fact that this man knew her name. What he must think of her after last night? How far she had fallen in such a short time.

"It was very comfortable, thank you," she said. "But I'm at a disadvantage. What is your name?"

"Donovan, madam," he said with another of those formal inclines of his head. "And I am at your service as long as you are a guest in this house."

She forced a smile. It was a kindness for him to act as though she were merely a houseguest. And one that would surely be gone before noon. "Thank you."

"Mr. Fitzhugh is waiting for you in the breakfast room. It is the third door on the left up the hall," he said, motioning to a long corridor behind the staircase.

She thanked him again and went on her way. Unlike upstairs, where the doors to the chambers were closed, they were open down here. She couldn't help but peek into each one as she passed. Curtains were thrown open in them all, flooding the chambers with light for the servants who were quietly cleaning and organizing.

It was a pretty place, indeed. Fine but understated. It certainly didn't reveal much about the man who owned it, though. Oscar Fitzhugh. She shivered as she thought of him, handsome and impressive and more than a little intimidating. She had no idea what to think of him. Perhaps that was his intention.

She reached the breakfast room and paused in the entryway. He was seated at the head of a small rectangular table, head bent into paperwork and an untouched plate of food at his right hand. He didn't appear to have noticed her yet, so she took that moment to look at him.

He really was a very handsome man. Even more so today than she had recalled. There was a little bit of a wave to his hair, even though it no longer looked like fingers had wended their way through it. His brow was furrowed in concentration and he had a hard, stern look on his face. She had no idea his age. It was hard to place, despite his salt-and-pepper beard and hair. Older than her own thirty-two years, she thought, but not fatherly. Oh no. Definitely not that.

"How did you sleep?"

His question jolted her out of her wicked thoughts, and she jumped in surprise as he glanced up at her, speared her with that dark and unassailable gaze. She clenched a hand against her chest and came into the room. "I…well, thank you."

He arched a brow as he rose to his feet. "*Well.* I don't think so. You had nightmares."

She worried her lip. "I hope I didn't disturb *your* sleep, Mr. Fitzhugh."

There was a flicker of something that came into his eyes. Eyes that flitted over her briefly. "Not at all. Even if you had, what right would I have to complain? I all but forced you here, didn't I?"

She smiled at the statement, a little teasing, she thought, though he still looked very serious, indeed. "You seemed to have the right motives at heart."

"Perish that thought," he muttered.

She shifted. "Are my servants well?"

"Yes," he said softly. "I had a man on your house within half an hour of your arriving here. He reports all is well there." He motioned to the chair beside his. "Sit, won't you? I wasn't sure if you had favorites, so I had my cook make up a small spread. May I get you a plate?"

Until that moment when Imogen looked at the sideboard, laden with delicious-looking food, she hadn't been hungry. But now the smells and sights assaulted her senses, and she nearly went weak in the knees. "Please."

She sat, watching him pick through the selection and load up a plate. He set it in front of her and retook his place. She had every intention of trying to speak with him politely, but her hands had begun to shake with hunger. She dove into the food as she tried to remember the last time she'd done so. The previous morning, perhaps? Or was it even before that? Money was so tight, she tried to keep her expenses, even food, to a minimum. And when she'd known she was returning to the Cat's Companion, she hadn't been able to muster an appetite.

Now, though, she shoveled food into her mouth. It was delicious, every bite. She had no idea how long she did so, but when she glanced up, she found Fitzhugh staring at her, those dark eyes glittering. She set her fork down and dabbed her mouth with a napkin as she shook her head. "I-I'm sorry. I'm being very rude."

"I don't think so," he said softly. "I asked you to eat and you are. Please continue. Can you talk while you do so?"

She nodded. "Yes. If I stop heaping everything in my mouth at once, I can talk."

There was a twitch at the corner of his lip, almost like he was suppressing a smile. "Can you tell me in as much detail as you can what exactly happened last night?"

"I feel this is unfair to you, Mr. Fitzhugh," she said. "I've involved you in my troubles enough and—"

"Tell me," he interrupted, his firm voice yanking her excuses out from under her.

She sighed and pushed the plate away, appetite gone once more. This was her private pain, her private story, and this stranger wanted to strip it from her. And yet he had earned it, hadn't he? Certainly he had saved her life when he pulled her into his carriage. Perhaps again when he allowed her to escape to his home rather than returning to her own.

And maybe it would just help to say it out loud. She hadn't really done that before. Oh, yes, she'd spoken to Aurora about it, but never in full. Her friend had her own problems.

"I-I suppose I should go back to the beginning," she said, hating that her voice trembled when he was so stoic and calm. "You must want to know why I went there, the widow of a third son of an important family."

He held her stare. "If you wish to tell me. But understand I don't judge you, whether you went to that place for gold or pleasure. Your body is your own."

She blinked. That would certainly not be the response of anyone else in her acquaintance. She cleared her throat nervously. "My husband left me with nothing at his death. His family has allowed me to keep the smallest of homes and two servants during my mourning, but nothing else, not even a carriage. Now that my mourning is coming to an end, they are already making noises about my needing to leave."

His cheek twitched. "They would put you in the street?"

"They would." She set her napkin on the table with a sigh. "I realized I would need to make alternate arrangements for my future. I thought of marrying again, but my own family is dead. There is no money. And my husband's family has hindered my ability to come back into Society."

"Why?" he asked, his brow furrowing again.

"They claim that seeing me makes it difficult," she said, trying to keep the bitterness from her voice. "And perhaps that is true. Perhaps I remind them of Warren and that chokes them in their grief. But they would destroy me for their comfort."

"Their kind always would," he said, a touch of bitterness in his voice.

"Personal experience?" she asked.

He shifted and was silent for a beat. "I know a great many of them in my profession."

She thought it might be more than that, but didn't press the subject. This man's history was none of her affair.

"I suppose you do." She worried her hands in her lap. "The next option for a woman like me was to become a man's mistress."

"That must have been a shocking decision to come to for a woman raised as I assume you were." There was no judgment to his tone, and that helped her feel less embarrassed by the confession.

"At first, yes," she admitted. "But I was not...*opposed* to what happens between a man and a woman in a bed."

His fingers clenched on the tabletop but he didn't react in any other way so she continued, "And I saw that some women were treated very well. I tried to make discreet inquiries."

"And used your real name," he said.

She nodded. "It made sense to do so since if I succeeded in obtaining a protector, I would be publicly seen as a kept woman. But it only caused me trouble. My husband's family was incensed. I was told in no uncertain terms that if I sought a protector, I would be put out of my home immediately and into the street."

"And you have no one to take you in?" he asked.

"My dearest friend is Aurora Lovell, another widow, also left destitute by her situation. She hardly has enough for herself."

"Viscount Lovell," he said, apparently pulling from a never-ending catalog in his mind. "Died of an apoplexy, wasn't it? In a bawdy house just barely better than the Cat's Companion."

"You are a wonder," Imogen breathed. "How do you keep your information organized in that mind of yours?"

He actually looked a little uncomfortable at the compliment. "It matters little. There must be other friends."

"There were. There are. But most have gone by the wayside. Some cannot afford to associate themselves with my fall. Some are not allowed. Some are fair-weather friends more interested in position than in helping." She wished she sounded less invested in that. Less hurt. "So I am on my own."

"How did you come to the Cat's Companion, then?" he pressed.

"The better places, someplace like Donville Masquerade or Vivien Manning's... I couldn't turn to them to find a...a..."

"Lover," he said, his tone suddenly rougher. "You'll have to find a way to say it, Mrs. Huxley."

"Please, won't you call me Imogen," she gasped. "It seems so wrong to talk about this while you use my husband's name."

Fitzhugh held her gaze a moment and then nodded. "Imogen."

She had heard her name said a thousand times, by dozens of different people. It had never sounded the way it did rolling off this man's tongue. She had never reacted the way she did now, her entire body pulsing with tension. Her sex clenching against nothingness.

Perhaps she should have learned to live with Mrs. Huxley because this was...so very wrong. Was she so far fallen that the first handsome man who showed her any kindness made her a wanton?

"I-I—" She struggled to find purchase against the tide of these unwanted feelings.

His pupils dilated slightly and he said, "You were explaining why you couldn't go to a more respectable place."

"Yes." She fought to regain her breath. "Yes. Places like those were crawling with people who might report back to my husband's family. I realized right away they weren't safe. So I started to go...lower. I was given a card for the Cat's Companion and so I went there."

"Not a very easy place to find a permanent protector," he said. "It's a brothel in the truest sense. Men there want a night, nothing more."

She nodded. "I know. Last night wasn't my first night there, you see. Still, I hoped that if I pleased one enough..." She trailed off. "I don't know if you can understand the kind of desperation I was facing. Perhaps it clouded my judgment. Perhaps it still does."

"I understand a little," he said. "How many nights did you go there, seeking out a savior?"

"Twice," she said with a shudder. "As I said, the first was a few days ago, but it...it didn't go well. He could not complete the...matter and got angry with me for it. He might have harmed me, I think, if he hadn't passed out drunk before he could. My friend Aurora was horrified. She begged me not to return. I should have listened."

He scrubbed a hand over his face. "So you've escaped with your life twice."

"Three times. The reason I ran away and saw the body was because the man I was meant to...to service sounded like an even more brutal one."

He pushed to his feet, his chair screeching across the floor as he did so. He paced to the window and stood there, broad back to her. She held her breath, for she didn't know if he had decided she was too much trouble or not.

"Mr. Fitzhugh," she said softly.

He faced her slowly. "How did you see the body?"

She shut her eyes, the images bombarding her again. She hadn't realized she was speaking, but she was. And she told him about running, about staggering upon the scene. About seeing that poor woman's body.

"What did she look like?" he whispered.

"Blonde hair," she murmured. "I couldn't see much else from that height and in the shadows."

That seemed to appease him and he moved back toward the table. "You said it was the Earl of Roddenbury down below. Are you certain?"

She nodded. "Yes. Maggie said his name. And he was a friend of my husband. I've seen him many times over the years, though we've rarely interacted. It was him, I'm certain of it."

His lips had pursed, thinning their full line. She drew a long breath.

"You saved me, Mr. Fitzhugh. I don't just think it, I know it. I owe you more than I could ever repay," she continued. "But I cannot impose upon your hospitality any longer. I will determine what to do to protect myself...somehow. Just have your man call me a hack and I can be on my way."

Saying those words was terrifying, but she had to do so. This was not this stranger's trouble to deal with. She had to manage it herself.

He tilted his head, his gaze unyielding. "You aren't leaving."

CHAPTER 4

T he shock that flooded Imogen's expression was obvious, as was the anger that followed. She lifted her chin, her jawline going harder, and Oscar saw a strength in her, that spunk that had been revealed only briefly last night. She had heart and he had always been attracted to that concept. Not that most men wouldn't be attracted to this woman.

That thought pulled him back. She might be desirable, that was a fact, but he couldn't afford to be drawn to her. It wasn't in the plan, for one thing. For another, what she needed was help, not some stranger panting over her. He had to get himself in line.

"You have no right—" she began.

He held up a hand. "Imogen, these people *killed* someone. And if you're right about Roddenbury, they are *powerful* people. Do you really think they'll let you skip off into the world where you might tell your tale and perhaps bring their house down around them?"

He saw that sink in. Saw her lose hope. He hated himself for being the one to do that to her, but what choice was there? She had to come to grips with the truth of the matter if he was to have any hope in helping her. Saving her.

He had to save her.

THE REDEMPTION OF A ROGUE

"We could...tell the guard..." she began.

He shook his head slowly. "Without any evidence, you're going to tell the guard that an earl murdered a woman who worked at the Cat's Companion? I have lived in this world a long time, my dear—I can tell you they'll turn away without a thought."

Her bottom lip began to tremble. "Because she doesn't matter."

"And he does."

"Then there is no hope," she whispered. "What would you have me do? Change my name and run away to the country? Look over my shoulder for the rest of my miserable days?"

He shifted because the fact was, it might turn out that way in the end. "Let me help you. I have resources—I'll work with them to try to figure out how to manage this. If we gather enough evidence, we might be able to stop these people. In the meantime, you will stay with me."

She had gotten up from the table and walked away while he spoke, and now she pivoted to face him. "No!"

He arched a brow. "That option is so distasteful to you?"

"No."

She stepped forward and he watched as her amber gaze flitted over him. She licked her lips, a tell that she wasn't immune to him, just as he wasn't immune to her. He ignored it. The circumstances were still the same, after all.

"No," she repeated, more softly. "I just...I can't...you wouldn't want..." She huffed out a breath in apparent frustration. "You are a busy man. You have a successful club built on catering to men like Roddenbury. And I am nothing to you. Nothing at all. Why would you do this?"

He gripped his hands at his sides. Confession wasn't in his nature, it never had been. It was too...dangerous. But these circumstances called for something like it. Some way to make her understand that he was on her side. That they would fight this together.

"There was...a woman," he said through clenched teeth. "She...she disappeared from the same brothel six months ago. There is evidence she is also dead."

Imogen's hand came up to cover her mouth and she moved toward him with a long step. "What did she look like?" she whispered.

He understood why she asked. The same reason he'd asked about the dead woman she saw. "Not the woman you saw last night," he assured her. "Louisa was red-haired."

Some of the tension left her face. "Her name was Louisa?"

He nodded. "Yes."

She reached out and touched his hand with hers. The barest of grazes of her fingers across his knuckles. A touch meant to comfort, and he supposed it did. But it also did something else. He stared down into her upturned face, and for a moment he felt nothing but desire for her.

It had been a long time since all the other emotions bled away. There was something peaceful about that, even if it resulted in a cauldron of need.

He moved away from her. He had to. And he cleared his throat. "I should have protected her and I didn't," he said. "But I will protect you. I will work out how to...save you."

"Can you?" she whispered, her voice a little rougher.

"Save you?" he asked.

She nodded.

He moved toward her then. He hadn't meant to. He hadn't wanted to, but he found himself coming across the distance between them in a few long steps. She reacted. A catch of her breath, a frisson of fear, but also something else. Something that called to the need in his own blood. Something that was so very unexpected.

"I swear to you on my own life that I will do everything in my power, Imogen."

She stared up at him, their gazes locked, and her breath shuddered. She opened her mouth as if to say something, and there was nothing in the world he wanted to hear more than whatever that was.

But he couldn't hear it. Couldn't want it. Couldn't pursue it.

He stepped back. "You must want to change," he said.

She glanced down at her dress. "I...yes. But how? Unless you are going to send someone to my home?"

He shifted. "I'm watching your house, but I assume I'm not the only one. Sending someone there would be too dangerous at present. But I..." He shut his eyes. "I have a few things here. They won't be a perfect fit, mind you, but close enough. I've arranged a bath to be drawn for you. You can tidy up while my staff finds those things and readies them."

When he opened his eyes, she was staring at him. For a moment, he thought she might speak. Might ask him something. But then she turned away. "Very well."

He grunted as a reply as she moved toward the door to the study. There she turned and speared him with a glance one last time. "Thank you again, for all your kindness."

She left before he could respond, which was a good thing because all he could do was let his breath out in a long stream. Had he been holding it? It seemed that was what he did whenever she came near him. Made him hold his breath.

Made him lose it. And it had been a long time since a woman made him do that. Which made Mrs. Imogen Huxley very dangerous, indeed.

Imogen sank down in the fine brass bathtub, letting the water cover her shoulders. It felt like heaven, for in her own home it was all basin washes for her. So this was a luxury. One she would have to thank Fitzhugh for later.

Her mind flitted to him, as it had been since she departed his company less than an hour before. Oscar Fitzhugh. He probably had a lot of women who sat in tubs thinking about him. Certainly he drew the attention if he was in a room.

Once he had it, he kept it. Those dark eyes always seemed to be boring into her. She had to assume it was the same with anyone else he encountered. She only wished she could read him. When he looked at her it was all endless depths, but nothing within them. Was he angry she was here disrupting his life? Was he happy to help her?

Did he only do so because of the woman he'd spoken of earlier? Louisa. The woman he...had he loved her? Imogen couldn't tell about that, either. He was, in short, a mystery.

Behind the screen, she could hear the maid tidying up. Imogen shifted a little in the water, grabbing for the fragrant soap that had been left on the ledge of the tub. As she lathered up her hands, she called out, "How long have you worked for Mr. Fitzhugh, Mary?"

"Oof, as long as I can remember. Me ma worked for him, and when I came of age, I was offered a job in the house, as well."

Imogen worried her lip. If she'd been raised in this house, the girl would have some insight into the man. For safety purposes alone, of course, Imogen had to know about him, didn't she? If she were going to truly put her life, her future, into his hands.

"What sort of person is he?" She wished she sounded less invested in the answer, but there it was.

The noise of tidying and arranging continued on the other side of the screen as Mary said, "I couldn't say a cross word about the man. When Ma died, he was kind as could be. Gave me all the time I needed."

Imogen swallowed hard. When her mother had died, Warren had expected her to be fine within hours. And he was her husband. Yet Fitzhugh had offered such grace and kindness to his servant. That certainly spoke very highly of him.

"What about his business?" she asked, knowing she shouldn't. It was none of her affair.

"Fitzhugh's Club?" the girl asked. "Though I've never seen it, it's very successful. He works himself ragged to ensure it. Eats at that desk of his more often than at a table. Spends plenty of nights there until two or three in the morning overseeing it. We're all very proud to work for such a dedicated person."

"Indeed, I have only heard good things about the place," Imogen murmured, but her mind was turning on this information. So the man was driven. Not a surprise. One could see that by just the way he held himself.

"Of course he's handsome as the devil," the young woman continued. "But you know that, of course. If you become his mistress, you will be well pleased."

Imogen jerked to attention and water sloshed around her. "His—his mistress!" she gasped out. "Oh no. I mean to say that isn't…"

Mary popped her head around the edge of the screen. Her cheeks were bright pink. "I'm so sorry, ma'am. I assumed. Please don't be angry."

Imogen struggled for calm. After all, how could it not be assumed that was what she had been brought here for? She and Fitzhugh had been alone in his house last night, unchaperoned, whether or not she had shared his bedroom.

"I'm not angry," she assured the young woman.

Relief washed over her face. "Very good. Th-they should have those gowns almost ready, Mrs. Huxley. I'll go check on them if you're well on your own."

"I am," Imogen said, forcing a bright smile so the poor girl would no longer look so sick.

She slipped away and as the door shut, Imogen rested her head back on the rolled towel Mary had placed as a pillow on the edge of the tub.

Fitzhugh's lover! What a thought. One she couldn't get out of her mind. What kind of lover would he be? Surely he would bring the command he exhibited in life into the bedroom. Those full lips would feel like heaven on her skin. Those strong hands would be like magic on her body.

She blinked up at the intricately carved ceiling above. Great God, what was she doing thinking such things? What was she doing feeling the pulse of need at those thoughts? A need she could easily slake by…

She slid her hands beneath the water, spread her legs a fraction and smoothed a fingertip across her entrance. She was wet, and from far more than the bathwater. Electric pleasure jolted through her. Her breath trembled from her lungs as she repeated the action.

Her whole body thrummed with tension. Both from the horror of her situation and a more pleasant kind. She knew release would help. It was something she'd learned over the lonely years of her marriage. She could make the pressure lift with a few strokes of her hand, even if the relief didn't last forever.

She shut her eyes and stroked harder, rolling her clitoris with her thumb. She let her mind wander and it took her right back to Fitzhugh. Back to his study when the air between them had felt so thick and heavy. What would have happened if she'd done more than take his hand for that brief moment?

What would have happened if he had tugged her closer like he had in the carriage? Or set her on the edge of the desk and stepped between her legs?

The pleasure mounted with that thought and she followed it even though she knew she shouldn't. Followed it to his hands pulling up her skirts. Followed it to his mouth on hers. To his cock sliding deep into her body as she clung to him helplessly.

She followed all her fantasies, as wrong as they were, until her legs began to shake and the pleasure roared up like a wave in the ocean. When it crashed over her, she arched, her toes flexing against the sensation. It was over too soon and she sank back in the rolling water, sated if only for a moment.

Lucky, too, for the door to the chamber opened and she slid her hand from between her legs as she heard the maid return. "These gowns are lovely, Mrs. Huxley. You'll look beautiful in them."

"Very good," Imogen said as she pushed to her feet and grabbed for a folded sheet of woven linen left by the tub to dry herself. She draped it over her body just as the maid came around the screen.

She was a pretty girl, with dark brown hair and a round, friendly face. "There now, you must feel better."

"Worlds better," Imogen agreed. "Almost myself again."

They walked around the screen together, and Imogen caught her breath. There were five gowns laid out on the bed, and each was more beautiful than the next. The finest of silks and satins, the most bright and happy of colors, the most elegant touches and embellishments.

"They're beautiful," Imogen breathed.

"Aren't they?" Mary clutched her hands before her. "The pink is too formal, I think. But the green is my favorite and it will show you to your best advantage."

Imogen stared at the beautiful gown and then stroked the fabric gently. It was the finest silk she'd ever touched. Finer than anything she'd ever worn, that was certain. And it was another woman's dress. What would Fitzhugh think when he saw her in it? What would he consider her best advantage?

Or would he consider it at all?

"Let us hope so," Imogen said as she dropped the linen cloth and picked up the gown. "I'm ready."

But as Mary began to prepare the dress, Imogen couldn't help but feel that statement was a lie. Whatever was about to happen, she wasn't ready.

And she wasn't sure she ever would be. She could only hope she would survive the next few days or weeks in this man's protection and not get too lost in his world. She had no place here, and she couldn't forget it.

CHAPTER 5

Oscar stood at the window in the dining room, staring out at the dark garden below. His thoughts ought to have been on his work. Normally that was where his mind always took him. How many times had Louisa chided him for it, asking him to come back to her?

He'd never been able to do it. Not enough for her satisfaction. And the wall had built between them and ultimately led to her death.

But tonight it wasn't his club that filled his mind. It wasn't even the arrangements he'd begun to make in his investigation of the murder Imogen had been witness to.

No, he thought other things. The woman herself. The slope of her neck. The curve of her jaw. The slant of her lips. Those things were... distracting. He shifted in discomfort and tried to push them away.

But before he could, the door behind him opened and he turned to watch Imogen, herself, step into the dining room. It had been hours since he last saw her. In his study, her chin had lifted in defiance and fear and strength as he wrecked her world. She'd been undone then, her hair barely tamed, her gown dirty and torn.

But not anymore. He caught his breath. The green gown had always been one of his favorites and she wore it well. The sleeves were a gauzy fabric and rather shockingly revealed the curves of her shoulders. The neckline was a bit low, and Imogen's bust was a little bigger than Louisa's had been, so the swell of her breasts edged at the neckline, forcing him to take in every inch of revealed flesh. Then the gown cascaded over her, the silk skimming her curves like it had been made to do so.

Her dark hair had been smoothed and lifted and spun into some fashionable confection, but for one errant curl that brushed the line of her jaw and made him want to sweep it away with the back of his hand.

"Good evening, Mr. Fitzhugh," she said as she stepped into the room, apparently oblivious to the impact she made.

She crossed to him and he tracked every movement, tracked the warmth of her as she stopped before him. Tracked the scent of her, something honeyed that reminded him of sweet treats.

"Good evening," he choked out. "I trust you feel better."

"Yes," she said. "Everything always looks better after a bath." He thought her gaze flickered lower when she said it, but then it was back on his face. "And the gowns are lovely. Thank you for allowing me to wear them."

He nodded as he held out the chair beside his. She took it and settled in, spreading her napkin across her lap as the first course was brought out.

When they were alone again, she took a sip of wine and said, "Were they hers?"

He had lifted his soup spoon to his lips, but now he froze there. As he slowly lowered it back to his bowl, he said, "Hers?"

As if he didn't know the *her* to which she was referring.

"The woman you discussed with me earlier. The one who disappeared into the brothel. Louisa."

His felt his jaw tightening. Felt the strong desire to dress her down for daring to ask that. Instead he ground out, "Yes."

She nodded slowly and ate a few bites of food. "Who was she?" she asked at last. "A sister?"

"No, Mrs. Huxley," he said softly.

Her gaze flitted down to her plate and her voice caught as she asked, "A—a lover?"

"Imogen," he rasped out because he couldn't find his full voice.

He thought she might stop then. Her cheeks flushed and he could see she was uncomfortable with pressing and poking and prodding. But then she slid her hand out and covered his for the second time that day. Her skin was warm and soft, the weight of her fingers somehow...comforting.

"I'm sorry," she whispered. "I only ask because I'm wearing her dress. And you say she disappeared into the very brothel where I nearly lost my own life."

"And you think you have the right to know," he finished as he slid his hand away and rested it on his thigh beneath the table. He flexed it because he could still feel the weight of her palm on his knuckles.

"Perhaps not the right," she said. "I suppose I don't have the right. But at present I feel so raw about what I saw, what I experienced. Nothing feels normal or right or peaceful. I can't even go home."

"And if you crack my chest open and spill some of me out, that will make you feel that the scales are balanced?"

Her eyes went wide at the image and she shook her head. "No, I suppose it won't. I'm sorry, Mr. Fitzhugh. You've been nothing but kind to me since I destroyed your peace by colliding with you last night. I won't pry."

She returned her attention to her plate, but Oscar couldn't do the same. He stared at her face, her lovely face. Her kind face. Her troubled face. And in that moment, he wanted to give her what she desired. Anything she desired.

He cleared his throat. "Louisa was a courtesan." Her gaze shot up and her dark eyes widened. "And for a while I was her protector. Her lover."

"It ended."

"Yes," he said. "Long before the Cat's Companion."

"Wh-why?" she asked, and then she shook her head. "I'm sorry.

That answer is certainly none of my affair. I shouldn't have asked it."

It wasn't her affair, but he had studiously avoided speaking to anyone about Louisa for six months. He spoke around her, but never directly about her. Now that he'd opened those gates, it was like he was compelled to walk through them.

"She wanted more," he said, trying not to think of Louisa's tear-streaked face as she told him that she loved him. As she begged him to feel the same emotion. As she realized he didn't. Couldn't, he had told her. "And I couldn't give it to her. So it ended. Badly."

Imogen had shifted, leaning forward, entirely engaged with him. Her steady stare should have made him uncomfortable, but instead it was...comforting. Almost a beacon in a storm that he'd been navigating for months.

"She disappeared a few months later," he said. "And I started looking for her. I heard she died. I know she died. And it is...my fault."

"Oscar," she whispered, using his first name for the first time since he introduced himself. No one called him that. Everyone called him Fitzhugh. Even Louisa had done so. Fitz, if she was being cheeky.

But hearing his real name, his given name, from this woman's lips was...intoxicating. Some of the pain of the past slid away when she said it, replaced by far darker and more desperate emotions.

Needs.

"I'm so sorry," she continued, completely unaware of what he was thinking.

She reached out and caught his hand again, this time with both of hers. She cocooned him with her warmth and his gaze slid to her lips.

Very kissable, full lips. He hated himself for noticing that in this moment of high emotion and tension. He hated himself for being able to divorce himself from what had happened with Louisa and instead focus on what his body drove for with Imogen.

"Be careful, Imogen," he said, his voice rough with desire.

Her eyes went wide but she didn't drop his hand. She just stared at him, her pupils dilating and her mouth slightly parted. She licked her lips before she said, "Why?"

He arched a brow. "You know why."

The door from the kitchen opened again, and she dropped his hand and leaned back in her chair as the soup bowls, largely untouched by them both, were taken away and the next course was brought in.

He never stopped looking at her as this was done. Not when the servants left them alone, either. She held his gaze, too. That shocked him, truly. Most women he'd known in his life had been startled by his intensity. Few had matched it.

And yet this woman held her own admirably.

"Let's eat," he said softly.

She nodded. "Very well."

Neither of them moved to do so, and he couldn't help how his mouth quirked up a bit in the corner. He blinked first, not because he needed to, but because he chose not to have this erotically charged battle with her tonight. He swept up his fork and began to eat, and she slowly did the same.

He changed the subject to books and watched her shoulders relax. But whatever electric moment had happened between them was still there, throbbing like a heartbeat behind it all.

He wasn't certain that could ever be forgotten.

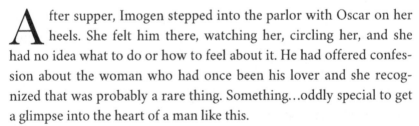

After supper, Imogen stepped into the parlor with Oscar on her heels. She felt him there, watching her, circling her, and she had no idea what to do or how to feel about it. He had offered confession about the woman who had once been his lover and she recognized that was probably a rare thing. Something...oddly special to get a glimpse into the heart of a man like this.

But then everything had shifted, changed because she touched him. And even though they had spent the rest of the supper talking of books and music and food, she couldn't pretend away the tension that arced between them.

He moved to the sideboard, and at last she could breathe because he was no longer marking and tracking her, like a hawk to her helpless rabbit. He poured them each wine, but as he pivoted and held out the glass, he frowned.

"I feel I owe you an apology," he said, those intense eyes settling firmly on hers once more.

She took a sip of the alcohol, wishing it shored her up more than it did. "About what?"

"Louisa." His gaze slid away and his frown deepened. "I think I may have been gruff about your questions. She is a...delicate topic."

She tilted her head, watching him. This was not a man accustomed to discomfort and yet he was allowing himself to feel it in order to offer her an olive branch of some kind. One she wasn't certain she was owed. After all, she had pried into a life that had nothing to do with her.

She smiled, perhaps the first real smile she had felt cross her face in weeks, even months. "Isn't gruff part of your personality? Your magnetism?"

His brow wrinkled. "Is it now?"

She nodded. "It seems to be. I'm certain many a person has looked at you and thought, 'what is that very gruff man thinking?' and then you speared them with a glance and sent them skittering away in nervous terror."

His eyes narrowed, and now she couldn't help but laugh.

"Oh yes, that's the glance." She lifted a hand to her chest. "And my heart pounds, just as you intended."

The corner of his mouth quirked slightly. Close to a smile, not quite one. She found herself wondering what he would look like if he did smile. Truly smiled.

"I am an ogre then, in your estimation. Is there a bridge I was meant to be guarding?"

"Not an ogre," she said with another laugh. "Ogres are ugly, for one thing, and you must know you aren't that. And cruel. Which *I* know for a fact you aren't."

At that, his expression hardened a little. The walls came back up. "A dangerous assumption, Mrs. Huxley. I suppose I can be as cruel as anyone else."

He turned away and walked to the fire. He stirred it, not because the dancing flames needed it, but she thought he might. He didn't like the playful connection, it seemed. It made him nervous. An odd thought that she could do that to such a commanding person with just a little playful teasing.

It made her want to press her luck, but instead she let out a sigh. "At any rate, you owe me no apology. I understand how the past one shared with another can be...difficult. Discussing it *delicate*, as you put it."

He pivoted at that. "Can you?"

She nodded. "My husband has only been dead a little over a year, after all."

He moved closer. "You two were close."

"What makes you say that?"

"Because you can't stand to have me call you Mrs. Huxley when you're talking about taking another man to your bed," he said. "That indicates some level of guilt at doing so. A betrayal you are loath to make. Hence, I make the guess that you were close. Perhaps you even loved each other, as seems to be the fashion in Society marriages at present."

There was something bitter about his tone, but she couldn't address it. Not when his words pierced her heart. Earlier she had prodded him about his past with Louisa and had been frustrated when he dodged the answers, even if she wasn't owed them.

Now he did the same and she felt a similar desire to push aside what her answers would reveal. But was that fair? In the privacy of this house, under these strange and trying circumstances...did she *want* to keep the barriers of polite lies between them?

It seemed her body would compel her to speak before she made a decision about that question, because she heard the words falling from her mouth. "I might as well complete my humiliation. Ours was an arranged marriage and it was...complicated."

Complicated. What a word to describe the push-and-pull between her and Warren.

"How so?"

She refused to look at him. She didn't want to see his face when she said the words that were perched on the tip of her tongue. "He had...many affairs," she said softly. "Often very publicly and never with any sense of shame or apology. But I was told, by him and by others, that it was the way of our world. That I should accept it because our marriage gave me opportunities."

Oscar's voice was strained and filled with disdain as he spat, "Opportunities."

She glanced at him then. His brow was low, his dark eyes penetrating as they focused on her. His lips were pressed hard together, making the full line of them thinner and white with pressure. He looked angry, but not at her. For her.

It gave her the strength to continue. "And to be...fair, Warren could also be affectionate. Kind. Passionate. Even loving when it suited him. We were not always unhappy. I often believed he did care for me, in his own fashion. And then he died."

"And you were left with nothing," he said softly.

"Yes. I was shocked." She paced away from him, to the window and looked out over the street below. Carriages danced by, it was early enough that people still strolled in the lamplight in small groups. Life went on. It always had.

"It sounds as though his family took advantage," he said. "From what you said this morning."

She nodded. "They did. I was told that if I had been a good wife, he would have made arrangements. That his lack of planning had to do with me, not him." Her jaw clenched as she ground her teeth. "And so here we are. He dug a hole and somehow I have managed to pull the earth down in around myself."

He made a low sound in his chest, and as she pivoted to face him, he came across the room toward her in a few long steps. Her eyes went wide as she watched him do so, confident and certain as a king. He reached for her, like he would take her elbow or her hand, but then he stopped himself and yanked his hand back.

"You cannot truly believe that it is your fault. From everything you've told me, you were put in an impossible situation by him, by his family, by every circumstance. You were doing your best to save yourself. Perhaps the decisions you made weren't perfect, but neither are anyone's. This is not your fault, Imogen."

Her lips parted. In all her life she had not ever had someone defend her so vigorously. Even Aurora, her closest friend and confidante, was not so bold. And yet this man, this near-stranger, demanded that she give herself grace. He sprinkled it over her without hesitation or demand.

"Oscar," she whispered, her voice barely carrying.

But he heard her. It was clear by the way his posture shifted, by the way his pupils dilated. He moved even closer, and now there was nothing but a sliver of space between them. She looked up into his eyes as he loomed over her and lost herself in the solidness of him, both in form and in how in control he was.

It almost felt like she could let some portion of control go and he would hold her and not let her fall.

As if he heard that thought, he reached out, and this time he did touch her. His fingertips grazed her own, and it was like lightning rushed up her arm, flooded her senses, settled in every space in her body that was responsive or sensitive. She heard her breath catch, felt herself sway toward him almost without meaning to do so.

He slid his hand up her bare arm, leaving fire in his wake, and then his fingers curled around her bicep and he pulled her against him. She gripped his lapels for purchase, lifting to him as he lowered to her. Their mouths met. For a moment, everything froze, like time had been stopped.

But then his tongue traced the crease of her lips and an explosion followed. She opened to him, lifting against him, making a hungry sound in the back of her throat that she had never heard before. He growled a response, crushing her against his chest. His whiskers were soft against her chin, but that was all that was soft about the kiss. He was firm, hard even, demanding, and she surrendered what he claimed without resistance.

His fingers slid up her neck, across her jawline. He forced them into her hair, tilting her head so he could deepen the kiss. And she was lost in it, lost in him, from the scratch of his beard on her chin to the taste of wine on his tongue. She was drowning and she didn't want to be saved.

She groaned again, and he froze. Time stopped a second time, and then he stepped away, balancing her gently before he released her and turned his back. His breath came short and hard, his hands clenched at his sides, and for a moment he said nothing. She *couldn't* say anything, so silence stretched between them for what like an interminable forever.

"I think we best not confuse things," he said at last, his voice lower and rougher than before. He faced her slowly and speared her with that mesmerizing gaze of his. "Do you agree?"

The words he said seemed very reasonable. And yet she didn't agree. But there was no use in saying it, not now when her mind was addled and her heart was racing. Not now when she couldn't come to her senses.

"Yes," she lied instead. "And I...I think I should probably retire to my room."

"That might be for the best. Good night."

She nodded her farewell and exited the room. But the moment she shut the door, she leaned back against it and sucked in air like she was coming up from an ocean riptide. In some ways she was. Oscar Fitzhugh seemed to be exactly that: powerful, overwhelming, capable of washing her away to where she might never return.

And for however long she stayed here, she was going to have to find a way to manage it that didn't include touching herself and fantasizing about the man every night.

CHAPTER 6

Oscar tightened his dressing gown around his waist and paced across his bedchamber yet another time. It had been several hours since his last encounter with Imogen Huxley, but he couldn't get the woman out of his mind. Or her taste off his lips.

He'd always been a man of control. In his business, in his life...in his bed. He chose lovers carefully and never allowed himself to be swept away except for that exact moment of release. He certainly couldn't recall the last time he'd kissed a woman when it hadn't been a perfectly planned moment. In the parlor after supper, he hadn't planned anything. He'd just looked down into Imogen's upturned face and his mind had...shut off. All that had existed was the driving need to touch her.

"Bloody hell," he muttered as he sat down at the table in his bedroom and slid an empty piece of paper in front of him.

If he couldn't control himself around the woman, then the least he could do was work to help her. He marked the number one on the sheet and began to write down a list of things he'd need to do. He had some contacts who might be able to help—he'd reach out to them. Roddenbury had once been a member of his club, so he'd search out those records.

He lost himself in the planning, his thrumming body coming under control by strategizing. He had very little idea of how much time had passed when a noise made him jerk his head up.

He focused, listening for it to repeat and it did. This time he recognized it. Imogen was crying out in her sleep, much as she had the night before. He'd ignored it then and the sound had passed swiftly.

Tonight, though, her moans and cries seemed louder. More pained.

He set his quill down and got to his feet. It wasn't his place to comfort her, of course. He didn't know her. He was helping her, but only because he had to. Common decency made it a requirement. And Louisa.

And judging from the way he'd lost control of himself earlier, he really ought not go any further than that.

"Please, no!" came her voice from the room down the hall.

He scrubbed a hand through his hair and then found himself moving toward the door. He stepped into the hallway, his bare feet silent against the smooth wooden floor.

She was so upset, she was bound to wake the rest of the house. For the sake of his servants, he ought to check on her. Soothe her.

That was it. He would do it only for the sake of his servants.

"Fucking liar," he muttered beneath his breath as he gently pushed her door open and peered into the room.

Her fire had died, but it still cast a glow over the bed across the room. She had flung the covers off herself at some point and was splayed across the sheets. Her chemise was shoved up around her thighs, her legs twitching as if she were running.

"No," she moaned.

He eased closer, and now the light hit her face and he saw her cheeks were streaked with tears. "Imogen," he said softly, hoping not to startle her. "Imogen, it's just a dream."

"Help me. Please," she whimpered, this time softer.

"I'm here," he said, reaching out. He touched her arm and shook gently. "Imogen, all is well. You're safe."

She jolted upright, and he caught her arms so she wouldn't flail off the bed. She swung at him, still asleep, fighting off an attacker that only existed in the dark recesses of her mind.

He levied himself up to the edge of the high bed and tugged her against him so she would stop trying to hit him.

"It's me, Imogen. Imogen, it's Oscar. You're safe, you're safe."

Her eyes fluttered open at last and she stared up at him. At first she was still obviously asleep and not truly seeing him, but then he saw her starting to come back to reality. Come back to him. Her lower lip trembled and then she leaned forward. Her head came to rest on his chest and he wrapped his arms around her, holding her close as she shuddered against whatever horrible images had haunted her dreams.

He could well imagine what they were, considering what she'd gone through. He lowered her back on the pillows, tucking her against his chest as he edged his way next to her on the bed.

Her breath came in great gasps and she lifted a hand to his heart. Her fingers slid past the closure of his dressing gown and rested, gently on the bare skin beneath. He never slept in anything—he was naked beneath the robe—and right now his body was very aware of how close he was to her in bed.

He pushed those thoughts aside. Incredibly inappropriate considering her state.

"I-I'm sorry," she whispered, her breath warm against his neck. "You must think me a fool."

"For having nightmares?" he asked, smoothing a hand over her hair. "Never. I'm not surprised at all by this reaction. You've gone through something terrible, Imogen. It's not over. I would be surprised if you didn't have a nightmare or two."

"I've always been an active sleeper," she said, her voice still heavy and sleepy. "Warren never slept with me during our marriage because I talked in my sleep and moved too much."

Oscar pursed his lips. The very idea that a man wouldn't want to curl himself around this woman all night every night, tradition or discomfort be damned, was...ridiculous. He'd hadn't often thought of

Huxley when he was a member of Oscar's club. He found himself disliking the man a great deal now.

"An active mind is a good thing, I think," he said. "You must work on a great deal while you sleep if you are so lively."

"You're very kind to say so, rather than chide me about disrupting your rest or upending the household with my screams," she murmured, and she lifted her head to look up at him.

Their faces were too close now. Just the slightest of angling and he could kiss her again. Everything in him wanted to kiss her again.

Which meant he had to get out of this bed.

"Now that you're well—" he began as he moved to part from her.

To his surprise, she grabbed for him, her fingers clinging to the lapels of his dressing gown. Color filled her cheeks, but she didn't release him. "Oh, please. Please don't go. Could you just...stay a little longer? Just let me try to go back to sleep before you—before you leave."

It was a bad idea. The worst idea. The longer he lay here, their bodies pressed together, the more the throb of wanting this woman built deep within him. Collected hard and heavy in his cock.

But how could he refuse her when she was trembling in his arms, begging him for just a touch of human kindness? How could he refuse her when the last thing he wished to do was leave her bed?

"Very well," he said softly, and reached down to tug the covers up. He pulled them over them both and shifted a little lower on the pillows.

She settled her head on his chest, her dark hair fanning over her shoulders and his hands like satin. They lay there together in the silence. She was awake, he could tell that from her breathing. He was *never* going to sleep in the state she was putting him in.

So it was to be torture. And he wasn't certain he could survive it, truth be told.

When she moved her hand again, the fingers flexing against his chest, he couldn't help the shuddering sigh that escaped his lips. She lifted her head a second time, looking up at him in the dimness, her gaze glittering. "You are…a very good man."

He flinched at that assessment. "I am not."

"You are," she insisted. "How many other men would have intervened on my behalf at the brothel, let alone taken me home and given me shelter and help once they learned my predicament? I do not think one out of ten would have done anything more than take advantage of my plight."

"Use it to bed you, you mean," he murmured, and watched as his fingers threaded through her hair. Had he meant to start doing that?

She swallowed hard and then nodded slowly. "Yes, I suppose that's what I mean. They would have—they would have wanted repayment of some kind…for their help."

He remained silent, all his control straining against his chest, straining against his dressing gown. Surely she must feel that as she was tucked against him. Surely she must know he was no better than those men she referred to in this speech about his supposed goodness.

"Imogen," he said, his voice rasping in the quiet. A warning, he hoped. Though it sounded more like a plea in the dark. A needy sound of desire and pleasure and everything he needed to rein in.

She shifted against him in response, her breath shaky as she slid her hand beneath his dressing gown entirely. Her hands traced his pectoral, fingers tangling in his chest hair.

"Why did you kiss me tonight?" she whispered.

"Because I'm *not* a good man," he retorted swiftly. "No matter if I try to help you, I'm not a good man, Imogen. You mustn't forget that. I'm ruthless and cold and unfeeling."

The last one wasn't entirely true. He was *feeling* a great deal right now. It was just all pulsing desire as she let her hand trail along his side and pushed his dressing gown open even wider.

"Be careful," he grunted, reaching up to catch her hand and hold it still against his hot skin. "Be very careful, Imogen. You push me too far and I might just take exactly what you said those other men would have wanted."

She stared up into his face, holding his gaze for an uncomfortably long time. He wanted to look away, but he couldn't. Not when those amber eyes held him steady.

"What if tonight I want that too?" she whispered. "What if when you kissed me it made me forget, just for a moment, everything else? And what if I knew that if you did even more than kiss me, it would erase it all just for a little while? And I want it to do just that, even if it's wanton and foolish and shortsighted."

He stilled, focusing on her face. They were opposites in some ways. She was asking him to shatter her with pleasure, strip her control away to make her forget. He had always clung to control as a means to feel...better.

Those two desires could absolutely work in tandem. Wrong or right. And did wrong or right matter in the quiet of her bedroom? With a woman who knew exactly what she was asking? A woman he wanted with a power that startled him. If he took, maybe that driving need would also fade and he could focus on matters at hand.

It could be helpful to both of them.

At least that was what he told himself as he leaned forward, cupped her chin and claimed her lips for the second time that night.

~

Imogen shuddered as Oscar's mouth covered hers. He was a very good kisser. That was the one coherent thought that fluttered through her heated mind. She'd been kissed a few times in her life. Warren, of course. Sometimes he was passionate, but often it was all perfunctory. Like she was a duty he had to fulfill.

Afterward, when she'd begun the business of seeking a protector, one or two men had put their lips to hers. Wet, on the whole. Somewhat unpleasant. Just a lot of thrusting tongue, which she supposed was meant to put her to mind of thrusting cock.

It hadn't had the desired effect.

But Oscar Fitzhugh kissed her differently. Like she was a banquet table laden with every treat in the world and he was a starving man. Like he wanted to savor her every flavor until the world spun into darkness.

She wound her arms around his neck, parting her lips and reveling in the soft abrasion of his beard on her chin. She made a muffled sound in her throat, a moan and a cry merged and desperate. It must have pleased him, for he maneuvered her onto her back and angled his head to kiss her even more deeply.

She drowned in him. That was the best analogy she could think of as he plundered her mouth, thoroughly exploring every nook and cranny until her head was spinning. She recognized his hands were now moving too. He cupped her jaw, thumb tracing the bone with feather-light gentleness. He slipped it lower, his hand covering her throat for the briefest of moments before he traced her shoulder, down her arm.

He was mapping her body with his touch, finding the places where she responded. She surrendered to the process, giving him everything he desired without hesitation or embarrassment. They were just two people here in the dark, both wanting the same pleasure.

There was no harm in that.

He pulled away from the kiss, his dark gaze spearing her, pinning her in place as he palmed her left breast. Even through the thin fabric of her chemise, she felt every ridge of his rough hand, every heated movement as he began to stroke her nipple, pinching it lightly between his forefinger and thumb.

She arched her back, her breath shuddering out. His intense stare was too much, so she closed her eyes and simply surrendered to the magic he was creating with his touch. She heard him chuckle, a low, possessive sound, and that only seemed to ratchet up the intensity of what his fingers did. He was a man stalking his prey.

She wanted him to catch her. To claim her. To make her give over everything she was, everything she could be, consequences be damned. Consequences were for tomorrow. Tonight was for something else.

His mouth brushed her throat, and she gasped as she dug her fingers into the thick waves of his hair. He sucked her skin, right to the edge of pain, and switched his hand to her right breast. She was panting by then, rising into him, as if she could find relief. But he denied it, instead building an increasingly high and heavy wall of sensation.

His mouth moved down over her collarbone, down the edge of her chemise, then crested over her breast. He sucked her through the thin fabric, and she ground up, desperate for more, for that release that would send her into oblivion for a little while.

His hand dropped lower, fingers splaying over her stomach, cupping her hip. He was sliding her now, pulling her tighter against his chest as he massaged her thigh. Her legs fell open and he caught the one closest to him, arching it up over his legs so that she was splayed lewdly on her back. He pushed her chemise up and she was revealed to him.

He made a small sound at the back of his throat. Something dark and dangerous that sent heat shooting through her veins. His fingers traced a path along her inner thigh, almost tiptoeing up her skin, closer and closer to her core.

When he touched her, she gripped at his arms, even though it was the most glancing of grazes along her entrance. She was so sensitive in that moment, he might as well have been doing far more.

"Do you want to come, Imogen?" he asked.

She let her gaze flit to his face. "Is that a serious question when I'm splayed out before you like a wanton, gasping and arching and shaking every time you touch me?"

"A very serious question," he assured her as he leaned in and nuzzled her neck, abrading her skin gently with his whiskers. "I want you to say it. Say you want me to make you come. Tell me that's what you want. Very simple, and you can have it."

She gritted her teeth at the demand, for that's what it was, no matter how sweetly it was supposedly requested. He was denying her

49

until she prostrated herself on the altar of his fingers. His mouth. Hopefully his cock.

"I want you to make me come," she said, forcing herself to meet his eyes. "Please, please make me come."

His pupils dilated to an impossible blackness. He cupped her chin, and this time when he kissed her it was rough. Demanding. Like stripping her control had somehow taken his own. She moaned against him, lifting into the devouring pressure of his tongue, warring with him in a battle for need and release and connection.

At last he broke from her mouth and panted down at her. He looked...angry, almost. Though she felt no fear for herself. But he didn't speak as he returned his hand to the place between her thighs. He laid the flat of his palm there, just covering her, and she ground into him out of instinct and desire.

"Don't push me," he growled. "Just *let* me. Close your eyes and let me."

She stared up into his face. Dark and intense and focused in the dying firelight. She could refuse him and she believed he would back away, exit the room, and they would probably never speak of this again. She didn't have the sense he was the kind of man who would force or even punish.

But he was still demanding trust. Trust a stranger who could hold her perfectly still with just a glare. Trust a stranger who was waiting, she would say almost patiently, for her to respond to his harsh order.

She settled back, dropping her hands away from his body, and shut her eyes. He grunted, almost another low laugh but not quite. What would he look like if he smiled?

She didn't get to think further because his hand moved against her sex. He peeled her open slowly, revealing her. Even in the dim light, he'd be able to see her. She felt heat flooding her cheeks and lifted toward him.

"Don't make me teach you how to behave," he breathed, but there was a catch in his voice that told her he was as wrapped up in the power of this as she was. If he drowned her, she at least forced him to take on water.

That was power in its own way, even if he was holding her down as he traced her entrance with his fingertip. She was wet already, felt herself close to dripping as he swiped his finger through her excitement a second time.

"Very nice," he murmured. "Look at me."

She opened her eyes and watched as he licked the proof of her desire from his fingertip. "Oh my God," she grunted, almost against her will.

His gaze narrowed and he held her stare as he dropped his finger back to her entrance, and this time he gently pressed himself inside. Inch by inch, to the first knuckle, to the second. He stretched her with his fingers and she flexed around him with a gasp of pleasure.

"It's been a long time, hasn't it?" he whispered.

"Y-Yes," she gasped. "I was looking for a protector but hadn't advanced this—this far with anyone yet. I only…with my hand…"

"Don't think about that," he whispered as he flexed his fingers and sent a jolt of sensation through her. "Just think about this."

"Yes," she murmured. "This."

He nodded. "I'm going to make that wait worthwhile."

He curled his finger inside of her, and she gripped the covers as a bolt of pleasure as hot and fast as lightning tore through her. He held her stare, punishing, hot and hard as he kept working her, grabbing her pleasure and pulling it from her with such expertise that she felt like a novice even after years of marriage that had been anything but celibate.

She flexed against him, gripping him with her body as she reached for more. For release. For everything.

He shook his head and settled his thumb against her clitoris, grinding against her there as he continued to pump inside of her, adding a second finger to stretch and tease her further.

She could no longer make coherent sounds as he forced her pleasure. As he created in reality what she had fantasized about when she touched herself in the bath what seemed like a year ago rather than a few hours.

And when the orgasm hit her at last, it was far more powerful than that release had been on her own. She bucked against him, grabbing for his arms, digging her nails in as she keened out all the pleasure. Wave after wave rocked her, too intense, too powerful, and never-ending because he forced her to continue to ride it out. He tormented, never letting up, making the moment last far longer than she'd ever imagined it could.

Only when she was limp and sated, still twitching, legs still shaking, did he withdraw his fingers from her. He never broke eye contact as once again he licked them clean of her essence. She shuddered as she watched. The man was a virtuoso and she wanted to be his instrument until he tired of her.

She opened her legs farther, ready for him to slake his own need by taking her. He obviously wanted her. That was clear by the way his cock tented out the silky fabric of his dressing gown.

But to her surprise, when he touched her thighs, it was to close them. He rolled her on her side so her back was against his chest and wrapped his arms around her. His breath was warm against her neck, her ear, as he whispered, "Sleep now, Imogen. I won't leave. Just...sleep."

She wanted to argue. To ask him why he wouldn't take what he so obviously wanted. She wanted to grind back against him and test the remarkable restraint he so obviously contained.

But she hadn't slept well in months. Certainly not in the last week or two. And with his arms around her, his warmth encircling her, her pleasure still thick in her veins, the exhaustion began to overwhelm her. All questions faded, all desires simply pulsed rather than throbbed.

And she slipped into sleep at last, with no answers, no certainty and nothing but pleasure and his body to keep her warm.

CHAPTER 7

I mogen jolted awake, and for a moment she had no idea where she was. She stared up at the intricately carved ceiling, so different from her own worn, leaky one, and it all returned to her in a wave.

She was at the home of Oscar Fitzhugh, the man who had drawn her to shattering orgasm not so many hours ago. But he was gone. She was alone in the comfortable bed, covers tangled around her bare legs.

She hadn't stirred when he left, which was a shocking thing because normally she slept so lightly that the tiniest sound or movement could disturb her slumber. She moved to the window and threw back the curtains, flooding the room with light from the sunny day. For a moment, the briefest moment, her troubles faded a fraction. Here, at least, she was safe. Here in these halls, she wasn't...afraid. Or at least she was less afraid.

She had Oscar to thank for that.

She worried her lip and got up to ring for the maid who had been helping her. Mary stepped into the room a few moments later, and her bright chatter as she helped prepare Imogen for the day put her at ease a little. Made her feel more herself than she had in a very long time.

"Mr. Fitzhugh is in the breakfast room," Mary said at last when

Imogen had been curled and primped and buttoned and looked presentable.

"Thank you," she said, smoothing the skirts that weren't her own. Trying not to blush or make it too obvious what she and Fitzhugh had been doing late into the night. She smiled at the maid and slipped from the room before she did anything to make it so.

As she meandered her way downstairs, her mind raced. On a good night's sleep, it was easier to think. To ponder both this specific situation and her life in general. Ponder what she should do and how she should interact with the man who had allowed her to take refuge in his walls.

She entered the breakfast room with a bright smile, ready to make the best of it all, but the smile faded as she stepped inside. Oscar was at the table, a paper in one hand, a plate before him. As she stepped inside, he lifted his thumb to his lips and sucked a smudge of jam from it.

Her body flexed, almost against her will. That was so much like what he'd done last night after he'd pleasured her. Licked her release away like it was as delicious as jam.

"Are you going to join me or gape at me all morning?" he asked, finally looking up from his paper.

She caught her breath, thrown off by him as usual, and hustled into the room. "Join you, of course," she said.

He motioned to the sideboard, and she moved there to peruse the wonderful selection of breakfast treats. "I'm sorry I started without you. I didn't know when you would rouse yourself."

She nearly dropped her plate, for she had been certain she heard him say *arouse* before realizing her mistake. She cleared her throat and went back to plating her food. "You owe me no disruption of your schedule," she assured him as she sat down at the place beside him and smiled. "You've had enough of those thanks to me."

He was staring at her as she spoke. His dark eyes focused on her face so intently she worried she had something on it. Or that he had suddenly decided he didn't like the angles of it. Or something equally terrible judging from the thinness of his lips at present.

"I asked you here," he said at last, and folded the paper and set it aside. "It's no trouble."

She laughed as she began to eat. "You are a very good liar, but a liar nonetheless. I know it's a great deal of trouble having a dramatic stranger in your house, demanding you take time away from your own business, calling out with nightmares in the night, dragging you from your own bed to—"

She cut herself off with a blush.

"It's no trouble," he repeated, this time his voice rougher.

She wrinkled her brow as she looked at him. He had held her against the mattress last night and taken her pleasure so easily. He had cradled her so gently afterward, comforting her enough that she could sleep for the first time in what felt like forever.

Today he certainly looked at her with the same intensity, but he made no attempt to discuss what had happened. Or push her to do the same.

Did it mean anything to him at all? Or was she just a reasonably attractive woman in a bed down the hall from him who fulfilled whatever needs a man like him possessed?

Only he hadn't taken her. He hadn't come. So what need had been fulfilled?

"You are staring at me again," he said, this time with a hint of humor to his voice, even if he didn't smile. "Do I have something on my face? Hate my beard? Wondering if these are my real teeth, or are they wooden?"

She bent her head and couldn't suppress a laugh. His teasing eased a little of the tension. "You don't have anything on your face. And I know your teeth are not wooden because we…er…that is we…"

"Kissed," he said softly. "We kissed, Imogen. That's the word for it."

"Yes, it is," she whispered.

"So it's the beard then," he said, leaning forward.

"No. The beard very much suits you." She fought the urge to lean up like he did and smooth her hands over the neatly trimmed whiskers. To trace the lines of white amongst the brown, just as she wanted to do with the gray at his temples. "It isn't much in style, though, is it?"

"I never cared about style," he said, leaning back.

"I suppose you wouldn't. I admire that. Style is sometimes all that is expected of a woman like me. Substance is considered a liability."

He draped an arm over the back of his chair. "By your husband?"

She shrugged, pushing away the pain of that question and the answer that would follow. "You live in the same world I do, Mr. Fitzhugh. My husband saw me as a decoration in his life. But so did my father. So does any man who considers me. That I am more is almost none of their business. I have substance for myself, not for anyone who cares only about style."

"You should find a man who appreciates substance," he grunted, but before she could respond, he pushed to his feet. "I have some matters to attend to, I'm afraid."

She swallowed hard. "About me?"

"Yes," he said. "About you. And other issues. I'll be gone most of the day, but you ought to explore the house at your leisure. The garden behind is a bit wild, but it should also be sheltered enough to be safe for you. My staff has been told to provide anything you might require."

She pushed to her own feet. "Anything?" she repeated.

His dark gaze dilated further. "Within reason. I'll see you later tonight." He moved to the door and there he paused, turning back toward her and letting his gaze roll over her in a slow wave. "Good day, Imogen."

"Good day," she repeated to his retreating back.

When he was fully gone from the room, she sat back down at the table with a thud. She was utterly confused. Fitzhugh was seductive and something close to kind, but he also shut her down with an ease that spoke of practice. He apparently had no interest in discussing what had happened between them the previous night. She had to assume that also meant he didn't wish to repeat it.

A fact that left her a little empty.

"A great deal empty. Foolish girl," she corrected herself out loud as she reached across the space and grabbed for the paper he had abandoned. She smoothed its wrinkled edges and tried to focus as she lost herself in the news of the day.

If he could be so nonchalant about the entire thing, so could she. It just might take a little practice.

~

Oscar stepped through the doors of Fitzhugh's Club and nodded to the butler who handled all the greeting and vetting. "Good afternoon, Goodworth."

"Sir," the man said with the stiff bow Oscar's patrons loved and he couldn't have cared less about. "Very good to see you again."

"How are things?" he asked. "I realize I was not here the past two nights."

A brief hint of curiosity passed over Goodworth's face, but he didn't pursue what had caused that unusual occurrence. "There is nothing of great interest to report, sir. The past two nights have been mostly quiet. A spirited card game last night, but nothing coldhearted."

"Excellent." He stepped from the neat foyer into the larger study where his patrons did their meeting in the late afternoons, their smoking and gaming in the evenings. It was perfectly put together, of course. That was what he expected.

"Is Will here?" he asked as he moved to the next room, the library. A footman was rearranging books that had been misplaced during the previous afternoon, readying the room for opening in an hour or two.

"Mr. White is in the private office," Goodworth said. "Awaiting your arrival, I think. He requested coffee—would you prefer tea?"

"No, coffee is fine," Oscar assured him. "Thank you. I'll have some things to discuss with you after I meet with him, I'm sure."

"I will not be far then," Goodworth said with another of those short bows before he strode away.

Oscar drew a long breath as he made his way down the hall. This was clearly what he needed, and he was glad he'd come, no matter how hard it had been to leave Imogen a short time before. But *this* was his life, not the stolen moments with her.

That was just fantasy. He had to remember that when her moans were stealing his senses and her bright smile was making him feel lighter. God, that smile. She hadn't flashed it until earlier at the breakfast table, and God's teeth but it lit her up. Made him feel like the sun had burst through the doors and into his house. Bright enough to burn everything in his life down.

He'd best be careful not to let her.

He opened the study door and let himself into the room. It was as fine as the rest of the club, though perhaps a little less ostentatious. Neither he nor his partner, Will White, were the kind of men who needed to show off for each other.

Will was sitting at his desk on one side of the big room, head bent over a ledger. Numbers had always been his strong suit, so he took care of all the books, from membership to financial. Oscar smothered a smile at the way his friend's gray hair was stuck up at an odd angle, probably from running his fingers through it while he concentrated.

Will was twenty years older than Oscar. Oscar had known him almost all his life, since he was eight and Will had briefly taken on the role of his mother's protector. While he often resented the men in and out of their home, ones who normally ignored him or were actively hostile...Will had been different.

Will had become a friend, a father figure. A partner eventually, when he asked Oscar to take a place at his side at his club. They'd renamed it Fitzhugh's, mostly because White's was already rather famously taken.

But Will was the heart of the place.

"Do you ever rest?" he asked as he entered the room.

Will looked up, a twinkle in his blue eyes. "Do you?"

"I've been away from the club for two nights, I will tell you," Oscar said as he sat down at his own desk across the room.

Will's eyes narrowed as he looked at Oscar. Even halfway across the room, he felt him judging. Reading. Will had been one of the few in his life capable of doing so. One of the few he trusted enough to allow it.

"You're troubled, not rested," Will said, getting up and crossing to him.

Oscar set his jaw as he tried desperately not to think about the reasons he wasn't well rested. Why he was *troubled*, as Will put it. But he couldn't help letting his mind wander to Imogen. To drawing her pleasure from her until his entire body shook with wanting her. To being taken in by that smile this morning.

He blinked to clear it all away. "I suppose trouble is a constant, isn't it?"

Will shook his head. "Not like this." He leaned forward. "What's going on? Club issues?"

"No. You run all the true matters so perfectly that I'm hardly more than a figurehead. The club is fine," Oscar said.

Will's lips parted. "Something with your mother, then? Is Joanna not well?"

Oscar smothered a smile. Will and his mother had parted ways decades ago, but Will had remained a friend. Perhaps the best one his mother had. He appreciated that. "Mama is fine. You probably saw her yesterday, yourself. You would know better than I her state of mind."

Will shifted slightly, but then his gaze refocused. "If it isn't the club or your family, then what is it?"

Oscar sighed. Will knew a great deal about his life. He'd always been a dependable confidante, and since what Oscar was doing might very well impact their shared business, he felt he owed it to him to be honest.

"I went back to the Cat's Companion two nights ago," he said.

The reaction was swift and emotional. Will pushed out of his chair and slammed both palms on the desk. "Oscar!"

Oscar flinched. Will only called him by his first name when he was in trouble. Rather like a child, actually, but he supposed old habits died hard.

"You don't need to give me the whole set-down," he said, holding up a hand. "I know your feelings on the matter."

"You know but you clearly don't care," Will said. "Louisa has been gone for months, Fitzhugh. She's been *dead* for months. Our sources are very clear on that, even if the details are fuzzy. What purpose can you have in going there except self-torture?"

"I want the truth," Oscar said through clenched teeth. "I want justice."

Will's expression softened. "You saw things as a boy that made you protective of women in your mother's position. I wish you hadn't. But you know, having grown up as you did, that sometimes there isn't justice available for women labeled fallen. It's incredibly unfair. But it is the way it is. Fight for laws to change it."

Oscar clenched his jaw and stared at his fist clenching in and out on the desktop. He was trying to keep his tone neutral as he said, "You may or may not be right. I'm not going to argue the facts with you. We've already done that so many times that I could probably tell you your arguments verbatim and you mine. I wouldn't have mentioned it to you at all except…"

He trailed off. Telling Will about most things was easy. But there was something about telling him about *her*, about Imogen, that felt much harder.

"Except?" Will encouraged, his tone gentle now.

"A woman ran out of the brothel and into my arms," Oscar admitted. "She'd witnessed a dead body, overheard that the Earl of Roddenbury had killed the poor girl. She was seen and had to run. And I'm… I'm protecting her now."

"Protecting?" Will breathed.

"Not a protector. Not like that." Oscar hesitated, for he'd certainly touched her as a protector would. Kissing her and touching all that lovely, silky softness was most definitely in the realm of lover.

As was his pulsating desire to do it again and again and again.

"True protection," Will said, oblivious to Oscar's thoughts.

"They want her dead, too," Oscar said softly, trying to push back the pure rage that accompanied that statement. "I've decided to take on her plight. Try to find a way to bring these bastards to justice at last."

Will flopped back in his chair and stared at Oscar for a long moment. At last he let out his breath in a long whistle. "The Earl of Roddenbury. Could that be true?"

"She seems certain."

"If he is involved—do you really think anyone will give a damn?" Will asked. "You know how that world works. They'll protect their own, justice be damned."

"I fear that may be the case," Oscar admitted.

"Then the best thing you can do for this girl is to help her make herself a new identity and get her out of London."

He flinched at the idea of that. Destroying her life to protect it. He didn't want it to come to that. "Perhaps *they* might believe her if I could find the right evidence. Or find the right person to tell," Oscar insisted. "She's a lady, Will. Or she...she was. She's the widow of Warren Huxley. He was a member here. Died last year."

Both Will's eyebrows went up. "I admit I don't have the kind of memory you do, where you can remember the details of a person with just one meeting. But I have some faint recognition of the name. How did she fall so far?"

Oscar flinched. "Bad husband. Bad family. The usual ways a lady falls." He frowned. "I know the guard is useless and that Society chooses what and who it deems important. It always has."

Will cocked his head. "You disdain them, but you make your money at their feet."

Oscar shrugged. "We often disdain what gives us advantage, I suppose. I never claimed to be better than anyone else in that regard."

"What do you need from me?"

He met Will's eyes. "You would help me even though you disapprove of this obsession." He shook his head before his friend could speak. "Of course you would. I admit I'll be...distracted by this for a while."

"I can be present here," Will assured him. "Would you like me to look at the records of members like Roddenbury and Huxley?"

"Yes, that would be helpful," Oscar said. "I doubt there will be anything there to assist, but more information is always good. I'll be making discreet inquiries, myself. So if you come upon any helpful connections I can seek out, I'll take those, as well."

"And what about this young woman, Mrs. Huxley?"

Oscar licked his lips without meaning to do so. There went his mind again, back to the weight of her leg across his own, to the way her back arched as he slid his fingers into her wet heat. To the shuddering pull of her body as she came against him. To the taste of her, sweet and salty as he lewdly licked her away and watched her tremble in response.

"I don't want to confuse things, like with Louisa," he said, his voice too rough.

"So you're interested in her, then?" Will asked gently.

Not gently enough. Oscar glared at him. "Don't go matchmaker on me," he warned.

"I wouldn't dare," Will said with a chuckle. "You're a bad catch, aren't you?"

He teased, for Oscar had said that many a time. Today it hit him in the chest and he nodded slowly. "I always have been. I'm going to gather a few things here, contacts and the like, and speak to Goodworth before I go. But I'll check in with you in a few days. Call on me or write if you find something in the interim."

"Of course," Will stood and extended a hand. They shook, and Oscar grabbed a few items from his desk before he headed for the door. As he reached it, Will called out, "Oh...and you should speak to your mother, you know."

Oscar pivoted back. Will was looking at him down his nose, a bit of judgment in his stare. "You were right when you said I've seen her more recently than you have."

Oscar rolled his eyes. "I know, I know. I'll call on her. Goodbye."

"Goodbye." Will's laughter rang in Oscar's ears as he walked away.

CHAPTER 8

I f Imogen had been confused when Oscar left her at the breakfast table, three days later she was absolutely flummoxed. The man had been almost invisible since their last passionate encounter in her bed.

Oh, she occasionally saw him as he slipped from the house, off to do some vague business, as the servants called it. Once he had passed her down a hallway before bed. She'd thought he might say something then. His dark eyes had tracked her as he said her name. But nothing. He had gone to his chamber and that was that. Certainly, he hadn't eaten with her. He hadn't spoken to her beyond a cursory 'good day'. He hadn't come back into her room to soothe her if she had nightmares.

It was almost as if he were hiding from her. This man who was so controlled, so commanding of any space he entered...hiding from *her*.

And what could she do about it? She couldn't go home. It was far too dangerous. She couldn't exactly receive callers here to pass the time or distract her from the odd dance she and Oscar had begun and that he had abandoned so abruptly.

Instead, she spent her time exploring the house and garden. Reading the man's books and examining any notes he'd made in the margins to try to determine who he was at heart. Asking questions of his servants, who were always incredibly kind, but also intensely close-lipped about the man who paid their wages.

"Good evening, Mrs. Huxley."

She started and turned from the fire where she'd been pondering her situation to find the butler, Donovan, standing in the doorway. "Good evening."

"I trust your supper was to your satisfaction," he said, as kind as always.

"Yes," she said with a smile to reassure him. "Mrs. Lesley is a fine cook and I've enjoyed all her wonderful food since my arrival. Tonight's pheasant was perfection. Please make sure you tell her."

"I shall, and I know she will be pleased to hear it. She enjoys cooking for a guest," Donovan said. He shifted as if uncomfortable. "Do you have anything else you require? There's a nice brandy there on the sideboard if you'd like a drink."

She pursed her lips. "No, thank you. Do you know if Mr. Fitzhugh will be joining me this evening?"

She blushed as she asked the question. One that revealed far too much. Donovan didn't react, though. Too well trained, she supposed, though she wondered what in the world the servants said about her below stairs.

"I'm afraid not," he said gently.

She folded her arms as frustration rose up in her chest. Dratted man. She fought to maintain at least an image of control as she asked, "Do you know why?"

"Why?" Donovan repeated, as if he didn't understand the question. She wasn't certain if he was being purposefully obtuse or if he truly wasn't accustomed to anyone questioning Oscar.

She pursed her lips. "Yes, *why*. I saw him arrive before supper and I don't believe he's left the house since then. Does he take his food in his chamber or his study to avoid me? Has he expressed displeasure in having me here, intruding upon his life?"

The butler's gaze flitted away a fraction, and that was her answer.

So she wasn't imagining things. Oscar *was* avoiding her. And it shouldn't have mattered. After all, she hardly knew the man. Their wildly inappropriate night in her bed aside, she had no attachment to him. He was helping her and that was all there was to it.

No, it shouldn't have bothered her, but she was bothered nonetheless. But that wasn't the poor butler's fault. He certainly didn't have the answers she required, not truly. Only Oscar himself could speak to his own mind.

"Thank you, Donovan," she said through gritted teeth. "You have been very patient and I don't need anything else."

He looked as troubled as he did relieved to be let off the hook in answering her. Still, he didn't press the issue and bowed away, leaving her alone. For a moment, she went back to staring the fire, clenching and unclenching her fists at her sides as she thought about Oscar creeping around his own house, trying to make certain she didn't see him.

It was ridiculous. If his mind or heart had changed when it came to housing her, she needed to know. She needed to make some other arrangement, whatever that might be.

She needed to understand if she'd done something to offend him. And the best way to handle all of that was head on.

She pivoted on her heel and strode from the room, down the hall and to his study door. It was closed, but she could see light dancing beneath it, which meant the fire was high and likely the lamps were lit. He was in there. Alone. And this was the perfect opportunity.

She lifted a trembling hand, girded all her strength, and knocked. There was a beat of hesitation, and then Oscar's voice came from the other side. "Enter."

She did so and took in a deep breath as she did so. This was one of the few rooms kept locked during the day, one of the few rooms she hadn't yet seen in her exploration of the house.

It was wonderful. Large and warm, with dark wood paneling, a fine expensive, wallpaper and a huge fireplace. Its mantel rose all the way to the top of the ceiling and was lined with stones. A dark and sophisticated room which fit the man sitting at the cherry wood desk, quill in hand, still focused on the papers before him.

"And she's fine, then?" he asked.

She blinked. He hadn't even looked up at her. He thought she was Donovan, and now the reason for the butler's concern for her was more obvious. Oscar had sent him to check on her.

"*She's* standing right here," she said softly. "Ask her yourself, or are you too cowardly for it?"

He jerked his gaze up and his knuckles whitened around the quill. He slowly rose as he set the writing instrument away. "Good evening, Imogen."

"Excellent," she said, pushing the door shut behind her and folding her arms. "You recall my name."

He arched a brow at her cheek, and for a moment she lost her breath. It was very irritating that he could spear her in place with just one look. With just one stern frown. It made her forget herself and in this situation that was not what she needed to do.

"So you are angry with me," he said, his tone not revealing his reaction to that observation.

"No." She shifted her weight. "Yes."

"Very confusing. Is it no or yes?"

"Yes!" she snapped. "I *am* angry. Or at least...irritated. Or maybe it's confused?" He was staring at her now like she wasn't making sense, and she supposed she wasn't. Drat and damn the man for being so disquieting. She drew a breath and started again. "I appreciate all you're doing for me. I assume you have been working on my...my situation."

A shadow crossed his expression, troubled and dark. "I have," he said softly.

"And that means a great deal. I'm not trying to be ungrateful."

"But..." he encouraged her.

"But I have hardly seen you in three days," she gasped out. "Not one shared meal, not one conversation. I'm going mad in these halls,

Mr. Fitzhugh, and I have no idea where I stand with you. Are you annoyed with me? Do you regret helping me?"

"No." It was one word, eased out slowly and with no other explanation.

She threw up her hands. "It's because of what happened between us, isn't it?"

The words left her mouth and she clapped a hand over her lips, but it was too late now. She had been imprudent in her irritation. Said the thing she'd promised herself she wouldn't. Brought up the moments that had been haunting her for three long nights.

He was stock still for what felt like an eternity. Then he slowly came around the desk and eased toward her a few steps. His gaze never left hers, and she was frozen by the force of that look and the powerfully attractive man behind it.

She'd never known anyone with such command.

"You want to talk about that night," he said.

"No." She said it as an instinct. "Yes. No."

"Confused again?" he teased, though it was gentle.

"If I am, it's because you make me so," she said.

He blinked and actually looked chagrined. He bent his head. "I *have* been avoiding you, you're not mistaken in that assessment."

"Did I do something...wrong?" she asked, and found herself moving a small step closer. Now they were no more than an arm's length apart, and it took all her will power not to reach out and brush the tips of her fingers along the hard angle of his jaw.

"No," he said. "*I* did. I shouldn't have come into your room that night. I certainly shouldn't have kissed you. I shouldn't have spread your legs and made you come. I shouldn't keep thinking about all those things. You are here for refuge, not for...not for all the things I want to do to you. So I'm avoiding you because if I don't, it will go far further than what happened the other night."

Her lips parted. She'd been picturing a hundred reasons for his distance, but never this. Never that he wanted her that same way she wanted him. Never that he was fighting that or that he was losing the battle.

She licked her suddenly parched lips and reached out. They both watched her seeking fingers extend toward him, and when she brushed against his hand, they let out a sigh in unison. She heard the ragged desire in his breath, saw it in his eyes, felt it in the way he leaned toward her. He was a coiled spring, wound so tightly that he could pop at any moment.

She trembled at the thought.

"I don't want you to avoid me," she whispered.

"I'm fire, Imogen," he said, and caught her seeking fingers. He threaded them between his own, unthreaded them, repeated the action. Such a simple touch, someone might even label it as innocent. But the reaction it caused was anything but. She felt like she was melting under the very heat he contained.

"I don't mind being burned," she whispered. "It's impossible not to want to risk it when you're standing there, staring at me like you want to eat me."

His pupils dilated. "Eat you," he murmured. "Now there is a wonderful idea."

He caught her waist and drew her against him. Her air left her lungs, but it didn't matter. Not when his mouth came down against hers. She didn't need air or water or food, just this. Just him and the way he pushed her back toward the desk. He was forceful, rough, and she had no choice but to simply fall into the current of his desire and let it sweep her away.

He caught her hips, dragging away from her mouth and watching her as he lifted her onto the desk. "You want this?" he rasped, his breath short, his voice dark and deep and dangerous.

Perhaps she should have hesitated. Perhaps she should have refused. But she didn't. "Yes."

He asked nothing more, but caught her chin and held her firm as he kissed her yet again. She lifted against him, clinging to the lapels of his jacket as he reached behind her and pushed the items on the desk away. He lowered her back on the hard surface, his mouth dragging to her throat. He sucked hard there, and she dug her fingers into his hair with a gasp, holding him steady against her flesh.

But he didn't stay for long. He dragged his mouth lower, over her still-clothed breast, her stomach, her hip. He hooked his hands behind her knees and tugged her to the edge of the desk. She leaned up on her elbows, staring at him. He held her stare with even certainty and she trembled from head to toe.

There was something infinitely wicked in those dark eyes that normally were so unreadable. Her sex twitched at the sight of it, her legs shook. She couldn't look away as he dragged a chair closer and took a seat. When he opened her legs and pushed up her skirt, she was bared to him. Right there at eye level.

She blushed, resting back on the desk a moment so she wouldn't have to watch him watch her in this most private place. She felt him do it, though. Felt the heat of his stare sweep across her with as much intensity as his fingers had a few days ago.

She flexed out of pure instinct and he made a rumbling sound deep in his throat. A growl, something possessive and animal. Then his mouth dropped between her thighs and he licked her pussy.

She jolted. If it had been a long time since she had a man inside of her, it was even longer since one did that. And her husband hadn't had the beard, which scraped along her sensitive flesh and brought her to the edge almost immediately.

He swirled his tongue around her clitoris, sucking until she gripped at the edge of the desk for purchase. Then he backed away, teasing and tormenting every fold of her flesh. She found herself lifting into him, sitting up to cup his head, hold him tight to her as she ground against him in desperation. He clenched her backside, rocking her more firmly against his mouth as he sucked and licked, spearing her with his tongue between tormenting her clitoris. The pleasure built, a wall he crafted with every sweep of his tongue. She wanted it. Wanted him to give her that release more than she wanted anything else in the world.

In that moment, nothing else existed but this. That was the true gift. When he did this, she forgot all the rest and surrendered purely to sensation.

"Please," she heard herself moan as she gripped his shoulders with her thighs. "Please, please."

He looked up at her without slowing his pace. Those dark eyes snared hers, holding steady, never wavering. She bucked against him, her entire body tingling, her legs shaking. And then he sucked her harder, faster, and the pleasure rocked her. She cried out, jerking against him so hard she feared she'd harm him. But he didn't slow. He gave her no quarter, tucking her tighter to his mouth, tormenting her even as she quaked and begged and wept with release.

It felt like it went on for a lifetime. That it would never end because he had no desire to end it, and she surrendered, relaxing back, smoothing her hands over her breasts through the silky gown as her moans eased and the twitching spurts of pure sensation slowed.

Only then did he pull away. He leaned over her, caging her in with his hands, his lips and beard glistening with her release. She reached for him, drawing him down to her, tasting herself on his mouth. She had no idea what would happen next, but she didn't want this to end. Even though she had no idea what that meant for her, for him, and for the future beyond the next moment.

CHAPTER 9

Oscar had been with a great many women. Sex had never been something he'd been taught to keep as a secret or a shame. When he wanted, he took. He'd kept mistresses and had shorter affairs over the years. He saw no shame in pleasure, as long as it was given and received by both parties.

But he'd never felt so out of control in any of those affairs as he did in this one with Imogen. Even now, as he caged her in on the desk, she didn't just kiss him. She licked her essence from his lips and his cock jolted. God, how he wanted to fuck her.

Instead, he pulled away, grabbed her hand and tugged her to a seated position. He couldn't think straight right now. He needed to think.

She shook her head as he reached out to draw her skirt back down over her legs. "I've never met a man like you."

He backed up a step. "I would wager that's true. You are accustomed to gentlemen."

"You think you're not that?" she asked, tilting her head and meeting his stare. There was nothing artful about her, it seemed. She was never trying to gain some advantage by anything she did. That was such a rare thing that he almost didn't know how to respond to it.

Perhaps that was why it was more prudent to walk away.

"I'm *not* that," he said. "I'm the first bastard son of the Duke of Roseford."

"Roseford," she repeated, and her surprise was plain on her face.

He tried not to let his pain be as plain on his own. "Ah, yes. The world knows of his twisted legacy. Of the bastard seed he spread all across the country. I am many things, but a gentleman is not one of them."

She wrinkled her brow. "Is that meant to…to shock me? To make me think differently of you? I really don't care about your birth, Oscar. And I think a gentleman is more made by his actions than his blood. You have shown yourself to be that by saving my life. And by the way you have pleasured me twice and seem to have no interest in claiming your own release, despite the fact that you are quite clearly…" She blushed and motioned toward his groin. "Aroused."

He tilted his head. This woman had done nothing but surprise him from the moment she'd careened into his chest and altered the very carefully charted course of his life. She was facing dangerous and terrifying circumstances, and yet she still maintained humor and elegance in their face. It wasn't out of some blindness to the situation, but it seemed her character was to make the best of whatever would come.

And she certainly confronted him without flinching. That wasn't something many men did easily. Oscar had ensured that, by creating a persona meant to intimidate. But she was waving at his cock without hesitation and calling him a *gentleman* of all things.

It was extremely unsettling. Not terrible. Just…unexpected. And it made him want her more, which was outrageous because how was it possible? Wanting her had become a constant drumbeat in his head, distracting him from everything else.

He cleared his throat. "You say I have no interest in fucking you." He used the lewd term on purpose, and she flushed at it, but didn't turn away.

JESS MICHAELS

"You haven't, despite multiple chances," she said. "What else am I to assume?"

"Assume nothing," he said. "Because you are very wrong. I *want* you, Imogen. I burn from wanting you. I cannot sleep from *wanting you.*"

Her lips parted and she sucked in her breath with the same little sound she made when he touched her pussy. God, how he loved that sound.

"Oscar," she whispered, and he reveled in his name rolling from her lips.

"I have avoided you these past few days not because I didn't want you, but because I fear I want you too much," he continued, because he needed to say it. To lay it out on the line for her so she could make an informed decision about what to do next. He owed her that, especially considering what she'd been through. "I have avoided you because I didn't want to...bully you into entering into an affair with me that you don't...want. That you feel you must be party to because you owe me a debt of some kind."

Her gaze softened and then slid down to look at him. His body. His cock, which was not helping the situation down there in the slightest. He felt hard enough to pound nails, it almost hurt.

"*Would* there be an expectation that I owed you, that it was a quid pro quo, if you...if you..." She huffed out a breath and her cheeks turned apple red. "...fucked me?"

He gaped at her a moment and then managed to get himself back together. "No. If we became lovers, it would be out of mutual desire. I wouldn't want anything less."

"Well, you know I...want you." Her voice got softer on those final two words. "You must see it. You must feel it. You're so much more experienced than I am."

"And I hesitate in part because of that. If we're to be lovers, you must know that I am *intense.*"

He looked down at her, his heart throbbing. To his surprise, she tipped her head back and let out a peal of laughter that echoed in the quiet room.

He pursed his lips, even though the sunshine sound of her laugh was fascinating beyond measure. "Are you mocking me, Mrs. Huxley?"

"Not at all," she said, smiling up at him, as if his stern command meant nothing to her. He'd never met a person who reacted to it that way before. "I only laugh because the fact that you're intense is fairly obvious. You acted as though that was new information and it is most definitely not."

He shook his head. "Intense when I look at you at supper and intense when I take you to bed are two different things, Imogen. In bed I like things...rough. I might hold you down, I might scrape my teeth along your skin until you feel the faintest bite of pain along with the pleasure, I might slap your arse until it burns, I might..." He stepped forward and extended a hand, letting his fingers rest against her throat. "I might do this, but a little harder, as I pound into you."

Her pupils dilated and she leaned into his hand, forcing his grip to tighten that tiny fraction that took it from gentle to something else. Her breath whispered from her lips in a soft sigh, and she nodded. "I... don't have experience in those things, you're right about that. But when you say them, I feel nothing but curiosity. Nothing but a desire that I suppose I should be ashamed of."

He dropped his hand away from her neck and tilted his head. "Why? Why should you be ashamed about wanting the same thing I've already confessed I want? Why should you be ashamed about what you want at all? You have as much a right to pleasure as anyone else, Imogen. Don't let anyone ever tell you otherwise."

Her mouth twitched, her expression softened, and for a moment it was quiet between them. He had no idea what was going on in that mind of hers, but at last she stepped forward, closer yet again to him. Almost tight to his chest.

"How long would an affair last if we were to enter into one?" she asked.

He cleared his throat, trying to find words around the lump that had suddenly formed there. "You were looking for a protector."

She nodded. "Yes. If I survive this—"

He flinched. "You will."

"*When* I survive this," she corrected gently, "my situation will still be the same as it was before. I need a protector, whether that is you or someone else."

"We could see how we suit while you are staying here," he suggested. "I've had mistresses before."

"Yes. Louisa," she said, her tone unreadable.

He ducked his head. "That would be another issue we need to address. Louisa wanted...she wanted something more than I could give. Perhaps it isn't something I'm capable of giving. And I never want to hurt someone like that again, I've seen the consequences."

"Love," Imogen said softly. "She fell in love with you."

He nodded. "Or she convinced herself she did. She wanted me to love her back. And while I was very fond of her, I considered her a great friend...it wasn't enough. She was hurt. She left. And the rest is...well, we're here. And she's gone."

Imogen reached up, cupping his cheek. God, how he wanted to lean into her fingers, to drown in this comfort she gently offered. Somehow he managed to keep himself still.

"I won't fall in love with you," she whispered.

His brow wrinkled at her certainty, and he found himself a little annoyed by the lack of emotion in that declaration. Why, he couldn't say. Her statement was exactly what he wanted. What he needed. If they were to have an affair, it had to be one that excluded the heart.

"If we try something and you don't like it, you need to tell me," he insisted. "If I want you and you aren't in the mood, you need to tell me. Sex should be something we revel in and celebrate and enjoy equally. Will you promise me?"

"You really are entirely unexpected," she said with a little laugh, he thought almost more to herself than to him. "But yes. I promise you I will only do what I like and I will only do it when I wish to. Are those all your terms, Mr. Fitzhugh?"

She extended a hand as if to shake on it, and he stifled a smile. Her cheekiness was so wildly attractive. He was pleased she was becoming comfortable enough, overcoming the terror of what she'd gone through enough, to show it.

He took her hand and raised it to his lips, kissing her knuckles before he traced one with the tip of his tongue. "All my terms. So we are agreed then."

"Are we lovers?" she asked, and looked genuinely confused.

"When we're lovers, I hope you'll be very certain of that fact."

She tilted her head, staring at him so intently that he caught his breath.

"What?"

"You are very handsome, Oscar. Really uncommonly handsome. It's distracting."

He blinked. He'd certainly been called handsome before, cooed over by women in bed or ones that he wanted to get there. But there was something different about this declaration of his supposed beauty. Something that made him turn away, back to his desk.

"I would like nothing more than to seal our agreement in a far more pleasurable way than with a mere handshake, but I wonder if you have some questions for me about your situation."

"Because you've been avoiding me, you mean," she teased gently as she followed him to the desk and blushed as he righted the items that had skidded across it while he pleasured her there.

"Yes," he said, lifting his gaze to hers. "Because of that."

"Have you determined any course of action that might allow me to not hide out for the rest of my life?"

He tried not to reveal his reaction to that question. She was being playful, perhaps to ease her fears, but the suggestion was a real one. It was entirely possible she would have to leave the city, leave her identity behind and anyone associated with it. It wasn't the solution he wanted for her, but there it was.

"I've been working on background on the players," he said. "Roddenbury was once a member of my club, so my partner Will White is collecting some information on his presence there. I've been working on the woman you mentioned, Maggie Monroe. I hadn't heard her name before in association with the Cat's Companion, so I'm trying to figure out where she fits into this mess."

"What will you do once you have the information you need?" she asked.

He clenched his teeth, because that was a more complicated issue. "Why don't we cross that bridge when we come to it?" he said.

She leaned across his desk, placing her hands flat on the top. "Oscar."

He met her stare, saw her fear and her questions. "I'm trying to figure that out, too," he admitted. "The guard is notoriously bad at what it does. And since we're talking about an earl in the mix of all this, it's also entirely corrupt."

She bent her head. "They won't care about the murder. Or about me," she said.

"But I do," he said, reaching out to trace the line of her jaw until she looked up at him with a shiver. "I promise you, Imogen, we're going to work this out."

She smiled at him, but it wasn't that bright sunshine expression he'd come to crave in the short time he'd been exposed to it. This was false, tight, meant to appease him.

"I know you'll try." She turned away and paced across the room to the fire. She stood there, silent, her shoulders rolled slightly forward in a position of defeat. Of exhaustion. Of fear.

He wanted so much to relieve it all. And since the answers he had couldn't do it, he had to do something else instead.

"Come to my bed," he said softly.

She pivoted toward him, her lips parting at his directness. "Oscar—"

"I can't solve the problems of the world tonight," he said as he crossed the room to her in slow, steady steps. "I can't promise you how this story will end. But I can ease the fear for a few hours, Imogen. I can give you pleasure. I can make you come until you're weak. Come to my bed."

He extended a hand, trying hard not to flex it with excitement as he waited for her to take it. She stared at it a moment, then touched her fingertips to his. She traced his fingers, then the back of his hand. It was all so slow, so gentle, that for a moment he forgot he was trying to seduce her.

Instead, *he* was seduced. He stared as she caught his hand between hers at last, lifting it. Her gaze caught his, holding steady as she kissed his fingertips, the back of his hand, the inside of his wrist. Then she pressed his hand to her heart. He felt it throbbing under the softness of her breast.

He wanted to make it throb even harder.

"Take me to your bed," she whispered as she lifted to her tiptoes and brushed her lips to his. "Please."

He caught her waist then, overcome by the desire she created in him. He dragged her hard against him, his fingers clenching against the middle of her back as she arched against him. He dropped his mouth, reaching for control, fighting for it with every part of his body. And then he kissed her. Soft at first, harder, then out of control as he tasted her tongue and felt the need in her grow as fast and as hot as his own.

"Come on," he gasped as he broke the kiss and threaded his fingers through hers. "Let's go."

CHAPTER 10

O scar hadn't stopped touching her the entire time they moved
through the house together. His fingers had gripped her hip,
he'd pinned her against a wall for another of those drugging kisses,
he'd brushed her backside with his hand until she stumbled. But now,
as he opened the door to his chamber, he stopped pushing and
allowed her to enter the room without him herding her forward.

She took in the room as she did so. Unlike the study, which was
done in dark tones, his chamber was unexpectedly light. White linens,
lighter woods, like this place was a reprieve from the mask he wore.
The one of command and control and dark intentions.

Dark intentions that became clear again as they looked together
toward the bed on the wall opposite the door. A very big bed, indeed.
Her breath caught as she looked at it, then at him.

"Still like the terms of your bargain?" he asked, arching a brow
almost in challenge. As if he expected her to find some means of escape.

Instead she began to unfasten her gown. "I suppose we'll find out
in a moment, won't we?" she asked.

His eyes went wide. "Far more than a moment, my dear. We really
must raise your expectations."

She laughed and her fingers fumbled against her buttons. She hadn't anticipated this side of him, playful, teasing...but she liked it. Possibly too much.

Luckily he didn't allow her any time to revel in it or explore it. He grabbed her elbow and tugged her against him. The playful lover was gone. The dark and dangerous one had returned, and she caught her breath just before his mouth found hers.

The kiss was knee-shaking. He'd kissed her before, of course. So many times in such a short period, and every time she'd been swept away. But this was different. This time when she kissed him, she no longer felt the wheels of his control holding them steady. He was no longer trying to protect her from his desires, from the ultimate end that would involve their bodies merged and their sweat combined as they writhed together.

His purpose was very clear and her knees went entirely weak, as if she were in some fairytale. But this wasn't a prince with his arms around her. As he tugged her hips tight to his and ground the hard evidence of his desire against her, she realized she was with the beast. A thrill of fear fluttered in her stomach at that thought, but it didn't make her want to pull away.

She liked it. All those dangerous things this man represented, all the desires he promised to stir with ruthless intent...she wanted it. She wanted him. She wanted it all now.

As if he sensed that, he pulled away from the kiss and stared down at her. His fingers wrapped around the edge of her gown, where she'd begun unfastening herself, and the fabric gaped. He held her stare and tugged, ripping the fabric, sending buttons flying.

"Oscar!" she gasped, half a laugh, half an accusation.

He tugged the fluttering fabric around her arms, twisting it just enough to trap her with it, but not enough to hurt. "I'll have another made for you," he whispered, his tone harsh in the quiet. "I'll have twenty of them made so I can rip them all off one by one."

She shivered at those words, at the utter disregard for propriety or expense or anything but what he wanted. He hesitated and his gaze softened. "Is it too much?"

She blinked up at him. "Why?"

"There is a strange expression on your face."

She smiled at his concern, the thing that belied his animal dominance in an instant. "I was just analyzing how much I enjoy having my clothing ripped off, even though I liked that gown," she admitted.

"Don't analyze it," he said, dropping his mouth into the crook where her neck and shoulder met and sucking hard enough that she gasped. "Just give in. Feel it. Enjoy it. You don't have to do a damned thing, Imogen. Just let me give you pleasure."

Her knees buckled, but she wasn't certain if it was because he was doing magical things with his tongue against her skin, or because he offered her a respite from having to manage her entire life. When was the last time someone had taken care of her? When she hadn't had a thousand duties or fears or obligations?

He was suggesting she could put it all down while in his bed. Suggesting she could be free of everything but sensation.

He reached around, and to her shock, swatted her backside. Hard enough to tingle, not hard enough to hurt through the fabric of her gown.

She jerked her face toward his and he arched a brow. "Stop thinking, Imogen," he ordered.

For a moment they stood there, eyes locked, and then she couldn't help but smile. "Yes, Mr. Fitzhugh."

"Bloody hell," he muttered beneath this breath. "Be careful with that, Imogen. I want to have a little control tonight."

He didn't allow her to respond, but tugged the rest of her torn dress away to flutter around her feet. The chemise beneath was short, just skimming her thighs, with thin straps and an extremely low neckline. She was practically naked now before this man.

And he was staring at her like she was a banquet to be savored. She swallowed hard under his stare. She'd been trained her entire life not to be too showy, that her nudity was a shame except in brief glimpses for a husband. She'd been fighting that as she tried to come to terms with a future as a mistress.

Right now she threw the entire concept out the bedroom window. When he looked at her, she wanted to arch her back. She wanted to let him see it all.

She trembled as she slipped the strap of the chemise off one shoulder. She watched him as she did it, watched his dark eyes dilate. Watched his hands clench at his sides. Heard his breath catch.

She tugged the chemise down, baring her breasts. Lowering it over her stomach. Shedding it at last and kicking it away.

She was naked. With this fully clothed man who looked at her like he could destroy her with a wave of his hand. That wasn't wrong. She already knew he could make her shatter with a curl of his fingers or a flick of his tongue.

She wanted much more than that tonight.

"Great God," he whispered, and reached out almost reverently. His fingertips traced her collarbone, crested down over her breast, fluttered against her stomach. His gaze darkened. "Get on the bed."

She didn't resist the order, just pushed herself onto the high mattress. She relaxed back on the pillows, watching as he divested himself of his clothing in what felt like lighting speed. She stared as each item fell away, revealing a little more of the man beneath the starched cravats and perfectly laid suits.

He was, in a word, a god. It was the only way to describe that lean, lanky frame, wiry with muscle. The kind of body that had been sculpted for years, art that ladies peeked at and giggled behind their fans, trying to determine if such a man truly existed in the world.

Imogen now knew they *did*, and bit her lip as he shucked his trousers down his legs and fully exposed himself.

"Oh," she squeaked, wishing she could be more eloquent, but her mind was addled at present. "That is something."

He chuckled as he palmed his half-hard cock and stroked it. It immediately came to full attention, curling up toward his belly. "You're going to swell my head."

"Which one?" she teased, and got to her knees, crawling to the edge of the bed.

He moved toward her, never looking away as she touched his chest. They both sucked in a breath as she slid her hand down, down over his stomach, down over the vee of his hips, and across the hard expanse of his cock.

His eyes came partly shut as she stroked him from root to tip and repeated the action a few times. He rocked into her, low, needy sounds coming from deep within his chest. She gobbled his reactions up greedily because they meant she had power. Power to move this remarkable man the same way he moved her. She wanted that tonight after twice having received pleasure without giving it.

She wanted so desperately to unwind this man, to shatter him like she'd been shattered. So she bent her head, letting her dark hair fall around them, letting it tickle his cock before she darted out her tongue and stroked him with it.

Immediately he made a hissing sound that sizzled like hot grease in the room. His fingers came into her hair, wrapping the long locks around his fingers and tugging gently. She felt him watching her as she sucked him, reveling in the warm, clean scent of him, the hard thrust of him as she drew him deeper into her mouth, the way he bucked when she swirled her tongue.

"Bloody fucking hell," he grunted as he began to thrust into her mouth. Slowly, gently, but enough to graze the back of her throat and trigger a slight response in her throat. She backed off, drawing away with a soft pop to look up at him as she continued dragging her hand over his now wet cock.

"Oscar," she murmured.

She didn't get to continue. He stepped forward, pressing his hands to her shoulders and making her fall back on the bed. She pulled her legs out from under herself and he collapsed over her, his mouth hungry for hers as he kissed her so hard and heavy that it felt like the ribbon of his control was stretched far too thin. Almost ready to break.

She wrapped her arms around him, letting her nails scrape his arms, his back, as she lifted up against him so that her pelvis ground against his.

He yanked his head back, and there was the snap of the ribbon. There was the beast hidden beneath control and cravats and careful planning and management of everything around him. She shivered to see that unleashed, shivered at what he might do.

What he did was devour her. He pressed her breasts together and bent his head to lick between them, scraping his teeth against the tender flesh as she writhed with the sensation of pleasure balanced on the edge of pain. He held her down as he dragged his mouth lower. He pushed her legs wide and found her center again, driving his tongue inside as he ground a thumb against her still-sensitive clitoris. She gasped, digging her fingers into his thick hair, grinding up to find pleasure.

But unlike before, he didn't give it to her. He knew how, he'd proven that, but as he smiled up at her, that didn't seem to be the purpose. What he was doing with his tongue, with his fingers, was drawing her up to the very edge of the pleasure. She shook with it, keened for it, her feet flexed as she reached for it.

And then he backed her away from the same edge until she was clawing at him, begging him, wanting what he could provide more than she wanted anything in the world at that moment.

He laughed as he licked her one final time, still not allowing the release. He caught her behind the knees, his fingers tracing patterns there as she writhed, and tugged her to the edge of the bed. He loomed over her, this naked man, his face cloaked in dark shadows that made his dark beard even more of a mask. He stared down at her with wicked intent as he aligned his cock to her ready sex.

He claimed one inch and she clenched at the coverlet with both fists. He was thick, and he stretched her, but it was such a delicious sense of sensation. He claimed another and another, and she lifted toward him, forcing yet more. She wanted all of him. All of him and then she wanted more still.

His expression shifted as he acquiesced. He was watching her so intently, his dark gaze flitting on her face, almost reading her or memorizing her in this moment when she was so damned vulnerable to him.

He dug his fingers into her hips as he fully seated himself, and shuddered out a sigh. The connection of their bodies was perfect, and she gave a sharp cry at how instant and heated the pleasure became. She could come in less than a minute if he kept doing that.

So of course he didn't. Still teasing, he ground against her, then pulled back for deeper thrusts. He fell into that rhythm. Grind, grind until she was desperately on the edge, then long thrusts. She was sweating, panting, calling out his name.

"What do you want, Imogen?" he asked at last, his voice impossibly rough and dark. "Tell me what you want."

"I want to come," she admitted. "I want to come and then I want to make you come."

His eyes widened slightly at the second declaration. As if she'd thrown him off his plan. But it gave her what she wanted. He braced himself on the bed, one hand on either side of her head. He never broke eye contact as he stopped the deeper thrusts and merely rolled his pelvis against hers.

She slid her hands along his spine, down to cup his hips, increasing the pressure of her fingers as if she could control what was happening. The pleasure was right there, so ripe for the picking, so close. But it had been close before and he'd denied it. Would he now?

He answered her question by grinding even harder, and the molten pleasure finally peaked. She jerked against him, her body clenching at his as she came. He continued to work at her, his gaze so focused on her face that she almost got lost in him as the sensation overwhelmed.

It was only when she relaxed back, sated, that he drew almost all the way from her and then took her with a full thrust again.

"You want my release?" he growled. "You want to make me come?"

She nodded. "I do. I want to see it."

He leaned farther over her, threading his fingers through hers as he held her down on the bed. His mouth claimed hers, punishing and hard and filled with all that passion he normally restrained.

And he took her. She'd heard the act described as that before, but had never experienced it in those terms. He *took* with hard and heavy and never-ending thrusts. She gripped her legs around his hips to find some purchase, angling her mouth to suck his throat as he grew more wild and needy.

She felt him close to the edge. His neck strained, his legs shook, and then he pulled out of her and stroked himself once before he came, his come splashing across her stomach as he called out her name into the quiet like it could somehow bring him home.

He collapsed over her, his mouth finding hers as they scooted up the bed, their arms and legs tangling. She cuddled into his side, reveling in the warmth of him, in the strength of his arms around her. In these moments, both the pleasurable and the quiet, it felt like she could be...still. Safe.

Even though she wasn't. She wasn't safe. This thing between them was an illusion in the end. Something temporary, something that would never involve heart or feelings or anything more than this magical meeting of bodies.

She couldn't ever let herself want for more. She'd learned the hard way what kind of pain that brought.

"Your thoughts are so loud," Oscar said, his fingers threading through her hair, stroking against her scalp. "Was I so terrible at bringing you pleasure that you immediately go into analyzing your next move?"

She rolled partially over, her hip thrown over his, her arms against his chest and her chin resting there as she looked up into his face. Good Lord, but he was handsome. Even more so with his hair mussed from sex.

"It certainly isn't that I wasn't well pleased," she said. "I don't think I've ever felt something like that before. Ever wanted release with such a keen sharpness. And when you gave it? I was floating, utterly weightless."

He arched a brow. "But?"

She sighed. "But the facts of my situation are still the facts, aren't they? I've been almost...*avoiding* thinking of them the last few days. Because when I did, I had the physical sensation that I could start screaming and never stop."

He frowned. "I'm sorry."

"It isn't your fault," she whispered. "However, after that...after what we just did, it's almost like the edge has come off the fear. I'm sure it's not permanent. I'm fairly certain that orgasms cannot heal all things."

"I'm willing to test the theory," he teased.

She smiled. "I look forward to that."

"I know what you mean, though. That physical jolt of pleasure..." He shook his head. "Sometimes it feels like it resets everything. If only for a moment. And if that means you can look at your experience without as much fear, then I'm glad of it. And what are your thoughts?"

She brought her attention away from his face for a moment, watching her fingers as she drew patterns across his chest. He was silent as she did so, not pressing her for answers, not demanding she give what she couldn't yet. He just...waited for her.

She appreciated that more than she might have been able to say out loud. To do so felt more vulnerable than spreading herself wide for him had been.

"I am grateful what you're doing for me," she said softly. "Using your time and resources to look for some solution to my predicament. But it is my life, isn't it? And since we have established that you and I can only be lovers, probably only for a short time, I can't just hide in your house waiting for you to sweep in like some hero in a story and save the day. It isn't fair to either of us."

He wrinkled his brow. "What are you suggesting? You can't do this alone, Imogen. You can't go home. It isn't safe."

She felt the harsh edge of panic thrum through her veins and drew in a deep breath to ease it. When she could find her words again, she said, "But I can help you, can't I? I must have a part in what you're doing, Oscar. I can't just wait and trust and hope."

She waited for him to dismiss that thought out of hand. That's what Warren would have done. Had done many times, when she dared to ask for a greater role in her own life. In his.

But Oscar seemed to be truly pondering the suggestion. She could see he was troubled. Of course he would be. The danger he spoke of was real. She'd seen its ultimate consequence.

At last he let out a long, low breath. "What you want is a fair request," he said slowly. "And having your input will likely make navigating this situation easier. I was..." He broke off and his lips pursed. "I have an appointment with a contact tomorrow. I'd like you to come with me. Would that help fulfill your desire to be a part of your own situation?"

She nodded. "Yes. I'd like that."

His hand had been resting against her back as they talked, and now he began to swirl his fingers against her skin in slow circles. She hissed in a breath at the gentle reawakening of her body.

"And now may I fulfill a few more of your desires?" he whispered.

She leaned up his frame, drawing her lips close to his without kissing him. "What did you have in mind?"

He didn't answer with words, but by cupping the back of her head and drawing her in for a kiss. She lost herself in him, forgetting her troubles once more. They would be there tomorrow. Tonight she just wanted pleasure.

CHAPTER 11

O scar smoothed his jacket for what felt like the tenth time since he'd entered the parlor less than five minutes before. It was the most foolish thing, how nervous he was in this moment. He was *never* nervous with the person he'd come to meet.

But then again, he couldn't think of a time he'd ever brought a lady with him to this place. Not that Imogen was with him in this particular moment. He wanted a chance to speak to his contact before she joined them, so she was out on the terrace, enjoying a breath of air before he called her in.

Before he opened her up, and himself up, to all the curiosity he knew would follow.

The door behind him opened, and he turned to face the person entering the room. She was lovely, always so lovely. A regal woman who maintained every ounce of her beauty, even as her hair went gray with the years. She had high cheekbones, the kind of skin women in the *ton* fought for and bright green eyes that at least one poet had written a popular sonnet about ten years before.

Oscar had always wished he'd inherited those eyes rather than his arse of a father's.

"Mama," he said as he crossed to Joanna Fitzhugh.

She had her hands extended and caught both of his, looking him up and down before she pecked first one cheek and then the other. "Not getting enough sleep, are you?"

He shifted under the regard that had always been able to catch him out. He'd been able to hide from anyone but her over the years. Yet another reason not to bring Imogen to Mama. At minimum she was going to know they were lovers without even looking too hard.

"It's not for entirely unpleasant reasons," he said with a chuckle.

She arched a brow as she motioned him toward the settee. She took a place there and patted the cushion next to hers. "I'm glad to hear it. I know you have some guilt about poor Louisa, but that wasn't your fault and I've hated to think of you drowning yourself in work and never just a little bit of fun or pleasure."

"Fun and pleasure," he said with a sigh. "You likely have enough for both of us."

She rolled her eyes indelicately and gave his hand a playful slap. "You just missed Will."

Oscar wrinkled his brow. "I hadn't realized he was calling on you today."

He knew all about their friendship, of course. He'd been very happy when they maintained it, as Will was his favorite protector and their own relationship meant so much to him.

"Was I supposed to keep you apprised of my schedule, love?" she teased.

He laughed at her quip. It was impossible not to. His mother had always been the one to make the best of things and never seemed to dwell overly long on the worst parts of her life.

"I don't think I want to know your schedule," he said with a wink. "I'm just glad you could fit me into it."

"Yes." Her lighthearted demeanor shifted a fraction and he saw the hint of worry she so rarely displayed. "Normally you just come without being so formal. I was a little surprised to hear from you yesterday. And you said something about introducing me to someone, yet you're alone."

He settled back in the settee. "My companion is here. I just asked her to wait on the terrace a moment so I could see you first."

"*Her*," his mother repeated. "The one keeping you up nights, I assume?"

He nodded, for again, there was no use at all in trying to hide the truth from her. "She happens to be the same, yes," he said carefully. "But that isn't why I'm bringing her to you."

For a moment, his mother actually looked disappointed, but swiftly wiped the reaction away. "Then why?"

"She's in a bit of trouble," he said. "And I thought you might be able to help."

His mother pushed to her feet. "You and your broken wings, Oscar. I adore you for caring, but I do worry that this obsession with acting a savior harms you. There must be balance in the world, my dear. One man cannot cure all the ills. Certainly he cannot save all the courtesans."

He pressed his lips together hard. This was an argument they'd had more than once and it wasn't one he wished to repeat at present, not when Imogen was waiting to join them.

"You can write me a letter then, with all your arguments, so I can read it over and over rather than forcing you to waste your breath," he said, flashing her a brief smile so the words would be teasing, not harsh.

"Would reading them help you take them in, I wonder?" she mused, and then let out a sigh of resignation. "What kind of trouble is this young woman in?"

"The kind that had her witnessing the aftereffects of a murder at a brothel last week," he said softly.

That got the response he had hoped for. His mother's eyes widened slightly and her hands clenched before her. "I see," she said softy. "*Real* trouble."

"Real trouble," he repeated.

"Well, let's see her then," she said, rising to ring the bell.

She spoke to her longtime servant, Teeter, when he arrived, and then returned to Oscar. As she looked at him, her expression was closed off. Her courtesan expression, Oscar had always called it. He hated when she used it on him, because it meant she was not allowing him to see her thoughts, but was absolutely making an attempt to read his.

"Don't pull that face," he said, wrapping an arm around her waist and squeezing gently. "I'm very well."

"Hmmm," she murmured, noncommittal.

But he couldn't argue further, because Teeter stepped back into the room and said, "Mrs. Huxley."

Oscar stepped away from his mother and caught his breath as Imogen entered the room. She was wearing yet another of Louisa's old gowns. He really needed to get her new ones, because these were a fraction too tight. Not that he didn't appreciate how they accentuated her curves. The color suited her, an olive-green silk that made her amber eyes jump out even from across the room. Her hair was pulled back, of course, which made him want to cross to her and thread his fingers through it. Take it down and make her messy. Make that nervous expression that was on her face clear away.

He hadn't yet told her who the contact they were meeting was, so he could see her surprise that he was standing so close to his mother. Perhaps a hint of jealousy as she looked from the strange woman she'd not yet met and back to him with question in her eyes.

"Oh, she's lovely," his mother murmured at his side, and then she crossed the room toward Imogen, her hand extended in greeting. "Mrs. Huxley, is it? I'm Joanna. Fitzhugh's mother."

Imogen gaped as the beautiful older woman grasped her hand and shook it firmly. She was stunning with her blast of beautifully styled gray hair and her bright green eyes. Her nose was like Oscar's, her mouth was similar too, except that she was actually smiling.

"I-I am pleased to meet you," Imogen said, and felt her cheeks heating.

"He didn't tell you he was bringing you to see me, did he?" Joanna pivoted away and shook her finger toward Oscar. "Naughty boy."

"I told her we were meeting a contact," Oscar said, looking past his mother toward her. Imogen could see his curiosity when he stared at her. He wondered what she thought of the perfumed cloud of a person standing before her.

"I suppose I am that," his mother laughed.

"Mrs. Fitzhugh—" Imogen began.

Her laughter grew louder at that, and she stepped forward and slid her arm through Imogen's. "Never married, my dear, and I *insist* you call me Joanna. Fitzhugh is correct that I could be a valuable contact into your...situation. After all, I've been a courtesan for decades."

Imogen's eyes went wide. Oscar had said he was a bastard son of the Duke of Roseford the night before, but that man was well known for taking his pleasure all over England. He'd never mentioned the origins of his mother.

"She's retired," Oscar said softly.

Joanna smiled at her and shook her head as she whispered conspiratorially, "I let him believe what he wants to believe."

Oscar let out a low sigh, but when Imogen glanced at him, his eyes were crinkled with humor. Not that she could blame him. This woman, his mother, seemed the kind who could draw mirth from anyone. She was a hurricane and she just swept others up in her wake.

"My head is spinning," Imogen admitted. "I have no idea what to say."

"Come and sit," Joanna suggested, and drew her to the settee by the fire. She all but shoved her into a position and crossed to the sideboard where she poured them all tea. When she returned, she glared at Oscar before she handed Imogen a cup. "Sit down, my boy. Next to the dear girl."

He shot Imogen a glance but did as he'd been told. The settee was so narrow, his legs were forced to bump Imogen's, and she froze when they did. When he even so much as brushed her, she was so aware of him. In his mother's house! On his mother's lounge!

Joanna returned with two more cups of tea, handed one over to Oscar and then settled into a chair that faced the settee. She sipped her tea and stared at them. "You do look well together," she mused. "I definitely see the attraction, Fitzhugh."

"Mama," he growled, and shot Imogen another apologetic look.

Imogen supposed she should have been embarrassed by this unfiltered woman's observations. After all, it was clear she knew Imogen was taking to her son's bed. And that she was tangled up in the worst of situations. And yet she didn't feel judged because of either of those things.

Joanna Fitzhugh was impossible not to like. Direct as she chose to be, she also had the strangest ability to make someone feel...comfortable. It had probably served her very well as a courtesan.

"How did you two meet?" Joanna said.

Imogen looked toward Oscar helplessly. She certainly didn't want to take the lead explaining that loaded subject lest she reveal something to his mother that he wanted to keep secret.

Luckily, he took the initiative. "I was sitting outside the Cat's Companion," he began.

Joanna's expression fluttered and her green gaze slipped down. The bright mask fell and true concern made her look more like a mother for just a moment. "Oh, *Oscar*. You didn't say which brothel."

He ignored the interjection. "And Mrs. Huxley burst out of the doors and into my arms."

Joanna flicked her gaze to Imogen and nodded slowly. "Ah, so you were trying to escape that terrible place. I see now why he might have come to me as a contact. Something happened to you there?"

Imogen shifted. "I...I didn't know how to go about finding a protector," she explained. "And I have fallen so far it is my only hope."

Joanna's expression softened even further. "I understand."

And it was clear she did, even without a bit of further explanation. When their eyes met, Imogen felt the bond between them. Of desperation turned to action. Of reaching for a slender reed of hope and trying to accept how it would change every moment of the rest of one's life.

"But the Cat's Companion is not a place to find a protector," Joanna said gently. "My dear, that is a hole of desperation and danger. A place for nightly pleasures, if you can dare call them that. Not for a permanent arrangement that offers safety and even satisfaction."

Imogen's breath left her lungs in a shaky sigh. "I recognize that now, of course. But I was so desperate and so innocent. I had no idea how to pursue a proper arrangement when my late husband's family was threatening me at every turn."

"Ah," Joanna said. "I see. From a good family then...a very good family. Their insistence at keeping their young women uneducated in the ways of the world is a danger to them in the end. I'm very sorry for your plight, Mrs. Huxley."

"Imogen, please," she said. "If you are kind enough to offer me such ease, I cannot stand not to do the same."

"Imogen," Joanna repeated, and cast a glance toward Oscar. "A very pretty name."

"What do you know about the Cat's Companion, Mama?" Oscar asked softly.

Imogen looked at him and found he had leaned back in the settee. He was the image of casual calm, but she could see the flicker of interest in his dark stare. The tension in his jaw and in the way his hand flexed against the settee back. The dangerous edge to him that was so...alluring.

"Aside from the more personal?" Joanna asked, and arched a brow at her son. "It is a terrible place. Where women go to disappear, at least sometimes."

Imogen caught her breath. "Like...like Louisa. And like that other woman I saw."

Joanna tilted her head. "He told you about Louisa?"

Oscar pushed to his feet and set his half-drunk tea down with a clatter on the side table. He paced to the fireplace and leaned a hand on the mantel. "Imogen saw a woman's body, Mama. Murdered, we think, by the Earl of Roddenbury. Only she was discovered in her attempt to escape."

"Roddenbury." The color drained from Joanna's face in an instant, and she leaned across to take Imogen's hands. "So you are in very great danger."

"And your son has been too kind in trying to assist me. But what can be done? If Society doesn't care about women who make their way on their backs—" She clapped a hand to her mouth as Oscar pivoted to face her. "I didn't mean to offend, Joanna."

Joanna shook her head. "You didn't. It is true that to be a woman in general means our lives are valued less by Society. When the woman spreads her legs to earn her way in the world, many think we are utterly disposable. It's why those in my profession have to look out for each other."

"It's lucky if you have people helping you," Imogen said, wishing her voice didn't waver. "When so few care."

"It is also lucky that not everyone even in the *ton* sees it that way. There has been talk for a few months about the Cat's Companion and those who perform whatever wicked acts there. I know of a pair in the War Department who are investigating the issue."

"Spies?" Oscar said. "The government has taken an interest?"

"Those who would do harm to women, sell them off against their will, kill them as Imogen has been witness to…do you not think they might be involved in other crimes more interesting to the Crown?"

Oscar's cheek twitched. "Of course they only care about that. But in the end, if it shuts down their house of horrors, if it stops the danger Imogen is in, I don't really care about their motives."

Joanna gave Imogen a half-smile. Almost conspiratorial again. As if they both knew that wasn't true. Oscar did care very much. Justice, it seemed, was important to him. And not just for those he knew. Imogen could see now he was frustrated by what ladies such as his mother endured. He must have seen a great deal in his younger life. Enough to make him a defender of those who needed one.

"And I've heard your new brother-in-law's partner has also taken on a related case," Joanna said. "He has that investigation firm, you know."

"Selina's husband?" Oscar asked, his tone suddenly tense. Imogen saw the flicker of interest in his eyes. He had not mentioned his siblings with any specificity before, though it was rumored they were legion, thanks to his father's ways.

"The very one. Derrick Huntington, I believe his name is. His partner's name is Barber."

Oscar's jaw set, and Imogen fought the urge to cross to him and question him further. He was close-lipped about his past, his family, anything personal at all. She wasn't likely going to change that by asking him about anything directly in front of his mother.

"I could reach out to them both."

He stepped toward her. "Mama, is that wise? We don't know any of these men well enough to trust their intentions. I don't want to bring Imogen's safety into question, or your own."

"No, I suppose you wouldn't." Joanna got up and moved to him, doing what Imogen couldn't let herself do. "What if I spoke to the spies, though? I don't have to bring up Imogen or anything about her. Just let me feel them out, since I've already heard some murmurings about them. Given my past, given my reputation, I'm certain they'd like to hear what the network of courtesans knows."

Oscar seemed to consider it. "Take Will with you. To be safe."

"I shall," she said softly.

"Would you like me to speak to him about it?" Oscar asked.

She shook her head. "No. I can manage that perfectly well on my own. But what about the other interested parties?"

"No," Oscar said, firmly and loudly. "I don't want any of my siblings near me. Leave them to their own devices."

He stepped away and went to the sideboard. Instead of getting more tea, he retrieved a bottle from the table and splashed a hearty dash of liquor into a glass. As he downed it, Imogen noted the white-knuckled grip he kept on the bottle.

All of this was very upsetting to him. She didn't fully understand why, but she wished so desperately that she could…help him in some way. Erase it somehow.

"When you do speak to them," Imogen said, "please tell them that the woman who seems to be in charge of things over at the brothel is named Maggie Monroe. She was with the Earl of Roddenbury and the body."

"Maggie Monroe," Joanna repeated. "I'll pass the information along, and do a little asking myself. I have some thoughts about that tidbit."

"Is that everything then?" Oscar asked. "Is there anything else either of you can think of?"

"Nothing comes to mind," Joanna said, and then she smiled at Imogen. "I would like to speak to this one by myself for a moment, though."

Imogen's eyes widened, but as Oscar stepped forward to argue, she shook her head at him. "I would be pleased to speak to your mother alone. She's been so kind as to help me, I have nothing else to hide."

Oscar glanced at her for a long moment, and then he sighed. He moved toward the door, but as he reached it, he turned back. "Be nice, Mama."

And then he was gone, his parting parlay leaving Imogen a little bit unsure of what she was about to face. Only she wanted this woman to like her. Not just because she was so charming, but also because of Oscar. And that was a dangerous desire, indeed.

CHAPTER 12

Oscar hadn't shut the door when he departed, so Imogen watched Joanna cross to the door and did so herself with a shake of her head. "Of course he wouldn't give us privacy," she said with a laugh. "As if he didn't know that I would take it. Silly boy."

Imogen couldn't help but smile. "It is difficult for me to think of your son as either silly or a boy."

Joanna speared her with a glance, even as she returned the smile. "Yes, he's very serious, isn't he? Very dark and dangerous. I'm sure it suits him well in the world. Woman always like danger."

Imogen set her teacup to the side and smoothed her skirts with both hands. "I was more relieved by the fact that he was safe. He has been exceedingly decent to me, Joanna. He is a very good man."

Her expression softened as she took her place across from Imogen again. "He is. I'm proud of him and what he has built himself up to be. He never allowed the past to hold him back. He always fought for more. His success is a great joy to me. Although I do worry about him."

"A mother's prerogative, I suppose," Imogen said.

"Do you know much about Louisa?" Joanna asked.

Imogen tensed. This must be why Joanna wished for privacy. "I-

I'm not sure it would be right to talk about her. She's obviously a diffi-cult subject for Oscar—Fitzhugh."

Joanna laughed. "I know you're bedding him, my dear. You don't have to stand on formality with me. I do admit it's interesting that he allows you to call him by his first name. No one does that, even me, as I'm sure you noticed."

"I did." Imogen blushed, but managed to clear her throat and continue. "As for Louisa, I think he wouldn't like me talking to you about her."

"But you're curious about her, aren't you?" Joanna pressed. "He mentioned her to you. Mentioned that she was lost at the same place you nearly were. That means something, you know. He doesn't talk about her to just anyone."

The meaning of those words sank into Imogen, and a rainbow of different reactions immediately formed. Part of her was warmed by the fact he had trusted her, even with the tiniest of facts, about some-thing he usually didn't share. But part of her was…jealous. She could admit that to herself, even if she wouldn't to anyone else.

Knowing that he cared so much for that other woman that he couldn't bear to speak about her made Imogen jealous.

"He told me he was her protector," Imogen said softly. "And that she wanted…more. She wanted him to love her and when he couldn't, she left. He feels guilty for what happened after, as if changing his heart would have made things different."

"He said that?" Joanna breathed.

Imogen shook her head with a blush. "No. I can just see it."

Joanna held her stare for what felt like a lifetime. Then she nodded slowly. "He holds Louisa up on a pedestal, I suppose because she disappeared…she died…in such a terrible fashion. But she wasn't perfect. And if he feels guilt, that is a shame, because he was never dishonest with her."

"Nor has he been with me," Imogen said. "He's been very direct and upfront with me about what he can and cannot provide."

"And is that enough for *you*?" Joanna asked. "Especially considering where you come from. What expectations you must have had for your life before."

Imogen wrinkled her brow. "How much did Oscar tell you about *me*?"

"Very little," Joanna assured her. "He is close-lipped with even his dear Mama. But if you plan on becoming a courtesan in the future, you will soon learn that divining the truth of those around you is part of the vocation. Would you like to hear my observations, and you can tell me if they're true?"

Imogen wasn't certain she did want that, but she found herself nodding nonetheless.

"You mentioned a husband. I would say dead a little more than a year. You no longer wear his ring, not on any finger and not on a necklace, at least that I can see. So there was perhaps no love lost, or at least there was disappointment in him."

Imogen's eyes went wide. "Yes," she choked out.

"You mentioned his family, their ability to control how you set out in the world to find a protector. And you said you were innocent. That makes me think you came from a family of wealth, privilege. But you are a missus rather than a Lady in your address. So a second or third son. Married off to the same."

"Yes," Imogen said, lifting a hand to her lips.

"You are afraid of changing your life by entering into the trade, likely because your family taught you that to fall is the worst thing that can happen to a woman," Joanna continued. "But I think you are a bit titillated by it too. The idea of pleasure, of freedom to pursue and receive it, is appealing to you."

Now Imogen pushed to her feet, cheeks flaming with heat. "I-I—"

"Too far," Joanna said softly. "My apologies."

"I'm simply not...not accustomed to such frank discussion," Imogen gasped out, pacing to the fireplace and wishing she could make her hands stop shaking. "I suppose I must become so if I truly wish to enter the world you have described."

"Eventually," Joanna said, her voice gentle. She got up and tilted her head, watching Imogen so closely that it felt like she was caged in by the stare. That was certainly where Oscar had learned the technique. "And what about my son?"

Imogen could hardly breathe. "What—what about him? He saved me and he continues to do so. I don't know why."

"Don't you?" Joanna said with a chuckle as her gaze flitted pointedly over Imogen's face. "But no. I think it's more than just your pretty face. There are a dozen pretty faces who could keep him company and *have* kept him company over the years. They never made him..." She trailed off and didn't finish that sentence Imogen suddenly wanted to hear. "I like you, Imogen. I read people, as you can see, because it keeps me safe. And I *like* you. But I can see you have a bit of a broken wing and that has been the kind of thing my son has always gravitated to."

Imogen straightened. "You fear I'm taking advantage?"

"Not exactly. I just hope that you will be able to see that he, too, isn't whole. He hides it very well. Perhaps together you could fill the hurt in each other. Help each other mend." Joanna held her gaze for a long moment, and Imogen realized she wasn't breathing. But at last Joanna blinked. "Don't mind me."

She stepped away, and Imogen sucked a breath into her suddenly burning lungs. Joanna paced back to the sideboard and touched Oscar's abandoned glass before she turned back and gave Imogen another of those dazzling smiles. All her worry was gone in that moment, wiped away and replaced by what felt like genuine kindness and brightness.

Another trick this woman had likely learned through the years of work. Please the companion. Make them comfortable in whatever way fit them best. Adjust to their needs so easily that they never saw the transition.

It was a skill that required a great deal of work, Imogen would wager. And she respected her companion for developing it.

"I am happy to help you," Joanna said. "Now, if you don't mind sending Fitzhugh in on your way out, I'll say my goodbyes to him and see you later after I've had a chance to make my own inquiries."

Imogen blinked. She was being dismissed, gently but firmly. Like a queen might do, actually. She barely kept herself from curtseying as she said, "I will. It was a pleasure meeting you, Joanna."

"And you. I mean it." Joanna's smile was real as Imogen nodded and exited the room into the hall.

Oscar was leaning against the opposite wall, and he straightened up as she stepped out. She blinked up at him, almost too discombobulated to find words. He shook his head at her expression. "Every time," he muttered.

"She—she wants to say goodbye to you," she said.

He snorted out a humorless laugh. "I assumed as much. Will you go to the foyer and ask that our carriage be brought?"

She nodded and tried not to stagger as she moved off toward the foyer. Her brain was spinning, not just with how easily Joanna had read her, but of the glimpses she'd gotten of the future she might live if she continued down the path she was on.

But also she thought of Oscar. Of the kind of man he had become after years of exposure to that life. And Joanna's statement that he, too, was broken under that hard façade.

It made her want to…help him. And that seemed a very dangerous desire, indeed.

"Were you truly compelled to stun the poor woman?" Oscar said as he reentered the parlor. "What did you say?"

He found his mother standing at the window, staring down into the street with a far-off expression. She pivoted toward him with one of her courtesan smiles, the ones that never reached her eyes. "Nothing, my love, I swear to you."

He edged closer. "And what do you think of her?"

She arched a brow. "You care, Fitzhugh?"

They looked out the window together. Imogen was standing on the drive with his mother's servant, talking to him as they awaited the carriage. She looked more on firm ground, at least. No longer so startled as she had been when she left the parlor.

"Of course I care, Mama. I value your opinion and I always have, even if I don't always take your advice."

"I think she is the first lover you have ever formally introduced to me."

He wrinkled his brow. Was that true? No, that couldn't be true. "You met Louisa. You met several of the women in my past."

"Because we ended up at the same opera or party," she corrected. "That isn't the same as bringing her to my home as you did today."

"Because she needs your help," he said, but that answer didn't ring entirely true. There *was* meaning to allowing Imogen into this corner of his life that had always been so private.

He wasn't certain he liked the meaning. The meaning felt too powerful.

"I suppose the more important question is: what do *you* think of her?" his mother pressed.

"She's...unexpected," he admitted, for it seemed the least revealing thing he could say about her.

His mother laughed. "Very good! Unexpected is one of the best qualities in a relationship." She leaned in and bussed his cheek, but when she stepped away, she caught his hand rather than letting him go, and clung a little too tightly. "Please be careful, darling. These people your Imogen has involved herself with...they are the darkest part of my world. It is dangerous, even for you."

"And for you," he said, squeezing her hand gently.

"Then we'll both be careful," she said. "I'll keep you informed about what I find. You do the same."

He kissed her cheek in return and then left her, heading out into the sunshine of the afternoon and the woman who was waiting for him in his carriage.

He only wished he could forget his questions about her, about them...about himself. But they lingered in the back of his mind, and he feared he had opened a box with Imogen that he could not close again.

~

I mogen looked across the carriage at Oscar as the driver turned them onto the main street and set the horses on their merry way back across Town to Oscar's home. In the shadows of the vehicle, his expression was unreadable. All she knew was that he was watching her. Intently. As always.

"I like her," she whispered.

His lips fluttered then, that little hint of a smile, and she could have sworn she saw relief pass over his expression before he pushed it away. It seemed he'd learned that ability at his mother's knee, as well. "I'm glad. She is wonderful. Not normal, but wonderful."

She heard the true affection in his tone. It warmed her. She had never been so close to her own family, nor felt affection between her husband and his parents or siblings. She saw glimpses of it with Aurora and her brother and mother. But even her friend kept secrets from those she loved, and that opened a gap between them.

"How did she—?" she began, and then cut herself off just as swiftly.

His gaze settled on hers, holding there, unyielding. "Become a courtesan?" he said to finish her question.

She nodded slowly. "It's not my business, I know. It's not my place."

"I dragged you to her lair and left you alone with her to be certainly scarred for life by her directness. I think you're owed a question or two. She would answer them as easily as I could. She doesn't consider her past a secret or her life a shame."

"Then how did it happen?" she asked.

"The beginning of her life wasn't that different from that of many girls. She was raised in a good family. They hadn't wealth, but they had some prospects. They were respected. It was assumed she would marry a merchant or a farmer or even a squire, if she was lucky."

His voice was steady and firm. It would have sounded strong to most who heard his words. But she heard something different. She heard the hint of pain there, under the steadiness. The telltale waver that said his mother was right. This man had broken pieces. He hid them well, as well as anyone she'd ever met.

But he was broken. And somehow that made her feel a little better. He was successful and strong and powerful. He'd become all those things even with the cracks. The pain. The loss. The breaks.

Which meant she could do the same. Perhaps they could do the same together.

But no. That was asking for the thing he'd already vowed he couldn't give her. He had asked to be her lover, nothing more. She had agreed to those terms.

"What changed her circumstance?" she asked, returning her mind to the subject of his mother.

"Well, that is all thanks to the great Duke of Roseford," he declared with a bitter tone. His hands gripped against his thighs, and she could feel the tension come off of him in a great wave. "It is, I suppose, thanks to *me*."

CHAPTER 13

There was nothing in the world Oscar wished for more than to be able to tell this story without hearing the crack in his voice. It was why he always avoided speaking about it. About the past. About his father. About his family, outside of his mother.

And yet this bewitching woman sat across from him and asked, just *asked* him…and he found himself telling the story nonetheless.

"He met her at an assembly he attended with a friend. Normally it was only attended by country folk. A baronet was enough to get their hearts to flutter, and here came this duke. One who had not yet cemented his terrible reputation, so he was welcomed."

"How old was she?" she asked softly.

"Eighteen, perhaps? Nineteen? She was out in Society, seeking a husband. And she was *beautiful*."

"She still is," Imogen said with a slight smile.

He shook his head. "She is. She turns heads wherever she goes. But when she was nineteen? She has a portrait of herself from right before she met my father, and there was no way a man like him would have been able to resist her. And in doing so, he condemned her to a much different life."

"Obviously, I only know your mother from a brief encounter

today, after a long life of experiences. So it's hard for me to picture her being taken in. She seems so certain of herself."

"She probably always was a little of that. But she was young. He had not yet married, so I'm sure he convinced her that she would be his bride. And so...she capitulated. She gave in after a short courtship. He had his prize. And he used her, giving no care to her future or her hopes or dreams. And then she found herself with child."

"You," she said, reaching out to cover his knee with her hand.

When she did it, he realized he'd been bouncing his leg up and down. He stared at her fingers, pale against the dark fabric of his trousers. Just the faint pressure of them, and he felt this strange sense of calm.

Enough that he could suck in a great breath and say, "Yes. Me. She begged him to do as he'd said and marry her so that she wouldn't be ruined. And he laughed at her."

Imogen flinched slightly and her fingers tightened against his knee, this time comforting, not just calming. "Poor Joanna."

"Indeed. He told her he would protect her if she chose to continue the affair, but that he would never marry someone with so little worth as she had. She turned to her family, but they were enraged with her for trading away the only thing of value they believed she possessed. She was thrown out on the street. And so, became my father's mistress."

"There must have been repercussions," Imogen said. "She had been of a good family and his seduction seems to have been somewhat public."

"Oh, there were. His reputation as one of the worst men in Society was born through his actions with her. And yet he was still a duke, wasn't he? Rich as Croesus and nearly as powerful as the king. He was untouchable. He used that to his every advantage. Meanwhile, she was labeled as fallen and had to leave behind everything and everyone she'd ever loved to move to a house in London and birth herself a son with a man she had begun to despise."

"But it is clear she doesn't despise *you*," she said. "Her love for you, her pride in you and your achievements, it shines all over her face. You cannot blame yourself for the circumstances of your birth. None of us are responsible for those."

"Perhaps not. But I sometimes wonder what she would have been able to do, what she would have been able to become with all her resourcefulness, if she hadn't had a bastard child to label her a harlot in the eyes of those who had power." He shook his head.

"What she became has power in its own right. It would be impossible not to see it."

That elicited a ghost of a smile to the corners of his lips. "Well, that is true, yes. She was always the kind to take her situation and make the best of it. She might have lost any love she felt for Roseford, but she very much hadn't lost sight of what she could do for herself as his mistress. She negotiated a hefty allowance for herself, and one for me after I was born. She forced him to gift her the home she resides in today, free and clear of his influence, so he could not take it away. It set her up so that when their arrangement ended, a year after I was born, she could have far more choice in what she did next and with whom."

Imogen smiled. "Very resourceful. And what did Roseford think of you? Were you his first child?"

"I was," he said slowly, for this was the part of the story he had never said to any other person. The part even his mother couldn't pry out of him. The part that affected so many of his choices and boundaries and relationships.

Perhaps she heard that in his tone. Perhaps she felt it in the tension that returned to his body, including the knee she was still touching so gently. Perhaps she just...*understood* because that was who she was.

"You don't owe me an explanation," she said.

He shrugged, wishing his feelings were as nonchalant as the action. "I was his first child, his first son. So even though their relationship had ended, even though she had affiliations with other men, he came to see me on a somewhat regular basis. It was made clear to me, even at four years old, that I was not ever going to be acknowledged publicly. But privately he even allowed me to call him Father...except when he demanded I call him Your Grace."

"Did it carry on then?" she asked. "That bond, insofar as it existed?"

"No," he said as he pulled the curtain back and looked out the window. "He married when I was six and had his Robert when I was seven. He told me there was no use for me now that he had his true heir. He never returned."

Her face twisted in anguish. On his behalf, though it didn't feel the same as pity. "Oscar, that is so cruel. I'm sorry."

He shrugged. "I learned to live with it. As did the rest of his illegitimate brood."

"And do you know them? I've heard..." She hesitated and blushed. "I've heard there are a great many."

"No," he said. "I don't see them. We aren't family, we just share blood. I have no interest in making their acquaintance."

"But Oscar—" she began.

He held up a hand to cut her off. "I think I've slit my chest open enough for you today. I don't want to discuss it further."

He had built a wall between them with that statement. He had meant to do it, though he hated to see the flicker of pain that crossed her face when he did so. Things were already getting complicated, even after just a few days. He had been trying to make sure that didn't happen.

He'd have to work harder at it.

Except she didn't seem willing to let him. She met his gaze, and the filtered light from the carriage hit her face, a halo around her like some kind of...angel.

She smiled at him. Playful again, beautiful. Putting him even further at ease without any effort. "Then what *do* you want?" she asked.

He stared at her. Was that innuendo purposeful? The tool she used to keep him from pulling away completely?

Did it matter? When he looked at her, so beautiful and so close,

JESS MICHAELS

he could scent the honey sweetness of her even from across the carriage. He wanted to taste it. Let it flow through him until the emotions that had been stirred today were dulled by pleasure and release.

He pushed across the scant distance between them, caging her in with a hand on either side of her head on the seatback. Her pupils dilated, but she held firm, not turning away, not drawing back. She met his gaze with a strong one of her own.

"You, Imogen," he said as he tilted his head and brought his mouth toward hers. "I want you."

He captured her lips then, hard and forceful. Almost daring her to withdraw or say no. To erect her own wall so he wouldn't have to feel quite so terrible about his own. Only she didn't. Instead she slid her hands along his chest, over his shoulders, and wrapped her arms around his neck to draw him even closer.

She was soft to all his hardness, open to his closed, welcoming to his prickly desire to keep the world out. He knew what could happen if he allowed too many people in.

Her acceptance made him waver, and for a moment, the kiss softened. But no, he couldn't do that. She was lovely and filled him with desire, but that was all he could ever allow himself with her. He couldn't let her make him forget.

The carriage was beginning to slow by then, turning into the drive for his home, and he pulled away, back to the seat across from her. They stared at each other, panting breaths matching, and he hardened his gaze purposefully. "We're going to my bed, Imogen. Unless you no longer want that."

She arched a brow, and for a moment it felt like she was the one with all the experience and he was a green boy again. Like she could see through him.

"I've made it very clear that what you want is what I want, Oscar," she said. "I'm not the one who keeps questioning it."

The carriage came to a halt and the door was opened by one of his footmen. She didn't hesitate, but slipped past him from the vehicle

and out onto the drive. He stared as she walked away, up the stairs and to the door where Donovan was waiting.

As she reached him, she turned back and smiled at Oscar. "Are you coming, then? Or are you just going to stare all day?"

She didn't wait for his answer, but went inside with a smile for his butler. He clambered out after her and bounded up the stairs. And he was at her heels when he realized that she had just called out "jump" and he had responded by asking "how high?"

And even though he couldn't stop himself as they entered his room, he realized that he was in a very dangerous position now. He would have to act carefully if he didn't want to hurt himself...or her... in the process.

~

B roken. Broken. Broken.
That word kept swirling around and around in Imogen's head as she walked away from Oscar, across the wide expanse of his chamber, toward the big bed on the opposite side of the room. Joanna had said something about the damage her son kept hidden. In the carriage, Imogen had felt it. Seen it in all the little tics and tells Oscar would hate himself for revealing if he realized he had done so.

Perhaps she should have been frightened off by seeing the soft underbelly of this man. Perhaps another woman wouldn't have wanted that when she could have only strength and heat and drive. But Imogen only felt closer to him as a result. They were, in some ways, similar. Both had experienced loss. Both had been abandoned.

And she wanted to offer him the same respite as he had for her.

She heard him coming after her. His breath was harsh in the quiet room, his footfalls heavy. His arms came around her from behind, dragging her back against his chest as his mouth found the side of her throat, and he pushed her to bend over the bed.

It was dizzying, his drive and passion. Intoxicating to feel how much this man who could have any woman wanted her. *Needed* her.

His fingers jerked against the buttons along the back of her dress. He fumbled as he parted her gown and then clenched his hands against the chemise beneath. "Fuck."

The word was said so quietly, she wasn't certain he realized he'd said it. But she'd heard it. She heard the feeling beneath it, too. He'd been vulnerable with her in the carriage, and now he desperately wanted to be hard again. To keep those walls up between them. Perhaps to even chase her away so she wouldn't see anything more than she'd already seen.

Only that wasn't his choice. She could see his drive and what was behind it, and just...refused to let it separate them the way he was hoping. She could embrace this side of him, accept it as she accepted the others she'd seen. Give him what he needed without allowing him to deny her what she wanted, too.

She softened beneath him, settling her head against the mattress, gripping the coverlet with both hands, lifting her backside in offering. If he needed to use her, at least they were both going to enjoy it.

"Imogen," he murmured, his voice sharp in the quiet. He pushed her skirt up, bunching it around her hips along with her chemise. Her backside was bared to him, and he cupped it with one hand, smoothing his fingers along the flesh.

It was so easy for him to make her want. The warmth and weight of his fingers against her bottom, stroking her skin, and all the nerve endings in her body felt like they fired at once. She pushed back against him, seeking his heat, and expected him to grind forward to meet her.

Instead he slapped her bare bottom with the flat of his palm. She jolted to attention and looked over her shoulder to stare at him in shock. He was watching her, reading her reaction as his hand returned to the place he'd slapped, and he stroked there again, gently.

"Did you just *spank* me?" she asked, incredulous and intrigued all at once. The initial swat had surprised her, but now her flesh tingled all the more where he was touching her.

"I did." His voice was a low rumble. "There's a line between pleasure and pain, Imogen. A little pain with the pleasure is…intoxicating. Even now…"

He smoothed his fingers and glided them into the cleft between her cheeks, skimming down as she writhed until he found her sex. He gently probed there, ignoring her as she tried to force him to press himself inside.

"Even now you're wet. But if you don't like it, I won't do it."

She wrinkled her brow. This man could take what he wanted. She would let him. She would very likely enjoy it. And yet as much control as he exerted, as much dark and dangerous energy as he exuded from every pore of his body…he still sought her consent. He still let her control the method in which he gained his pleasure.

That was the real power. That was full control. And a thrill worked through her body at the idea she held anything close to that over this man.

She licked her lips, and his pupils dilated to an impossible darkness. "Are you punishing me for anything in particular?"

His mouth twitched, another hint of a smile that never went further. "You pushed up into me when I wasn't *ready* to grind against you. I suppose that is reason enough to teach you how to behave. But mostly I slapped that delicious arse because you are irresistible. I like the way it sounds as my flesh meets yours. I like that little pinkness your flesh gets. The bite makes the lick a little more…soothing."

She shivered. "I like the lick, I've probably made that clear to you. I don't mind the bite. But perhaps just…ease me into it?"

"Of course. Maybe someday I'll spank you raw so you'll feel my handprint on your arse the next day and it will remind you of me fucking you until you were weak." He leaned over her, curling his body around her, drawing her back and grinding against her from behind until her fingers tangled in the coverlet for purchase. "But for now, we'll go slow."

He pulled away, leaving her cold where his warmth had been. He caught the back of her gown, tugging her to a standing position. Her skirt slipped back into place around her legs and she frowned. One slap was all she got after all that discussion?

"Don't make that sound," he said as his hands slid into the gap he'd created when he unbuttoned her dress a moment ago.

"What sound?" she asked, lolling her head back against his shoulder because his fingers were like magic against her skin.

"That disappointed little grunt," he said. "I'm going to make sure you are *very* satisfied, Imogen."

She laughed, but it faded as he tugged the dress down, baring her from the waist up. He cupped her breasts from behind as he flattened his still-clothed chest against her back. His thumbs strummed her nipples, he squeezed her breasts, a little roughly even, and she felt her knees starting to go weak as sensation rippled through her.

"I believe you," she gasped.

He kissed the side of her neck, sucking hard enough to give that little flash of pain he'd been describing earlier, then licked gently to soothe. Her sex twitched, and she understood. And she wanted more as he ground against her, trapping her between the bed and his body, forcing her to be captive to his whims.

He pulled the dress again, and nudging it down between them until it hit the floor at her feet. He pressed a hand to her back, pushing her into her original position, bent over for his pleasure. Now she braced, ready for the slap again.

"You're not going to know when it's coming," he promised, as if he could read her mind. "That's part of the pleasure."

"For you," she choked out as a laugh.

He chuckled in response. "I know when it's coming. Now...please behave, Imogen."

She found herself lifting up on her toes, seeking what he was resistant to giving. "I'm sure you'll make me."

That did earn a slap, a little harder than the first one. Her bottom tingled for a moment and her fingers clenched at the sensation, especially when he cupped the place he'd struck, tracing the mark he'd surely left with his fingers.

He reached between her legs with the opposite hand and pressed a finger to her clitoris, flicking the hood away and exposing the nerve. She bucked against his hand, squirming against the pressure as pleasure mounted between her legs. He increased that pressure in response, stroking her as she ground against him, rocking herself toward release. Just when she was right on the edge, ready to fall, he slapped her backside once more, and she jolted against him with a cry.

The pleasure was so intense she almost pulled away from it, but he held her firm, continuing to play her like an instrument. And then she felt it, his thick cock at her entrance. She had been so lost in her release, she hadn't even realized he'd freed himself from his trousers, and now he slid in inch by inch, her still-clenching pussy welcoming him.

The sensation changed with his cock to grip on. She pushed back, taking him to the hilt and pulsing against him as she buried her cries against the mattress. She felt the tension in him, even though she couldn't see him. Felt him trying to maintain control over himself, over her. But the more she keened and ground against him, the more his fingers tightened at her hip, clenched against her clitoris.

He started to thrust with a harsh moan, and as he took, he slapped her backside. Over and over. Gently, but continuously, punctuating each swivel of his hips with the contact of his palm. She met his thrusts with wild ones of her own, never letting him fully control what was happening, and surrendering herself to every sensation overloading her mind.

When the second orgasm hit her, fast on the heels of the first, she didn't care if she screamed the house down. She bucked, squeezing so tightly she feared she'd hurt him, letting her fingers join his on her clitoris. His thrusts grew deeper and harder, the slap of skin on skin now his pelvis hitting her backside rather than his hand. Only when she collapsed against the edge of the bed did he withdraw and come against her back with a grunting sound of relief and pleasure.

They leaned there together a while. She had no idea how long, still suspended in pleasure and release. Eventually, he pushed away from her and she rolled over to look at him. He was still fully dressed but for the fall front of his trousers, and she licked her lips at how lewd that felt. To be naked and covered in sweat and his release while he stood there looking almost pulled together. He had done this animal thing with her, but he still looked like a gentleman.

Almost a gentleman.

"Look at me like that and you might not like the results," he growled.

She reached up to catch his lapels and brought him closer, leaning over her, caging her in. "I think I proved I like the results just fine, Mr. Fitzhugh. Are you certain *you're* not the one afraid of what will happen if I keep testing your control?"

He didn't respond. His nostrils flared and his expression hardened before he dropped his mouth to hers for a fast, punishing kiss. She surrendered to it, and to him as he pushed her further up on the bed and stepped away to strip out of his clothing.

For the moment, at least, all the vulnerability he'd shown in the carriage was gone. She had allowed him to hide it back under this shield of passion and pleasure and command. It didn't mean, however, that she had forgotten what she'd seen. Or that she didn't know that the bond they had begun to forge on the ride from his mother's wouldn't eventually have consequences. It was plain it would for them both.

Only she didn't want to think about that now when he was offering her pleasure so they could both forget the past, both forget the pain...both forget anything but how perfectly their bodies moved together. The rest would come later.

CHAPTER 14

I mogen looked up from her coffee cup with a smile at the maid who had entered the room to take her plate. She had to resist the urge to stretch like a decadent cat. After all, she'd slept most of the morning away thanks to a very long and passionate night with Oscar.

He'd been gone when she woke, though, and she hadn't seen him yet today.

"Do you know where Mr. Fitzhugh is?" she asked as she handed over the empty cup to join the rest of the breakfast dishes being cleared.

"In his study, I believe, ma'am," the girl said, and for a moment her gaze flitted over Imogen.

She shifted beneath the look, subtle and gone almost immediately. Still, the stare was easily read. Her affair with the master of this house was common knowledge belowstairs, it seemed. Not a shock in such a small environment.

The Imogen of a week ago would have blushed at the realization. She knew she would have felt some shame at being seen as wanton or wild. But today she felt neither of those things. Oscar kept telling her that her desire and her pleasure and the things she wanted when he touched her were all natural. She was beginning to believe him.

At any rate, she would end up someone's mistress one way or another when this was all over. She had to start becoming comfortable with the judgment that certainly came with it. Her goal was to one day be as confident and untroubled as Joanna seemed to be.

"Thank you," she said with a smile as she got up and walked down the long hallways.

She took her time as she strolled, for she was in no hurry to see him. She knew what awaited her, after all. Smoldering heat and unfettered need and a man who made her feel both exhilarated and...safe. How those two emotions existed together, she wasn't entirely sure. It was a dichotomy, just as the man himself was.

She reached his study door. It was closed, and she knocked gently. She heard him moving around, and then a curt, "Enter!"

She smoothed her skirts and did so with a bright smile. Oscar was seated behind his desk, bent over some paperwork. He didn't look up. "What is it?"

"It's me," she said.

He glanced toward her, his gaze washing over her as it always did. Then, to her surprise, he returned his attention to the items on his desk. "Yes, I know. Did you need something, Imogen?"

She blinked at the cool and almost dismissive tone of his voice. After yesterday, both in the carriage and in his bed, she was certain things had shifted between them. Yet he offered her no connection today, not even the barest hint of one.

She cleared her throat and forced herself to be as detached as he was. "I have been thinking about my situation and I know my staff must be concerned about me."

"They've been informed of your safety and I have paid their wages for the next month," he said, again not looking up. "Your home has been closed up and your mail forwarded to a solicitor in my employ, and will thus be forwarded to me. Untraceable, or at least not easily so."

"Why wasn't I told of this?" she asked, stepping farther into the room. "I would have wanted to pass a message of my own to my people. And I would like to see my correspondence."

He arched a brow as he looked at her again. "Expecting invitations, are we?"

She pursed her lips at his dismissive tone. "You know that isn't my concern. I may not have many people who care for me in my life, but I *do* have Aurora. She must be sick with worry. Normally we correspond at least twice weekly, and she hasn't heard from me!"

He let out a long sigh and got up. He crossed to his sideboard and opened the top drawer. "These were forwarded today."

He held them out and she took them, flipping through the slim number of items that had come in her time missing. That there were so few made how alone she was in the world a stark thing, indeed.

"Did you plan to tell me these had come?" she asked. She found three letters from Aurora in the stack and clutched them to her breast as she discarded the rest: an old invitation to a tea and a letter from her former brother-in-law that could only be rude and foreboding.

"Of course," he said, his tone beleaguered as he retook his place at his desk. "Apparently you think me a controlling ogre and you might not be wrong in that assessment. But you were still abed when I received your mail this morning. I did not think any of it was pressing enough to have you roused, given how little you slept last night."

"That was your fault," she pointed out as her cheeks grew hot.

"It was my pleasure, I assure you," he said. "And the additional fact is that you *cannot* write back to Lady Lovell or any of the others, even if you wished to do so."

She shook her head. "What are you talking about, Oscar? Why can't I write back?"

He fisted his hands on the desktop and looked up at her slowly. "Because those who would wish you dead are likely watching any friend or family member who might receive a message from you. If they intercepted a letter from you, they might use it to track your whereabouts."

That made her stomach drop in her chest, but Imogen managed to keep her countenance clear. "So the only option is to allow my friend, my dearest friend, to believe me possibly dead?"

He pushed to his feet and she saw how carefully he was controlling his reaction. His gaze was bright with frustration and concern, even though his hands didn't waver. His voice was even and calm. "Is the better alternative for you to actually *be* dead?" he asked. "Just another body in the courtyard for Maggie and Roddenbury and God knows who else to dispose of in the river?"

She flinched, but he didn't stop. "Is that what you want for yourself? Because if suicide is your goal, I won't allow it. I...*can't.*"

He turned away at that last word and paced to the window. For what felt like a very long time, they were both silent. At last, she let out her breath. "Oscar—"

He held up a hand. "I do understand your concerns," he said softly. "I will try to find a way to communicate your safety to Lady Lovell that will not endanger either of you. But for now, you cannot write to her. You will not."

"I think you are confused," she gasped as she shoved her letters into her pelisse pocket and crossed the room to him. "You might bend me to your will in your bed, but outside of that room, you cannot control me."

"I'm not trying to control you," he snapped as he caught her hand. "I'm trying to save your life."

She pulled away from him and took a long step back. "It's hard to tell the difference, Mr. Fitzhugh. I'll just take my letters back to my cell now. I appreciate you allowing them through your blockade at all. Good day."

She pivoted and left the room, knowing she was performing a massive fit of pique but unable to care. This man made it clear he was not going to care for her beyond as a sexual plaything, but in the same breath confused everything between them with this show of overprotectiveness.

It was frustrating as could be. And for the moment, she had no idea what to do or how to give herself enough space so she didn't end up confused, hurt and ultimately...alone.

~

A s Imogen slammed the door behind herself, Oscar spun away and stood at the window. He slammed a palm against the glass, feeling the cool surface reverberate beneath his palm. "Bloody hell," he muttered.

He returned to his desk and sat back down, but now the items there swam before his eyes. His focus was gone, flounced out the door along with Imogen. Now he could only think of her.

Although someone might look at her and judge her to be simply one thing. He knew full well what that was: a pretty prize on a man's arm, whether that was a husband or a lover. In the time Oscar had been acquainted with her, he knew that wasn't true. Yes, she was beautiful. So beautiful. And yes, she had an air about her of refinement and propriety, despite what arrangements she'd been trying to make at a brothel or the ones she had made with him. That might be a shock to some, but not to him. He'd been raised around courtesans, and he knew most of them were more clever, well-read and interesting than the most properly educated person in high society.

Beyond that, there was even more to Imogen. She was sunshine, with her easy laugh and bright personality and ability to adjust to and make the best of any situation. Even here in this house where she felt trapped and in a situation she certainly couldn't have chosen for herself, she very rarely complained.

She was kind, too. His servants were people to her, not just a means to get what she wanted. She was certainly thoughtful when it came to him. Gentle even when he was not. She had listened to his tale of his childhood, drawn out of him by just how quietly she accepted it. Had she judged? No. Had she offered some empty platitude? No.

She'd just taken it in, taken some of the weight of it from his shoulders, if only for a moment.

And then there was her passion. Taking lovers was something common for him. Sex was a natural desire, and he indulged in pleasure when he needed it. But he'd never had a lover like Imogen. Not the most talented bawd had ever drawn his desires to the surface like she did. He looked at her and he wanted her.

Even when she was calling him her jailor and flouncing out of his study.

He shook his head. "This is not good," he muttered to himself.

And it wasn't. He knew what was happening between them, even if he would never, could never label it out loud to her. She was getting too close. No, *they* were getting too close, because he felt himself leaning into her the same way she leaned into him.

It was like what had happened with Louisa all those months ago. She'd wanted more. He'd pulled away from that want and hurt her. And now he was doing it all over again with a different woman.

He didn't want to hurt Imogen. He longed to fix what he'd already done to hurt her. A dangerous prospect, especially since the reason he wanted to fix it was because he desired the sunshine she brought back in his corner of the world a little longer.

Even if it couldn't be permanent. Shouldn't be. Wouldn't be.

"Damn it," he muttered as he got up to ring for a servant. He had some arrangements to make. Ones that would do nothing to protect her heart, nor his own. And in that moment, it didn't matter.

As she walked down the long hallway toward the back parlor, Imogen stared at the letter in her hand. Just holding it made her feel a tremendous rush of guilt.

It had been a few hours since she'd left Oscar's study with her back up and her hands shaking with frustration. And pacing around her room reading Aurora's increasingly terrified correspondence had not helped. The last letter, at least, had contained a kernel of respite. Aurora had gone off to a brief country gathering with some new friends, though she pleaded with Imogen to write and had left a forwarding address for that very purpose.

And so a plan had hatched. Oscar had said Imogen couldn't write to Aurora because someone might be watching her home to intercept such a correspondence. But there was no way they would be doing so out in the country at some party so totally divorced from any connection to Imogen.

She'd written her letter, ignoring the guilt she felt at defying Oscar's direct order for her not to do so. And now she slipped into the back garden for what she hoped would be the second part of her plan.

Oscar's garden was as wild as the man's own heart. A bramble of wildflowers and weeds, trees and unkempt bushes. During her time here she had found a few tools hidden in a small shed at the back of the property and had spent some of the hours slowly beginning to bring the garden back into order.

Which was when she had noticed that the same little boy rushed past the back gate at the same time each day. She edged to the gate, trying to look as though she was just fiddling with the garden if someone were spying on her from the house. Within moments, there came the rushing footsteps, and she pressed herself to a knot in the wood.

"You there, boy!" she called out.

He skidded to a halt in his running and looked around. She could see him in a partially obstructed view from the hole in the gate. He looked to be around eight or nine, with a dirty face and no shoes.

"You a fairy?" he asked as he looked around for where the voice had come from.

"Of course not," Imogen said with a laugh she couldn't suppress. "I'm here, behind the gate."

He leaned in and her eye met his through the knot in the wood. His face twisted in uncertainty and he eased a little closer. "Seems a fairy thing t'do, you know. 'ide behind a gate and call out. Me ma says the fairies steal children's souls."

Imogen twisted her face in horror. "I don't know if that's true, but I know I'm not a fairy. Just a woman with a request and a coin for someone willing to fulfill it."

He stepped up closer and pressed his eye to the knot. She stumbled back at the unexpected closeness and he looked around the garden. "I know this place," he said. "This is Fitzhugh's 'ouse. You one of 'is servants?"

"Something like it," she said, because she certainly wasn't going to go into the intricacies of her odd arrangement with the master of this house with a child. "I need to send a letter, but I'm not able to do it myself. Would be willing to post it if I give it to you?" She dug into her pelisse pocket and held up the letter along with her last silver coin. "And this?"

He eyed the coin, and she could see his interest. "You a princess trapped in a tower?"

She blinked. "N-no."

"You look like a princess," he muttered.

She looked down at herself in the fine gown, and sighed. It wasn't even hers. It had belonged to the last princess who holed up in this tower with this man...prince or beast might he be.

"Will you do it?" she asked.

He shrugged. "No skin off my nose. Give the coin over then," he said, and held his hand beneath the knot. She shoved the coin against it, and it wedged, but with a few taps of the edge, it pushed through. For a moment she thought he might just run with the money, but then he waved at her. "Now the letter."

She rolled the folded pages into a scroll and pushed it through the opening, as well. "You'll do it today?"

"On me way 'ome," he said, though she wasn't certain if that meant right away or later. Beggars, of course, could not be choosers, though, so she nodded.

"Thank you. I do appreciate it."

He grunted some version of farewell and then rushed off again, racing down the alleyway behind the house and disappearing out of her sightline in the narrow hole.

She drew in a long breath once he was gone. She had no idea if he would truly post the letter, but at least she had tried. And knowing she could ease Aurora's fears should have made her feel a little better.

Instead, she felt terribly guilty for going against the directive Oscar had given her a few hours before. She owed him so much. But he had made it very clear that he wasn't meant to be a permanent fixture in her life. Aurora was.

She had to focus on that in the end, and not tell herself stories about the prince masquerading as a beast who had trapped her in his elegantly appointed tower and seduced her with his library. This fairytale could certainly not end well if she let herself forget that the final chapter would not be a happily ever after, at least not for the two of them.

CHAPTER 15

In the three days since Imogen had flounced out of his study, Oscar had been more confused than he'd ever been in his life. He felt her pulling away. During the day, she stayed out of his path. She read in the library, she worked in his garden, she sequestered herself in her room.

She was doing as he asked. She was keeping up a barrier between them. He should have been happy. But he wasn't. He found himself shadowing her. Watching her from the window above when she was in the garden. Sneaking peeks of her in the library when she wasn't looking. Standing at her chamber door, talking himself in and out of knocking.

And yet at night...oh, at night everything changed. She slipped into his room, never mentioning the gulf that lay between them. She came to his bed and sank into the pleasures they could share. When he dominated, she submitted. When he pressed her boundaries, she opened herself to him.

And when she occasionally took the lead, he found himself fighting all the urges within him to fall to his knees and spend the rest of his life worshipping her.

He shook those troubled thoughts away and continued on his way through the house. He hadn't seen her since she left his bed last night to return to her chamber, and now it was late in the afternoon. The plans he had been formulating for days had finally come through and he almost vibrated with excitement as he exited the house and looked down from the terrace over the garden below.

She was there, a basket in one hand and clippers in the other, trimming his rosebushes. His heart leapt before he jerked himself back from the pleasure he ought not feel and made his way down the stairs to the garden to join her.

She lifted her gaze to his as he came down the last step and strode across the lawn. Her expression revealed nothing of how she felt to see him.

"Good afternoon, Imogen," he said as he reached her. "What are you doing?"

She glanced at him again and then went back to trimming the dead heads off his roses, this time with a little more...violence than a moment before.

"I'm making the best of things," she said as she wiped her cheek and left an adorable smudge of dirt in her wake. "I've been cooped up inside for nearly a fortnight and I feel I shall go mad. I hope you don't mind my attacking your garden to fill the time."

He looked around. Where once his garden had been a mess of brambles and weeds, interspersed with flowers worth looking at, she had really made progress in her short time here. There were paths under the mess, it seemed. And flowerbeds. And bushes.

"It's wonderful, Imogen," he said. "Truly lovely. I appreciate you spending your energy on this. And as for making the best of it, it seems you always do that, don't you?"

If he expected her to smile at that observation or agree, he was taken aback when she made the most unladylike snort he'd ever heard and tossed the clippers down with more than a little force.

"Ah, yes," she retorted. "That's me. Accepting everything, no matter what the cost. From my family. From my husband." She looked away from him. "From you."

He stiffened at the comparison to those who had never had her best interests at heart. "It isn't the same."

"No," she mused softly, and once again her gaze found his. "No, not entirely, I agree. At least you have my pleasure as a goal, if nothing else."

She bent to retrieve her abandoned clippers with a heavy sigh that made her frustration apparent. He reached for her, intercepting her before she could return to her work, and turned her back to him. He forced her to hold his gaze, and yes, he saw her frustration. But he also saw her exhaustion. Her worry.

How he wanted to protect her from all that. Or at least take it away temporarily.

"I'm...sorry, Imogen. I realize this is difficult for you. I realize I have perhaps made it more difficult," he said, and her eyes widened as if she hadn't expected that acknowledgment.

She swallowed, and he followed the motion with his gaze, wishing he could follow it with his lips. But he had to do more than seduce her in this moment. For once he had more to offer than physical pleasure.

"What is it you wanted, Oscar?" she whispered, her tone slightly gentler than it had been. "You normally don't pursue me during daylight hours."

He suddenly felt nervous and cleared his throat as if that could change the emotion. "You feel trapped here and I don't feel good about that. So I found you to ask you to go out with me."

Her brow wrinkled. "What happened to your edict that I was not allowed to leave these walls? That if I did so, it would mean certain and immediate death?"

She was teasing, but he tensed at the words she chose. "Please don't joke about that."

Her gaze flitted down. "Of course. I'm sorry. So you want me to go out into the world with you. When? Where? Why?"

He stifled a laugh at her barrage of questions. It so reflected her spirit when she did that. She questioned without even knowing she was doing it sometimes, and he often found himself caught up in the spell of her curiosity. It made him see the world in a new way, when she questioned it and him.

But today he couldn't answer that barrage without revealing too much of his surprise. Instead, he straightened up and said, "You'll have to wait and see. Just dress for a pleasant afternoon and meet me in the foyer in an hour."

"Oscar—" she began as she wiped her dirty hands off on her pelisse.

He reached out and caught those hands. They were warm and soft in his own, and as he drew her a little closer, he caught a whiff of her honey sweetness that always made his cock very aware of how close she was. Today he ignored it.

"Please," he said quietly.

She blinked up at him at the *please*. He understood why. He wasn't a man who asked for much. He claimed more often than pleaded.

She nodded slowly. "Very well. An hour."

She extracted her hands from his and gathered up her basket of clippings as she headed back toward the house. At the bottom of the stairs, she stopped and looked back at him. Her face was lined with confusion, but he thought also little excitement, and he barely held back a smile.

If things went well, she was going to enjoy this day a great deal. He hoped she would. He depended on it, despite the dangers that fact created. But in that moment nothing mattered aside from seeing her pleasure, and not just the physical kind this time.

Imogen sat in the carriage across from Oscar, watching him closely. He seemed...nervous as they rode along toward whatever mystery destination he had in mind for her, and that was rare in itself. Still, he had his usual, serious expression on his face. The one that made his brow lower and his eyes dark and his mouth almost disappear in his beard.

"Do you *ever* smile?"

He tilted his head. "Do you mean am I *capable* of it? Physically?"

She huffed out her breath at his teasing. "You must be capable. I've seen you *almost* do it a few times."

"Have you now?" he asked, and there was one of those hints again, just the slightest flutter at the corner of his lips.

Which only drove her harder to make it happen fully. "I just wonder what could draw such an expression out. What if you...won a thousand pounds at cards?"

"A thousand?" he repeated, and shook his head. "Such high stakes are not in my blood. I gamble only to make my club patrons feel unjudged, and never with that much. So it isn't possible, thus I would not smile."

He was playing with her, and she lowered her eyelids in a glare. "If you found an adorable puppy in the park," she suggested.

"How adorable?" he asked, that serious expression never wavering from his face even as he toyed with her.

"Like a tiny little bear," she said, and leaned closer to him, batting her eyelashes to mimic some sweet little puppy. "With folded ears and eyes that gazed up at you and whispered, 'Take me home, Mr. Fitzhugh.'"

He swallowed and shook his head slowly. "If he was so adorable, surely he would belong to someone else. A child, perhaps. You wish me to take pleasure in depriving a child of his beloved pet, Mrs. Huxley? Very cruel."

She flopped back against the carriage seat with a laugh. "You are impossible. But I *will* discover something, I assure you."

"I look forward to the attempt," he said, and pulled the curtain back once more. "We have arrived."

She leaned forward and looked through the glass. They were approaching a building, but the sign was obscured by the angle of the carriage before it turned and they pulled around the back, away from the busy street.

"Oh, I feel you are doing this on purpose, to make me nervous," she burst out.

"That I would never do," he said as the door opened and he stepped out.

He turned back and extended a hand to help her. She looked down at him, into that face, so handsome even if the harder years this man had lived had given him gray in his beard, had made his expression always dark and dangerous. He looked so cold, and yet he wasn't. Not in his heart.

She shivered as she touched him, taking his hand and reveling in the electric spark that always flowed between them, even if she was wearing gloves.

She stepped into the alley and managed to tear her attention away from him and toward the nondescript building instead. "Will you tell me now where you've brought me?"

"Welcome to the Carlton Museum, Imogen," he said, and he seemed to be watching her face for every nuance of her reaction to this news.

She didn't hold them back—she couldn't have even if she wished to. She clapped her hands together. "Oh, Oscar! The Carlton Museum! I've *always* wanted to go here. I've heard the displays are beautiful."

"They are," Oscar said as he guided her toward the stairs at the back entrance. "When the Levarian Museum collection was broken up and auctioned off ten years ago, Carlton bought up as much as he could. It is almost fully intact. He's agreed to close up an hour early, and we are being given a private tour."

Imogen lifted a hand to her mouth and stared at him in wonder. Her husband had never encouraged her interest in the world and had scoffed at the idea of coming to this place while he still lived. Since his death, she hadn't had the funds for even the modest admission fee Carlton charged to see the exhibits.

"Oscar," she breathed, reaching for him again. But before she could say or do more, the door at the top of the stairs opened and a smartly dressed man closer to Imogen's age than Oscar's stepped out.

"Ah, Mr. Fitzhugh," he said in friendly greeting. "I'm so pleased you have arrived. This must be Mrs. Henderson."

"Er, I'm—" Imogen began in confusion, but Oscar caught her stare and gave a slight shake of his head. Ah, so he had given a false name, probably to protect her. She really could learn from that. "Yes, Mrs. Henderson."

"I am Edward Carlton, madam, at your service."

Imogen extended a hand in stunned greeting. "Good afternoon, sir."

"Mr. Carlton is a member of my club," Oscar said, answering one of the questions she had not been able to ask before they were interrupted.

"And when the great Fitzhugh asks a boon, it is a rare enough thing that a man cannot refuse," Carlton said with a laugh. "It looks to be a treat since he has brought such a lovely companion."

Imogen blushed at the compliment. This man was younger than she would have thought him to be. After all, everyone knew Carlton was a captain of industry, working alongside such respected gentlemen as Grayson Danford on canals and who knew what other kinds of things.

"Thank you," she said softly. "Both for the compliment and for the offer of a private viewing. I'm so excited to see the exhibit."

"Then let us not delay your pleasure even a moment more," Carlton said, motioning them in. "Let me show you my collection."

He offered an arm, and Imogen looked back at Oscar. He was watching them, the usual unreadable expression on his face. And yet for a moment she thought she saw a flicker in his eyes. But then he motioned her as if to give her his blessing and followed her and Carlton into the museum.

They had toured the museum for two hours. No, that wasn't correct. Imogen and Carlton had toured the museum for two hours. Oscar had trailed after them, watching her rather than taking in much about the exhibits, regardless of his interest in nature.

She was a pure pleasure to observe in this environment. Bright and excited, intelligent and engaged. She was more drawn in by each and every new exhibit than she had been by the last. It was enchanting. *She* was enchanting.

Not that he was the only one to notice this. Edward Carlton seemed equally taken in by her, if his rapt expression and unwavering attention was any indication. The burning sensation of jealousy that rose up in Oscar's chest every time the man took her elbow to direct her to a new exhibit was something he fought to control.

He'd brought her here, after all. He'd wanted her to enjoy herself, and she *was* enjoying herself. Carlton was never untoward and his interest was understandable. It could even be…helpful to her. Carlton was rich and successful, exactly the kind of man who could be a powerful protector if Imogen wished to pursue that road.

He could even be more if it came down to it.

"…Fitzhugh?"

Oscar blinked and found that as he stared at Imogen, Carlton had actually separated from her and come to his side.

"Woolgathering, I apologize," he choked out. "What is it?"

Carlton glanced toward Imogen and back to him, and then cocked his head. "Of course. Woolgathering. I was only saying that I need to take care of one item of business before we end our tour. May I leave you here in the bird room and come back for you in a moment?"

"Of course," Oscar said. "Imogen is so taken by the tableaus, I'm sure she'll enjoy the extra moment here."

Carlton arched a brow but said nothing else, and simply bowed from the room. It was the first time Oscar had been alone with her since the carriage ride, and he moved toward her like a magnet to iron, drawn helplessly to her.

JESS MICHAELS

"Oh Oscar, look at this beautiful bird," she said, pointing to one of the main tableaus that filled the room. The birds were from all over the world and had been carefully preserved through highly skilled taxidermy and placed in detailed dioramas to add to their beauty and appeal.

In the one she pointed to now, a red-faced crimsonwing if the signage was correct, from the African continent, was balanced delicately on a piece of foliage, its little face turned toward the observer in curiosity.

"The red and green are startling," she continued. "Almost like a holly bu—" She pivoted toward him, and he thought she would say more, but her eyes went wide and she cut herself off.

"What is it?" he asked, taken aback by her expression of what seemed to be shock.

"You...you are *smiling*," she said, and she lifted her hands to his cheeks, her fingers caressing there gently.

He blinked. He hadn't realized he was smiling, but indeed he was. He felt the expression on his face as he looked down at her.

"I told you I was capable," he teased in an effort to reduce the power of this moment. But it didn't work. It was undeniable what this meant—she saw it and he felt it.

"You're smiling at...at *me*?" she asked.

He cleared his throat. He should step away from her, push off what was happening and pretend it meant nothing. But when her hands were on his cheeks and she was looking up at him in the same wonder she reserved for the natural beauty captured in this museum, it was impossible. She was undeniable, no matter how much he knew he should deny her and himself.

"I suppose," he admitted slowly. "That seeing your...your pleasure and enthusiasm at the exhibitions makes it impossible not to be drawn in."

Her expression softened slightly. "This was a wonderful surprise, Oscar. A perfect day, and I'll never forget it, no matter how long I live."

Her fingers brushed against his jawline, and in that moment he felt the smile she was so enthralled with fall slightly. When she touched him, it was impossible not to shift into something far more driven, far more needy. She inspired that as much as anything else.

He bent his head, and she lifted to him. They kissed in the middle of the exhibition hall in front of the staring birds, and it was like the first time. Her lips were soft beneath his, her fingers gripped against his shoulders as she made a soft sound in her throat that he knew all too well. He had lived to inspire that sound since he first took her to his bed. That raw expression of desire and pleasure.

He traced her lips with his tongue and she opened to him, but he didn't delve too deeply. He didn't surrender to everything he wanted. They didn't have time, this wasn't the place. But he needed to taste her as much as he needed food or water, so he did so gently. Time and location blurred as he held her closer and lost himself in all she was and all she made him be.

It was only the clearing of a throat at the door that made them part. Imogen ducked her head behind him as Carlton re-entered the room.

"Pardon me," he said with a slight smile toward Oscar.

"Pardon *us*," Oscar returned with a shrug for the other man.

Imogen was blushing dark red as she finally allowed herself to meet their host's gaze. He was kind enough to say nothing else about what he'd interrupted and instead said, "I hope you enjoyed my collection, Mrs. Henderson."

"I did," she breathed. "Oh, it's so entirely lovely and you were a wonderful guide. Thank you again for allowing us this private showing."

"Many come through these halls and just wander through the rooms and look but never *see* what is right in front of them. You, on the other hand, seemed to treasure these items as much as I do, myself," Carlton said. "And so you are welcome back any time. You may even bring your grumpy friend, but only if he can promise me a discount on my club membership in return."

Oscar shook his head. "We'll see."

Carlton laughed and motioned them to follow, leading them back to the same back entrance they had come in hours before. "I had your carriage brought 'round while I tended to my other errand. Good evening, Fitzhugh." The men shook hands, and then Carlton reached out to take Imogen's hand. He lifted it to his lips and kissed the top gently. "Mrs. Henderson."

She blushed again. "Good evening, Mr. Carlton. And thank you again."

He waited until Oscar had handed Imogen up into the carriage to wave and go back inside the building. Oscar let out a sigh as he followed her in and settled in across from her. As the carriage began to move, she clasped her hands in front of herself. "That truly was a treat. Thank you again."

"I was happy to do it. Sometimes being in my position has its benefits," he said.

"Because you know Mr. Carlton from your club." When he nodded, she smiled. "He was very kind."

"He was very flirtatious," Oscar corrected. "Surely you noted that."

She shifted slightly. "He didn't make me uncomfortable, though."

"He's a good man," Oscar said, flexing his hands against his thighs and trying to keep his voice light. This was, after all, an opportunity to distance himself. One he should take to protect Imogen. To protect himself. That moment in the museum had been too close. "I would guess he might offer to protect you if you were interested once we manage this mess with the Cat's Companion."

Her smile, which had still shone on her face, faltered at those words. "I...see. Did he tell you that?"

He shook his head. "No."

She rubbed her temples briefly. "Please tell me you didn't act as my agent in some way and tell him I would wish for that kind of offer."

"Of course not," Oscar said. "I am not your agent, for one. And I wouldn't act as such unless you told me specifically to do so. I only pointed out the obvious so that you might see your situation is not as hopeless as you've thought. With the right introductions and connections—"

She turned her head, her lips thinning. The good will he had renewed with her that afternoon seemed to have faded away entirely. "Well, thank you for that lesson," she said softly. "I suppose I will have to consider it once we resolve my current dilemma."

He frowned. He'd brought up the subject, but now that she had agreed, even in theory, he couldn't help but picture what that future would look like. Imogen as another man's lover. Perhaps even as another man's love.

He shook off the unwanted feelings that accompanied the thought and instead changed the subject. "At any rate, it's nearly time for supper."

"Back home?" she asked, and though she looked at him again, he felt the walls back up between them. There was regret that accompanied their return.

"No," he said. "We'll be meeting with my mother, actually. She asked us to return to her, I believe she's done some looking around for you."

Imogen's annoyance left her face and she straightened up. "Then I look forward to seeing her. I'm sure you do, too. You must be ready to be rid of the burden I've put on you."

He hesitated, because what he wanted to do was reply instantly with a passionate *no*. But when she turned away again to look out into the fading light of sunset, he instead said nothing. And wished he was capable of saying more.

Wished he were capable of anything more than what he could give.

CHAPTER 16

Imogen tried to keep her expression serene as Oscar led her down the hall and into a parlor at his mother's home. He was so capable of divorcing himself from his emotions—she would do well to practice the same response.

Only it was so difficult. There were moments where she glimpsed something deeper in him. Like when he'd smiled at her at the museum and she'd thought she'd seen...

Everything.

She'd seen everything. But he'd pulled it back swiftly enough and he was always very clear that the future would not hold some connection between them. What they were sharing was purely sexual and absolutely limited to however long the investigation lasted. God's teeth, he was already trying to find another lover for her. A *protector*, he'd said.

She'd be a fool not to consider the suggestion. After all, Edward Carlton was intelligent, friendly and handsome. A few weeks ago, she would have jumped at the opportunity to become his mistress and get out of her terrible situation. Today?

Well, today the idea that Oscar could push her in that direction without feeling anything about it stung.

He released her as they entered the parlor, and walked over to the sideboard. "Drink?" he asked.

"I could use one," she mused, and watched as he poured her a splash of sherry. He didn't even have to ask what she liked anymore. He knew. And he would take Scottish whisky, just as he did any time he had a drink before supper. But he sipped it, never overindulging. No, Oscar Fitzhugh did not do that. He was always in control.

She frowned as she took the sherry and moved to the window to look out onto the busy street below. All these people buzzing from place to place, happy or not, but not trapped. Not in danger to be murdered if they so much as left the protection of four walls.

She felt those four walls closing in even now.

"Good evening!"

She pivoted back to watch Joanna step into the room. She was beautiful, of course, but Imogen found herself caught off guard by it again. It was as if she somehow forgot it or softened it in her mind, and then she saw Joanna and her loveliness rushed back.

Joanna kissed her son's cheek and then crossed to her, arms open in greeting. "My dear. Oh, you look lovely. That blue suits you."

Imogen glanced down at the gown she wore. Very pretty, yes. And still the left-behind dress of a dead woman who haunted Oscar. Drove his every decision, including the one never to let Imogen near. She almost hated the pretty outfit.

"And this is our dear friend, Will White," Joanna said as she parted from Imogen. She'd been so distracted, she hadn't noticed another man come into the room behind Joanna. He was tall, though not quite so tall as Oscar, who he was standing beside at the sideboard. He was very handsome, with gray hair, a defined jawline and bright blue eyes that flitted over Imogen before darting to Joanna. He smiled slightly at her and their connection became palpable, if only briefly.

"Will is my partner in the club," Oscar explained as Mr. White crossed to Imogen and shook her hand in greeting.

"A pleasure."

"And he was once my protector," Joanna added, never one to shy away from awkward subjects. "And he remains my dearest and truest friend."

"Very nice to meet you," Imogen said.

He shrugged. "The two of them have never been the kind to mince words. Any friend of Joanna or Fitzhugh is a friend of mine. I'm pleased to make your acquaintance after hearing so much about you."

Imogen blinked toward Oscar. "So much about me?"

"I mentioned you to Will after our first meeting," Oscar explained softly. "And I would assume he also heard about you from my mother." He glanced at Mr. White again. "You did go with her to Donville Masquerade and wherever else she was seeking her contacts?"

Mr. White opened his mouth to answer, but Joanna held up a hand. "There is plenty of time to discuss that after supper. By the way our poor Imogen is gripping her drink like a lifeline, I can see she would rather have a break from such dark topics. Am I wrong?"

Imogen stared at her white knuckles. She hadn't even realized how tightly she clung to her drink. Leave it to Joanna, master of finding all the answers, to see it.

She glanced toward Oscar. She was still so...turned upside down by everything that had happened between them at the museum and since. To now be asked to focus on news about her desperate future did feel like too much.

"A respite might be nice," Imogen admitted softly. "It's been a long day." Oscar flinched slightly, so she rushed to continue, "To be able to pretend things are normal for a while would be good. To pretend that this is just a supper amongst...amongst friends."

"Then it will be that," Joanna assured her as she slipped an arm through hers. "You will have the very best meal tonight, dear girl. My cook has made roasted pheasant in Will's favorite presentation. We all bend over backward to please him whenever he comes around, so it should be delightful."

Joanna led her from the room, and Imogen couldn't be sorry she'd done so. It allowed her not to look at Oscar. Not that she couldn't feel his stare on her. Not that she couldn't feel the weight of the future

already pressing down. The one that would answer life versus death…
and the one that would ultimately take her from his side, one way or
another.

~

J oanna had not been wrong: the pheasant was perfect. As was the
company. When Imogen mentioned Carlton's Museum, Will
White had become animated about his love of the natural
history exhibits. The bright conversation that followed had allowed
Imogen exactly what she'd said she wanted.

For an hour, she felt normal. Like this supper was just with
friends. And with a man she…well, she could say she cared for Oscar,
couldn't she? That wasn't breaking the rules between them. A person
could care for a friend. Or for a man who had saved that same person.
Caring was a *positive* thing, not a negative.

She only wished she were more certain of that. One thing she *was*
certain of, however, was that Joanna Fitzhugh and Will White were *far*
more than friends. She caught them looking at each other across the
table. There was a lightness when they said each other's names. And
the palpable connection that moved between them was something she
recognized. Something she felt when she glanced at Oscar and
thought about all the wicked things he could do if they were alone.

Even now, as the foursome moved down the hall back to the parlor
after supper, she couldn't help but notice how Joanna rested her hand
on White's inner elbow. How her fingers clenched gently as he leaned
down to say something private to her.

"Imogen?"

She jerked her head toward Oscar. He walked beside her, but
didn't hold her arm or offer his. "Hmmm?"

"You looked a little lost," he said. "Are you well?"

"I'm fine," she said. "I was just thinking how well they look
together. And how happy they seem to make each other."

Oscar glanced ahead to where his mother and White were

entering the parlor. His brow wrinkled, as if he hadn't noticed their closeness before. He shook his head toward Imogen. "My mother was very lucky to keep him as a friend after their affiliation."

She stopped and lowered her voice. "But they are more than friends now."

He stared at her, looked toward the parlor and then stared back at her again. "No, you're mistaken. My mother is a flirt with every handsome man. It's part of her charm, her nature. Will is a friend to her, nothing more."

Imogen tilted her head. She saw a kind of desperation in his eyes before he covered it. "Do you not wish them to be together?"

He blinked. "N-no. Of course not. Will is the best of men. He treated me like his own though I was not. When they ended their relationship, it was heartbreaking to me as a nine-year-old. But he continued to treat me well even after it ended. And her. Still, if they were together again, I would know. I would see."

There was that hint of desperation again, this time in his voice. He covered it by running a hand through his hair. "Come, they're waiting."

He walked toward the parlor, forcing her to hop to it to keep up. They came into the room together to find Joanna pouring the port as Will held the glasses. They were laughing together. Oscar stopped at her side and stared, then shook his head and walked away. As if that could stop what she'd suggested.

"It was a fine meal, Mama," he said, taking the port Will offered him. "But we've put off the inevitable long enough. We must talk about your contacts."

Joanna glanced toward Imogen, and there was concern on her face. Imogen's knees almost went weak at the sight of it. She'd not had anyone care for her except for Aurora in so long. And her friend had her own troubles, so Imogen sometimes kept her fears and worries secret.

"I suppose we cannot pretend away the inevitable forever," Joanna said with a sigh. She crossed to Imogen and took her hand, guiding her to the settee and motioning her to sit. As Imogen did, her heart leapt. There was something so...troubled on Joanna's face.

"What...what is it?" Imogen asked. "Why do you look at me that way?"

Joanna caught both her hands and held tight, never breaking eye contact with her. "Will and I went to Donville Masquerade two nights ago and met with Marcus Rivers."

Imogen swallowed hard. "I-I've heard of it," she admitted with a quick glance toward Oscar.

He held her gaze evenly, and heat flooded her cheeks with a blush she couldn't control as she thought of the palpable sexuality the underground club created, even when people just spoke of it. It was known as a den of sin on every level, but was considered a safe haven for those who came there. When her husband's family had made it clear she would be banished if she made an attempt at such a conspicuous place, she'd been lost.

She wished she could have gone there, sought her protector there instead of making the terrible mistake of going so much lower and endangering herself. But then again, she wouldn't have met Oscar if she hadn't, so...it was hard to regret everything that had come out of that terrible position.

"Rivers and his new bride are both decent. He's always run his club by a very strict set of rules. Because of this, he's a wonderful resource for knowing who is *in*decent. I explained your situation—"

Imogen pushed to her feet. "Oh no!" she gasped.

Oscar jolted as if he would move toward her, but Joanna held up a hand to stave his advance. "I didn't use names," she promised Imogen as she caught her hand and drew her back down. "I simply explained the basics of the situation. He was troubled. He's heard rumblings of..."

She trailed off, and this time Oscar did step closer. "What? What could be so terrible that even you would hesitate?"

"Women of my position, women in worse positions, they are

always in danger. Men have power, and if a person is judged important, then they can get away with anything."

"Even murder," Imogen breathed, her mind spiraling her back to that dead body. That poor woman, snuffed out so cruelly and treated like refuse. Who was she? Did someone look for her? Miss her? Or had her life been like her death...lonely. Empty.

She shivered at the thought and the grief she felt for that woman.

"Yes. I suppose all women walking this earth are somewhat aware of that fact. We walk on guard at all times." Joanna shifted. "But this is...different. Rivers says that there are rumors of more than just a random killing here and there. They are...forcing women into the trade."

Imogen drew back. "What?"

"Yes." Joanna shook her head. "Even kidnapping some of them. Which is why the War Department has become involved. When I mentioned Roddenbury, all the color went out of Rivers' face. The earl is at the heart of this, it seems. Profiting off the trade of these women both here and on the continent. Apparently he's been doing so for years, using the power and protection of his title."

"Why has no one stopped him?" Oscar asked.

Joanna glanced up at him, and her expression softened. "You know why, love. You know why more than most."

Oscar's cheek twitched, and Imogen bent her head. Roddenbury was titled. He could get away with anything if he managed it correctly, just as Oscar's father had done for years.

"Bloody hell," Oscar growled, and paced off to the fire to stare into the flames. His hands flexed at his sides, his rage barely contained.

Joanna sighed. "In truth, he has been stopped in some ways. The courtesan network, it's been whispering about him for years. The rumors and warnings about his cruelty and danger are probably why he's sunk lower, down to women with far fewer resources. Places where he believes he can buy his way out if he gets in trouble."

Pressure spread through Imogen's chest and her hands shook as she slowly stood. "But...but these agents of the crown..." she whispered.

"They do seem serious about the pursuit," Joanna said gently. "But..."

"But what?" Imogen asked, her voice barely carrying.

"It seems one of the agents is titled, as well. It's rumored a duke," Will White said, and his gaze cast away from Imogen, as if he couldn't bear to see her face when he gave that news.

Oscar pivoted away from the fire, and his face was dark with anger and frustration but also...fear. Seeing that fear flicker over his face in that moment nearly dropped Imogen to her knees.

"So they'll protect each other," he snapped. "As they always fucking do."

Imogen stared at him and his words sank in. She had always been on the outer edges of that world. The daughter of a second son, the wife of a third. Far enough to not reap the greatest benefits of title. Close enough to see the damage. To see how those men with title had been allowed to harm others, to lie, to cheat, to get away with anything they wished and have it covered up.

Of course that was what would happen here.

"But..." She was almost unable to form words when her throat was closing up at such a rapid pace. "Is there any way to address this? To make it right again for those women? For...for me?"

The entire room was staring at her. But no one responded, and their hesitation gave the response their voices wouldn't.

She nodded. She couldn't stop nodding, like her head was on a hinge, and backed toward the door. "I-I need a moment," she gasped out, and then ran from the room.

Only it was hopeless. There was nowhere to run to. And the future she'd had the tiniest hopes for seemed to vanish before her eyes, leaving only destruction and terror in its wake.

∼

O scar had carefully crafted his life so that he no longer had to feel helpless as he had as a boy. But as he watched Imogen stumble from the room, all color gone from her cheeks, her eyes filled with tears and her hands shaking, all those powerless feelings had flooded back.

"God's teeth, that poor woman," Will muttered, and crossed to the settee to place a hand on Joanna's shoulder.

Oscar glanced at them together and shook his head. That was a topic for another day. Right now he had to focus on Imogen. Imogen was all that mattered to him.

"Well, follow her," his mother said. "It's all you want to do, I can see it."

He nodded and looked at the door where Imogen had departed. "I am."

But he didn't move. He just stood there because he felt utterly toothless. Completely ineffective. He wanted to save this woman. To protect her in every way. But aside from offering her shelter, what else could he do?

His mother got up and came to his side. She touched his arm, and he looked at her.

"Oscar," she said, using his first name as she so rarely did. Only Imogen did it regularly. Hearing it from someone else's lips jolted him.

"What can I do, Mama?" he asked. "What can I possibly do? We all know that men with titles will always win. I've watched them do it all my life."

"And yet you've never stepped down from a fight," she said softly. "Because of that, those men *haven't* always won. You've climbed over top of their barriers and made a life for yourself that your father would have denied you, *tried* to deny you. Sometimes we only win by inches, love. But inches add up over time. Don't lose hope. Grab onto it with both hands and then go out to that woman and offer it to her as a lifeline. She needs it. She needs *you*."

He looked down at her and felt the truth of that. It was a heavy weight on his shoulders, but one he wished to carry. For Imogen he would carry the world.

He nodded and said nothing else, but departed the room and moved down the hall. He had a feeling she had gone out onto the terrace to get some air. After all the time he'd observed her in his home, he knew she often went outside to clear her head. It was why she spent so much time tidying his hopeless garden.

He went to the parlor where he could access the terrace and stepped outside. There she was, haloed by moonlight, staring up at the stars. He stared because he couldn't help himself. She was so lovely standing there. If he hadn't known her, he would have said she was a beautiful woman enjoying the night and nothing else.

But he did know her. So he saw her rolled shoulders, the tremble of her hand at her side, the way her breath was slightly labored as he came closer. Her pain seemed to come off of her in waves, her fear a companion standing at her shoulder.

"Imogen," he said.

She pivoted, and there were tracks of tears on her face as she stared at him. She was silent for what felt like a lifetime, and then she stepped forward into his arms. He held her as she leaned against him, supporting her weight, if he could do nothing else. He smoothed her hair gently, over and over, memorizing the silky texture as it grazed his palm.

At last she looked up at him. "It's all ruined, it's all over."

"No," he whispered, but he knew it was quite possibly a lie he told to make them both feel better in this impossible position.

She knew it too. She shook her head slowly. "I'll never be able to go back to how things were, will I?" He hesitated, and the silence answered her question just as it had in the parlor a few moments before. She rested her forehead on his shoulder and gripped his jacket tighter.

"We'll find a way," he promised.

She laughed, but there was no humor to the sound, only pain.

"What way? How do I exist if this man and his...minions can destroy me with impunity? Do I change my name? Do I leave London? Do I leave the country entirely?"

"No!" he snapped, too quick, but the suggestion had hit him so hard in the chest he almost couldn't breathe with the thought of it. "No," he repeated, this time more gently as he held her tighter. "We'll work it out, I swear it to you, Imogen."

She lifted her face again, and her amber eyes sought his in the moonlight. She sighed. "You can't swear it, Oscar, because you can't work it out. You can't fix this."

His lips pursed. She was saying his worst fears out loud. That he would be rendered impotent thanks to a cruel man with a title high enough to give him immunity against any crime. That any influence and power Oscar had built for himself, against all odds, would not be enough. Not for her. And in this moment, she was all that mattered.

"That is not acceptable," he said. "And so I do not accept it. I swear to you under these stars, by the light of this moon, that I will do everything in my power, I will bring all I've built to bear and I will find a way out of this that doesn't involve you being taken from—" He broke off and shook his head. "That doesn't involve you losing it all. I swear it, Imogen."

Her lips parted, as if the passion of his words had surprised her. Still, she nodded absently. Then she let out another great sigh. "I do not think I'll be a very good companion anymore tonight."

"Neither will I. Will and my mother will understand, I think, if we depart early." He stepped away from her only far enough to tuck her hand into the crook of his elbow. She flexed her fingers there, and he felt the pressure of her grip in every bit of his body and soul. "Come, we'll say our farewells and I'll take you home."

"Home," she repeated as he drew her inside. But she didn't argue, not with the suggestion and not with the label. Even though he should have clarified, he didn't do that either. He just kept her close and prayed he could fulfill the promise he had made to her.

For both their sakes.

CHAPTER 17

I mogen opened her eyes and looked around. She was in Oscar's
room, which was not an uncommon place for her to wake. The
more uncommon element was that he was still abed beside her,
despite the light coming in around the corners of the curtains, which
told her it was late in the day.

They had not made love the night before. He hadn't suggested it,
she hadn't the energy to do so, but he'd still taken her to his bed,
helped her undress and held her. Held her all night, soothing her
when the nightmares raged.

She rolled over now to face him and found he was watching her
through a hooded gaze. Her entire body twitched with desire, despite
the terrible circumstances. She ignored it and reached up to trace the
angle of his jaw. His whiskers tickled her palm, and she smiled at the
sensation. "Good morning."

His lips were tight as he nodded. "I would ask you if you slept well,
but I know the answer, I fear."

"My nightmares troubled you," she said with a shake of her head.
"I'm sorry. I should sleep in my own room rather than keep you up all
night."

He lifted his fingers to her lips and pressed there gently. "It isn't about my quality of sleep, Imogen. It never was. I rarely sleep more than a few hours any night, whether you are here in my home or not."

"Why?" she asked, tilting her head at the thought.

He shrugged. "My mind is too busy, I suppose. Or maybe I don't like my dreams, either."

"What do you dream about?" she whispered.

He eased onto his back and hauled her tighter against his side. As he stared up at the ceiling above them, she remained quiet, hoping whatever space she gave him might encourage him to let her in just a little.

She needed that.

"My father," he said at last. "I often dream of the last Duke of Rose-ford. I dream of the day he left. I dream of looking in the mirror and seeing his face."

Her brow wrinkled. "Your father's reputation is still spoken about in hushed whispers in the circles that matter. And there is nothing I've seen in you that has ever reminded me of the rumors about him."

He shrugged, but despite that, it was evident this topic meant far more to him than he was allowing her to see. "Perhaps. I've worked hard not to be anything like him. But the blood breaks through, I fear, from time to time." He let out a long sigh. "Whenever I hear those whispers, the ones you talk about, I cringe. Whenever some fop comes up to me in my club and starts in on how much he looked up to the last Duke of Roseford and his never-ending quest for pleasure, my stomach turns."

She traced her fingers along his chest. "I wonder how your brother feels. The one who holds the title now."

"Robert?" Oscar said slowly, as if saying the name was difficult. "He was like him. So much like him. And then he...wasn't anymore. Just like that, like some kind of lightning bolt hit and changed him."

"Love, they say," she whispered, thinking of the rumors that had run wild a few years ago when the new Duke of Roseford wooed and wed his duchess. Imogen had waxed romantic about it one day, and

Huxley had made some sharp comment about love not existing. Just another reminder that she couldn't have what she wanted.

Now she looked up at the man who held her, and wanted...

No, she wouldn't let herself think that. She wouldn't let herself crave the lightning bolt he described. Those sorts of things only existed for a few lucky souls, and Oscar was nothing but clear to her about his boundaries.

She snuggled a little closer and his arms tightened around her. He was warm and solid and whole, that was what mattered right now. He was here and he would protect her, if nothing else.

"Did you enjoy your day out?" he asked. "Despite the end?"

She lifted her head. "I did," she said. "It's a funny thing. In my heart, I am not the kind of woman who craves parties every night or to have a dozen friends. I've always preferred a quiet night in reading a book to bustling about constantly. But being here, not being able to leave for my own safety, it has made me realize how much the choice of staying in or going out means. That moment when I realize I can't just stroll over to the park or call on a friend...it hits me. So I very much appreciated you allowing me that moment of normalcy yesterday."

"I'm glad," he said, and there was that flutter of a smile around the edges of his mouth again. "It was a pleasure watching you. I know I've been hard on you about staying in or not contacting your friend. So I was happy to have the connections required to allow us a private showing of Carlton's collection."

She worried her lip as he continued. He didn't know that she had thwarted his order and reached out to Aurora. Here he was going on about offering her a respite and being apologetic about his stiff rules, and she was lying to him.

She didn't want to do that. Especially since he would find out soon enough. Aurora had said in her letter when she meant to be back in London, so Imogen had asked her to meet as soon as she returned. Just a few days now, for she knew Aurora would do everything in her power to make that meeting. Oscar would have to know about those plans at some point.

She cleared her throat as she sat up and stared down at him. The moment she moved, his gaze narrowed and his mouth tightened. "Imogen…" he said.

She worried her lip. "Can you read me so well?"

"I can see your expression filled with concern and guilt, so yes, I suppose I can." He folded his arms, and all it succeeded in doing was making his chest ripple, which did not help her concentrate on what she had to do next.

She shifted and forced a smile. "I might have a small something to feel guilty about. But I'm about to tell you what I've done, so that's something, isn't it? Confession of a wrong deed is a very important step in rectifying—"

"Imogen," he interrupted. "What did you do exactly?"

"You told me not to reach out to Aurora," she said softly. "But I…did."

"What?" he burst out, throwing the covers back and padding, utterly naked and deliciously distracting, away from her. He pivoted as he caught his dressing gown and threw it over his shoulders. "When? How?"

She explained to him how she had smuggled her letter out, and its contents. His jaw tightened with every word she spoke. "What were you thinking? You know how dangerous your current situation is. What if that boy was working for Roddenbury?"

"The eight-year-old child who uses the space behind your home as a way to cut through to the opposite street?" she asked.

He shook his head. "Children go to work at far younger than that, my dear."

"If that were true, it would mean Roddenbury would already guess I was staying at your home, wouldn't it? To send his child spies in the hopes I might slip one a letter and the last coin to my name? In that case, we would already be dead, I assume."

She shivered, and his body tensed. "I suppose," he conceded through what sounded like clenched teeth.

"I was *careful*, Oscar," she assured him. "I made my handwriting on the outside of the letter look different. I left no indication of where I was in the address or in the letter, itself. I simply asked Aurora to meet with me on Friday and told her I would give more direction when the time was closer. I need to see her. Especially if it might be the last time. I need to see her and show her that I'm fine. I need to…"

She bent her head. He moved forward, his expression softening. "You want to say goodbye."

"If I must," she choked out. "And I think I have to consider that might be true. I need to come to peace with that."

He scrubbed a hand over his face, and she could see his frustration, though it no longer seemed to be directed at her. He nodded. "I do understand. And while I wish you had been more up front with me, allowed me to help you, I cannot fault you for your desire to see someone you love. So we have a few days until this meeting, then?"

"Yes," she said. "I asked her to write to me when she returns to London on Thursday night, knowing it would be forwarded here and I would give her a location for the meeting on Friday. I'll let you choose it for highest safety and…" She trailed off and felt heat come to her cheeks.

"And?" he encouraged.

"I'd like you to meet Aurora," she said. "She is my dearest friend and you are—" She cut herself off. "I'd like you to meet her."

"I will," he said after what felt like the longest hesitation in the history of hesitation. "I would very much like to meet her."

"Good," she said, and meant it. She had so few people in her life that she cared for. She wanted them to know each other and like each other. She wanted to see Aurora's reaction to this man and all his command and kindness and passion.

"Imogen," he said, and took a long step toward her. "I know the conversation with my mother and Will last night was upsetting to you. I know this all feels…hopeless. But we will work it out."

She smiled, but in her heart it was hard to believe him. She knew, after all, that there were some things that could not be resolved. A murderous man who could destroy with immunity seemed like one of them.

If he sensed her hesitation, he said nothing further on the topic. Instead he drew in a long breath. "I have something I need to do today. Will you be all right by yourself? Should I have my mother visit and keep you company?"

"No," she said. "As much as I would enjoy her, I think I'd like to be by myself. I have a great deal to think about."

He held his stare on hers for a moment, then nodded. "Very well. I'll step into my dressing room to ready myself, but I'll come back to say goodbye before I go."

She forced a smile as he moved into the adjoining room and closed the door behind himself, but his words rang in her ears. Say goodbye. In the end, that was what they had to do. They had to find a way to say goodbye.

And she feared that moment was coming far more rapidly than she was ready to face.

～

O scar smirked as he looked around the smoky gentleman's club near Charing Cross. The place was fine, but Oscar's club was finer. He took some small pleasure in that as he took in all the details, from the livery of the servants to the placement of the chairs and tables throughout the hall.

But celebrating the comparative quality of his business to this one wasn't why he'd come here, so he pushed those thoughts aside and drew a deep breath as he looked around.

This was a gaming area of the club, but in the afternoon it was mostly quiet. Two tables with two pairs of men playing. He moved farther into the room, noting when the gentlemen's eyes came up. Some seemed to recognize him and registered surprise that he would be here.

He ignored it as he moved toward the table all the way in the furthest corner of the chamber. He didn't recognize the man facing him, but the one with his back to Oscar raised his interest. After all, his quarry was supposedly in this room, and since he saw him nowhere else, this had to be him.

He stepped up and cleared his throat. The gentleman turned his face upward, and Oscar's entire body stiffened, as much as he tried to maintain calm on his face.

Roddenbury.

"Good afternoon," he said as coolly as he could manage. "I see you're playing vingt-et-un. Do you have space for another?"

The man who had been playing against the earl seemed to sag with defeat and he looked at Roddenbury with pleading. "You can't bring in another. You need to give me the chance to win back what I've lose."

Roddenbury sneered in plain disgust. "You couldn't win against a child. Go home, Evans. If you didn't want to lost what you gambled, you wouldn't have played with what mattered."

Oscar straightened, for this wager seemed to involve far more than the pile of blunt in front of Roddenbury. The man, Evans, bent his head and got up. He looked at Oscar and his expression was so hangdog and pitiful that Oscar turned away.

"Better luck to you, sir," Evans said as he trudged off.

Roddenbury snickered as he gathered up the cards and motioned to the seat across from him. "I hope you have the blunt to truly wager."

Oscar sat and reached into his jacket pocket to withdraw the blunt he'd brought for just this purpose. A large amount of it. A thousand pounds in notes. He couldn't help but think of Imogen and her teasing him about winning just this amount as he placed it on the table. Perhaps he'd picked the sum on purpose. For her. All of this was for her.

"Excellent, a real game with high stakes," Roddenbury said, his eyes shining with greed as he sized Oscar up.

Oscar refrained from pointing out the stakes were higher than Roddenbury realized, and held out a hand for the cards. Roddenbury handed them over, and Oscar began to shuffle as he looked over the earl. He was a young man, perhaps a handful of years younger than Oscar, himself. He had dark hair and brown eyes that held a hint of the cruelty this man was capable of.

Oscar supposed some might call him handsome. He was certain many a lady had cooed over Roddenbury, hoping to gain his favor… only to realize she had made a terrible mistake the moment they were alone. This was the man who had chased Imogen, who threatened her life and their…*her* future. What Oscar wanted to do was come across the table and strangle the life out of him.

Roddenbury arched a brow. "Deal or leave, sir. I don't have all day."

Oscar dealt out the first hand and they settled into the game, each trying to get the titular vingt-et-un or as close to it as possible. The skill was knowing when to take a card or when to wait. Oscar had to fight his careful nature to risk the blunt he'd brought and maintain Roddenbury's interest.

They'd played for a quarter of an hour before the earl tilted his head and snagged Oscar's gaze. "I know you."

"And I know you, my lord," Oscar retorted. "I suppose we are both infamous men."

Roddenbury chuckled. "For very different reasons, I think. My title gives me some of my notoriety."

"And how you use it," Oscar offered.

Roddenbury's eyebrows lifted. "That too. As for you, I suppose you have two things that make you someone Society talks about, *Mr. Fitzhugh.*"

Oscar inclined his head to acknowledge the recognition. "And what are those?"

Roddenbury dealt the next hand before he answered, "Your club. And the fact that you are one of the Roseford Bastards."

Oscar flexed his hands against the table before he flipped the cards in front of him. "Most don't have the audacity to bring up that subject with me."

"Well, I suppose I do so because I admire your late father,"

Roddenbury said, and tapped his fingers on the wood to indicate he would draw another to try to make his quinze closer to a vignt-et-un.

"Of course you did," Oscar said, and saw the opportunity this man's poisoned words created. He leaned closer and smiled as Roddenbury went over the limit. He pushed his money forward with disgust and glared as Oscar said, "I've heard rumor you might have some of the same interests as the late duke."

"Women, you mean," Roddenbury chuckled. "Don't we all?"

"A good many men are enthralled by the charms of ladies, of course," Oscar said as he tried, once again, not to think of Imogen back at home. Maybe still in his bed. Waiting for him to find a way to save her. He shook the distraction away. He'd come here with a purpose in mind. He had to focus in order to fulfill it.

"But I've heard it goes further than that," he continued. He drew a deep breath and met the other man's gaze. "I've heard you have women…available. Or can make them so."

CHAPTER 18

O scar watched for any tiny indication of Roddenbury's feelings on the question, but the earl was a good card player. He didn't respond for a moment, though his gaze remained heavy on Oscar as he pushed the deck over for him to deal. Oscar shuffled as the tension between them ratcheted up. Roddenbury didn't know what to think of him and he wasn't inclined to trust. In some ways, that was smart. Wicked men did wicked things, but most would draw the line at kidnap, murder and forced imprisonment of women. The earl would be a fool not to look for traps at every turn.

"Are you looking for women, Fitzhugh?" he asked, his tone suddenly heavier, darker.

Oscar cleared his throat. "I'd like my club to be more…competitive with some of the hells. Perhaps some willing women would make that happen."

Roddenbury snorted out a chuckle. "How about less than willing? Though they do tend to come to heel given enough time and incentive."

Oscar swallowed past the bile gathering in his throat. He wanted to hit this man so badly he could almost feel the crunch of his cheek beneath his fist.

"You look angry, Mr. Fitzhugh. Do you not approve of my methods?" Roddenbury leaned forward. "Or is it more personal?"

Oscar thought of Louisa. He thought of Imogen. "I suppose everything is personal in the end, my lord."

"Deal the next hand, Mr. Fitzhugh. And why don't we raise the stakes?" He pushed his money to the center of the table. All of it. "All in."

"No matter the hand?" Oscar said.

"Life isn't worth anything without risk," Roddenbury said with a thin smile.

Oscar shoved his own money in and dealt the cards. Roddenbury motioned to him and Oscar flipped his cards. Two kings. He arched a brow at Roddenbury and waited as the other man flipped his own cards one at a time. A queen. And as he picked up the other card and looked at it before he showed it to Oscar, the earl smiled.

Oscar's heart sank. He turned the card and revealed an ace.

"I believe that's the game."

"That was good luck," Oscar mused as he watched his money get pulled away by his companion.

"Or something like it," Roddenbury said with a chuckle as he cleared the table and got up to walk away.

Oscar gripped his hands against the tabletop. So Roddenbury had cheated. And giving that fact away through inference was some odd way to show his dominance, that he was unbeatable. That he was unstoppable.

Oscar couldn't let that stand.

He stood up and followed Roddenbury, turning him back toward him and yanking him closer. Roddenbury jerked back, cocked his fist and punched Oscar straight in the face.

He reeled at the unexpected attack, at the pain that shot through his cheekbone and around the eye that would surely be blackened in moments. From the corner of that throbbing eye, he saw others coming toward them. He wasn't a member of this club, but Roddenbury was. Given that fact and their disparate places in Society, he was surely about to be kicked out.

He jerked Roddenbury closer. "I know what you are, Roddenbury. I know what you do. You will be stopped."

Roddenbury staggered back and held up a hand to stay the men who were coming to intervene. He stared at Oscar for a moment, his gaze moving up and down his frame. Then he shook his head. "You don't appear to be a foolish man, this little interaction aside. And I certainly hope you haven't done something you might regret, sir. Because if I find out you have interfered with me...if I find out you are working in league with *anyone else* to harm me or my business, I will destroy you. I will destroy everything you have, everything you are, I will destroy everything you love. And she...if there is a she...will still suffer. So that loss will be *for nothing.*"

Oscar's stomach turned. Roddenbury was talking about Imogen. He guessed, though he might not be certain, about Oscar's involvement. And so he had come here to feel this man out, to try to uncover if he could be stopped...and instead he had done nothing but bring him ever closer to Imogen.

"I don't know what the hell you're talking about, Roddenbury," he grunted. "I just meant you were a card cheat."

"I hope that's true," Roddenbury said. "Take this riffraff away."

Oscar felt the men grabbing for him and yanked from their grip, smoothing his jacket as he pivoted on his heel and strode from the club on his own volition. But as he threw himself on his horse and rode toward home, his stomach churned.

He'd always controlled his emotions for this very reason. And now because he couldn't stop thinking of Imogen, of helping her and taking the fear from her eyes, he'd probably only made things worse. He might even lose her because of what he'd done.

The thought of which turned his stomach and drove him even harder to get to her.

I mogen was curled up on the settee in Oscar's library with a book she had been trying to read for over an hour. Only she couldn't concentrate. Every time she started to lose herself in the tale, she would think of Oscar. She would think of Aurora. She would think of that poor dead woman whose murder had changed her life forever. She'd been searching the papers for days, trying to find some indication her body had been found. Mourning her even if no one else did.

She threw the book aside and got to her feet just as the door to the library opened and Oscar stepped in. She took a step toward him, about to welcome him home with a kiss, when she noticed the circle of a bruise around his left eye.

She rushed forward. "Your face!"

He flinched and lifted a hand to it. "I knew it looked bad when Donovan's eyes went that wide."

"What happened?" she asked as she caught his hand and drew him to the settee. He allowed her to force him into a seated position and didn't argue when she tilted his head to the side to see the injury better in the lamplight.

"I could tell you I walked into a post," he suggested.

She scowled at him. "For weeks you grumble around here like an ogre guarding his bridge and *now* you have jokes?"

He pursed his lips. "I'm not an ogre and I don't even own a bridge."

She pulled away and shot him what she hoped was a withering look. "Oscar!"

He bent his head and the way his gaze moved away from hers made her stomach plummet.

"Oscar?" she repeated, this time on nothing more than a breath.

"I went to see the Earl of Roddenbury," he said, and got to his feet to pace away.

Her mouth dropped open, and for a moment she was struck mute with shock. He didn't fill the silence, and so the only sound was the crackling of the wood on the fire until she managed to find some words. *Any* words.

"Please tell me this is a nightmare," she said as she got to her feet and followed him across the room. She caught his elbow and forced him to turn back toward her. "Please tell me what you just said to me is a lie or a bad joke."

"It's neither," he said.

"Why would you do that?" she asked. "Especially after lecturing me about reaching out to Aurora! Why would you immediately leave our bed and march off to find a man who wants me dead?"

"Because I hoped to get some information out of him," he growled, and yanked away from her. "I hoped that we might come to some kind of understanding that could help you."

"But he punched you," she said.

"He cheated at cards," he explained, but there was something in his eyes that let her know it was more.

"Oscar," she snapped.

He glared at her. "You can't manage me, you know."

"You *need* to be managed, apparently." She shook her head. "*Why* did he punch you?"

"Good Lord, you are unstoppable." He shook his head, but he didn't sound angry at that fact. "In my attempt to wheedle the truth out of him, I have...likely only raised his suspicions about me. I let emotion take over and I revealed too much of my hand, my strategy. I...lost control."

She wrinkled her brow at that idea. This man didn't lose control. He didn't get swept away by emotion. He was careful not to do either of those things.

"What do you think he'll do?" she asked.

"I'm not sure," he admitted. "Perhaps nothing. Perhaps he'll decide to do more than punch me in the face. Either way we'll have to make some contingency plans. He might start watching me after today, which means I'll make arrangements for you to be moved somewhere safer. Perhaps out to the country, after we see your friend in a few days. I'll have Will take over the club until this dies down."

"I suppose I understand that," she whispered.

He nodded. "We'll do what must be done."

"What I don't understand is why would you risk yourself in this way? Why would you run after a man we already know is violent and vile? One who could ruin you or worse?"

His eyes lit and he caught her elbow, hauling her a little closer, molding her against his chest as he towered over her in a way that should have been intimidating. But it wasn't. Because this was Oscar, and she knew who he was. What he was. She knew his edges, as well as his curves and she knew she never had to fear him.

"Why do you *think* I did it, Imogen?"

She gasped at the implication. The tension that had been hanging between them, forever unnamed but for desire, seemed to increase even more. There was hardly space to keep them apart. His lips so close she could feel the heat of them linger on her own.

"Oscar," she whispered, and felt him tense as his arms came around her.

"No," he murmured back, and then his mouth found hers.

~

Oscar wasn't proud of the tactic he had employed against Imogen, but what choice did he have? His overly emotional response had caused trouble not just with Roddenbury, but now he'd been on the verge of the kind of confession to Imogen that would be incredibly dangerous. If they brought their hearts into this matter, there would be no end to the damage.

So he kissed her. But when her arms wound around his neck and she gasped out a moan against his lips, strategy was forgotten. Everything was forgotten but her, just as it always was. The woman could do that, more than any other before her. She could tie him up in knots with her smile or laughter, or just by looking at him from across the room. And yes, that had everything to do with how much he wanted her. And it had everything to do with so much more than desire.

But he pushed that away. He had to push it far away. Concentrate on the element he could control. The element he could accept and separate as something different. Something less dangerous.

Even though it was just as potent. When Imogen's fingers bunched against his back, when she lifted toward him with a mewl that vibrated on his lips, his body's response was more than potent. What he felt was powerful, changing. A need unlike any other because in the past need had been about pleasure. This need was specific to this woman in this moment, and nothing else in the world mattered.

So he backed her across the room, toward the settee they had abandoned a few moments before. He tangled his fingers into her hair, holding her steady as he lowered her onto the cushions. When his weight covered her and she lifted against him, he nearly came unmanned right then and there.

But this was about regaining control, not surrendering it further, so he resisted the urge to just take, and instead continued kissing her as he hitched her skirts up. When his fingers brushed the fabric of her stockings, his nails lightly abrading her skin through the silk, she jolted beneath him and let out a gasping cry that hit him directly in the cock.

God, how he wanted her. In his blood, in his skin, in his mind and every inch of his body. Only having her would stave off the need, and only for a short while. That desire would return, as hard and as heavy as the first time, within hours, sometimes minutes.

"Fuck," he muttered against her throat, and then he began to kiss lower. He let his mouth glide over her breasts, still hidden beneath her pretty gown. Over her stomach as he slid to his knees on the settee before her. Down to her thighs as he dragged her to the edge of the couch and pushed her dress up onto her stomach.

Her tugged the slit on her drawers wide and sucked in a whiff of her sex. Clean and sweet, musky with her need. He wanted to taste that flavor on his tongue. He wanted to feel her ripple with release as he ate her.

She stared down at him from her perch on the settee. Their eyes met, and he saw the wicked spark in her eyes. She pushed her legs open wider and reached down to spread herself for him.

He was fully clothed and had hardly touched her, but he could have spent in that moment. Instead he leaned in and pressed his fingers against hers, forcing her even wider before he leaned in and licked her.

She jolted against him with a gasp, and he doubled the pressure of his tongue as he repeated the action. How fast could he make her come? That was the question. He counted the seconds in his mind as he sucked her clitoris, swirling his tongue around the nub just the way he knew she liked it. Her breath shortened and she began lifting into his mouth, seeking what he offered, grinding to garner more pleasure.

She jerked against him at last, the waves of her release rippling on his tongue as he continued to stimulate her and force her to cling to the edge of the settee. At last she fell back, panting with relief. Only then did he unfasten the placard on his trousers, freeing himself.

She looked down, licking her lips as he stroked himself once, twice. She opened wider, a wicked groan exiting her mouth as he aligned his hard body to her slick one. He entered her in a long thrust. She was tight around him, perfect and heated and made for him.

He braced himself against the settee cushions, lowering his face close to hers but not kissing her, even when she lifted toward him. He expected her to whimper or demand, but instead she chuckled. A low, rough sound that made him grind his hips in a circle against her.

"Hard," she demanded, meeting his gaze. Her voice was softer now, more tender despite the question. "Hard, please."

He lost all sense at that demand, said so sweetly. He lost control for the third time that day. But this kind of surrender was perfect. He tangled his fingers into her hair, tilting her head back so she'd watch him the entire time he took her. He placed his opposite hand against her throat, squeezing ever so slightly and loving how her body tightened around him as she moaned.

And then he did as she asked. He fucked her hard, losing himself in the never-ending edge toward release, losing himself in how her eyes glazed over and her cries echoed in the library. He lost himself in the grip of her pussy and the slickness as she came a second time, clawing at him and screaming his name.

His own pleasure arced, like lightning in his veins, and he only barely withdrew from her and came against his hand, making a keening cry that joined with hers before he collapsed against her and kissed her once more.

If he expected her to perhaps broach the topic of Roddenbury or the future or his emotional reasons for seeking out danger, she didn't. She just wrapped her arms around him, holding him tightly. As if she knew as well as he did that nothing good could come from exploring a future that couldn't be. A surrender that couldn't be.

A love that couldn't be.

And even though he should have been pleased by that silent capitulation, even though it should have made him feel better that she wouldn't find a way to break both their hearts, there was something hollow about the victory. Somehow he'd lost, even if he'd won.

But there was nothing he could do about it now. All he could do was plan for the meeting with her friend in a few days, and how and where he would put Imogen next in the hopes of saving her life.

CHAPTER 19

The three days until her meeting with Aurora both flew and dragged. Dragged because her lockdown in Oscar's home had become far more desperate. Even the gardens had become off-limits, and she could see he got nervous when she even put a toe on the terrace. Flew because she felt her time with Oscar swirling away like sands through an hourglass.

He kept talking about sending her away from London after she met with Aurora. He said it was temporary, but they both knew better. She'd already begun to come to terms with the fact that her life as she knew it was very much over. Whatever happened next, it would be a different chapter. Perhaps it would come with a new name and ultimately a new home. A new life. As what, she couldn't imagine. She'd be useless as a servant thanks to her privileged upbringing. She had no idea how she would ever land a position as a lady's maid without references or a history.

Perhaps if she went to the continent, she could continue with her original plans to become a courtesan. Only when she thought of another man touching her ever again…not Oscar, who knew her body like it was an instrument and he a virtuoso…

Well, she wasn't thrilled by the idea. How could she pretend when all she'd do for the rest of her life was compare every man with the one who made it clear he didn't want her, at least not forever.

But now here they were in his carriage, on the way to his club, where he'd agreed to let her meet with Aurora. Imogen sighed and hoped she was keeping her maudlin thoughts from her face. Oscar was staring out the window, but that didn't mean he wasn't entirely aware of her. He always seemed to be.

"We're here," he said, his voice rough.

He leaned away from the window, and that gave her a place to look. She leaned in as the carriage pulled up to a beautiful building with intricately carved pillars and a sweeping marble staircase that led to a red door. She looked across at Oscar.

"It's wonderful," she said. "You must be so proud of it."

He blinked as if he were confused by that statement for a moment. "I didn't build it. I just bought it. With my father's payoff."

She shook her head at the bitterness that laced his tone. "You made it a success without any help from him," she insisted. "Even *I'd* heard of your club before I met you and not just because Huxley was a member. It's the place to be, even more than White's. Your salons are more whispered about, your intellectuals more…"

"Intellectual?" he filled in with that flutter of a smile that made her heart leap and long for the very rare full expression.

"You have the *most* intellectual of them all, I've been assured," she teased. Then her own smile fell. "Truly, Oscar. You should be proud of what you've built for yourself."

He shifted as if her praise made him a little uncomfortable. The door to the carriage opened, and he motioned for her to exit first. "Wait until you see the inside of the place before you judge. Perhaps it's shabby."

She took the help down from the footman as she laughed. He followed and they walked up the stairs together. A butler was waiting at the door. He was stuffier than Oscar's private butler, Donovan, who was everything proper but still friendly and capable of a smile from time to time. This man had no hair out of place and his tone was filled with gravitas as he intoned, "Mr. Fitzhugh, welcome back, sir. And welcome, madam."

Oscar inclined his head. "Goodworth. Have all the arrangements been made?"

"Yes, the club was closed an hour ago and the last of the patrons left a quarter hour ago. There was much complaining, but your decree that we would provide a free entertainment next week was met with great enthusiasm."

"Excellent. Mrs. Huxley's guest should be here shortly. Please send her to us in the great parlor. We'll await them there."

"Very good. There is tea already there for you."

The butler gave a smart bow as Oscar took Imogen's arm and guided her down a long hall past multiple meeting rooms and parlors and into a large chamber with giant windows that overlooked the street below.

She gasped as she looked around her. She had never been in a men's club. It was forbidden. But she had always pictured them as stuffy places, thick with smoke and wrinkled newspapers and monotonous voices droning on about politics and the prices of barley.

But this hall was light and airy, tables spread through it and comfortable leather chairs and a settee by the fire and more chairs overlooking the windows. A sideboard was set against the wall opposite those same windows, with a wide selection of bottles lined up in perfect order.

"Oh, Oscar," she breathed. "It's wonderful."

She pivoted to face him, hands clasped together, and found his cheeks were actually bright with color. He was blushing, and she found it almost as charming as those rare hints of a smile he sometimes allowed.

"Thank you," he said softly. "We have worked hard to make it thus. It was Will's club to begin with. It was struggling and I bought in as an owner. We changed the name to Fitzhugh's because, obviously, White's was already very much taken."

She smiled at the quip. "Do you like the work?"

"I do," he said, and he looked around almost as if he were seeing the room for the first time, too. "The membership is more diverse than in other clubs. We have the titled, of course. There is no avoiding that if one wants to be successful, but I'm much more interested in catering to those without title or family connection. Men who are building themselves up through industry and science, freedom and justice. If our salons are spoken about, as you said in the carriage, it is because our membership is collectively great of mind."

He was passionate as he spoke, as passionate as he often looked when he touched her, took her. His dark eyes were bright and intense and his hands moved in animated fashion.

She smiled because she couldn't help it. His enthusiasm, so often muted by design, was impossible to deny.

"Why are you looking at me that way?" he asked, shifting slightly.

She shook her head. "You're very charming, Mr. Fitzhugh."

He choked out a laugh, and for only the second time since she met him, a broad smile broke across his face. Her heart stuttered once again at seeing it. Like finding the most beautiful pearl in an oyster, it was a rare and valuable thing.

"Don't spread that around," he said. "If it is true I'll have lost all my powers to impress those who require me to be dark and brooding."

"I won't say a thing," she said.

He moved to the sideboard and fiddled with the bottles. "Tell me more about Lady Lovell. We can trust her, can't we?"

She nodded without hesitation. "Of course. We met at a soiree years ago. She had only recently married, I had been unhappy for a long time. We latched on to each other, told each other secrets no one else knew. Until you, that is." She blushed, because it seemed she was now incapable of doing anything but revealing herself to him more and more.

Even if she knew that it could end in no good.

"You are more like sisters than friends," he mused as he looked at her with a troubled gaze.

Those words soothed her a little. "We truly are. I'm so lucky to have her in my life. I don't know what I'll do if I—" She bent her head and drew a few long breaths before she spoke again. "If I cannot see her ever again."

He stiffened and pivoted away. She saw the flex of his shoulders. The tension there. For her, about her, because of her. It felt like a wall between them, and she faced the fireplace slowly, creating her own distance between them.

She lost herself in the flames for a moment, trying to settle her mind. It was only a sound from the door that shocked her from her troubled reverie. She pivoted toward it and her knees went weak.

Aurora was standing at the door beside a handsome gentleman holding a cane. Her friend met her eyes, lifting her shaking hands.

"Imogen!" she cried out as she released her companion and rushed across the room. They launched themselves toward each other at the same time, and Imogen clung to her in the tightest hug she'd ever shared with her friend.

They parted, and she looked Aurora up and down. She had always been exquisitely beautiful. She had honey hair and green eyes, high cheekbones and a full, curvaceous figure. She was the kind of woman men turned to look at on the street. But she had never looked more beautiful than she did in that moment and Imogen recognized, with instant power and clarity, that it was because Aurora was in love.

Out of nowhere, everything became so overwhelming. She glanced at Oscar, who was still standing at the sideboard, hand clenched against the tabletop, not looking at her. Putting up the wall that always came between them. She buried her head into Aurora's shoulder and burst into humiliating tears.

"I'm sorry, I'm so sorry I frightened you," she murmured as Aurora stroked her hair gently, offering the comfort Imogen needed, but perhaps didn't fully deserve.

"What the fuck are all of *you* doing here?"

She jerked her face toward Oscar and followed his gaze toward the door. Now it wasn't just Aurora's companion, the one Imogen was certain she was in love with, in the doorway. No, the room was now filling with people. Two white couples and a tall, handsome Black man had all filled the room and stood silently.

And Oscar stared at them, all the color draining from his face, even as he glared in that commanding, almost menacing way he could sometimes muster. He looked truly troubled and she realized he *knew* some of Aurora's friends.

If his anger was any indication, he knew them very well.

His attention broke from them and pivoted to her. The betrayal was lit in his eyes. "Imogen, this was *not* our arrangement."

～

A s Oscar stared at her, Imogen caught her breath. He still couldn't tell if she'd known about this ambush all along, or if it was a surprise. Still, when she stepped away from Lady Lovell and toward him, her hands shaking as she lifted them in silent entreaty, he wanted so much to reach for her. He had to fight that desire with all his might, fight to keep his gaze on hers, but not soften it.

"I didn't know," Imogen said, softly but firmly. She was all but willing him to see it was true. He could read it on every line of her face.

But he still wasn't certain. After all, this roomful of people weren't just some random collection of individuals. The man Aurora had come into the room with at first was Oscar's half-brother, Nicholas Gillingham. One of the other women at the doorway was his half-sister, Selina Oliver...Huntington, he thought her married name was.

And the other couple with them was the Duke and Duchess of Willowby. Old friends of his brother, the newest Duke of Roseford. In fact, Robert was the only one missing from this merry band of intruders.

This connection between Lady Lovell and Imogen, that she'd brought his family, the one he'd banned from his life, along with her...

That couldn't be coincidence. And the only one he'd told any version of that story to was Imogen. So how could she not be involved?

"She *didn't* know," Lady Lovell said firmly as she crossed to stand beside Imogen. She really was lovely, though her beauty dimmed a fraction when next to Imogen's light.

He also had no idea if she could be trusted. But she certainly surprised him when she examined him closely for a fraction of a moment, then held out a hand to Oscar.

"Mr. Fitzhugh, you have no idea how much I owe you for helping my friend," Lady Lovell continued. "I could *never* repay you."

Oscar took her outstretched hand at last, shaking it gently. "There is no repayment necessary. It was my pleasure."

His gaze moved to Imogen, and now she blushed. He had gone too far, revealed too much before this audience and embarrassed her. He had no idea why he'd done it. Why he'd felt a need to reconnect with her when he didn't even know her intentions.

Lady Lovell squeezed Imogen's elbow gently, and he saw Imogen straighten a little, as if she had been buoyed up by her friend's support. That made him like the viscountess even more.

Lady Lovell cleared her throat and said, "But I swear to you that Imogen had no idea I was bringing this small army with me." Oscar met Imogen's eyes and she nodded slightly. Lady Lovell continued, "I thought you might not see us if I told you I was bringing help. But that is what this group is. Everyone here wishes to assist with this investigation. Help Imogen."

Oscar jolted. Could that be true? Was none of this sudden arrival of his family about him after all, but...her? And if so, how could he refuse that assistance if it might save her life?

"I suppose I understand that," he said reluctantly. He faced the gathered crowd. "I think most of us need no introduction."

"Yes, you wrote us off long ago, didn't you?" Selina said as she glared at him and folded her arms. She looked so much like their late father in that moment that he nearly flinched. "So why waste time on pleasantries now?"

"Selina," the man beside her said softly, his hand coming to the small of her back. Then he nodded toward Oscar. "I am Derrick Huntington, Mr. Fitzhugh. Selina's husband."

"Selina is my sister, Imogen," he said.

Imogen caught her breath and stepped forward, her hand fluttering out like she wanted to touch him, comfort him, but not quite doing it. He found himself wishing she had in this dizzying moment. "What?"

Oscar ignored the question and gave a slight nod for Huntington.

"This is my partner and fellow investigator, Mr. Edward Barber," Huntington continued, motioning to the Black man who was coming forward, hand extended.

"A pleasure," Oscar said, and meant it, for while he might have issues with Selina and Nicholas, he had none with her companions. "I've heard good things about your investigative prowess, gentlemen."

Lady Lovell moved to the door and took Oscar's brother's hand. Nicholas didn't take his eyes off Oscar, but allowed her to draw him to Imogen. "This is Nicholas Gillingham. Nicholas, this is my best and truest friend, Imogen Huxley."

"He's also my brother," Oscar interjected, and for a moment he thought Imogen might fall over from the shock of it all.

"Nicholas who you…" Imogen whispered, and Lady Lovell nodded to fill in a gap Oscar didn't understand. "I-I didn't know he was related to Oscar…Mr. Fitzhugh."

"Neither did I until Mr. Fitzhugh's name came up in your letter," Lady Lovell said, and glanced at Oscar.

Nicholas came forward, slow with his cane. Oscar found himself glancing at his leg. Everyone knew Gillingham had nearly died in the war. Now he found himself wondering more about him. He'd always all but ignored his existence, going so far as to ban him from his club.

"We've never met," Gillingham said as he extended a hand. "Nicholas Gillingham."

It was a firm handshake when Oscar took it. His brother didn't posture or pull. And when he let him go, his gaze wasn't cold or cruel, rather kind but also curious.

Oscar cleared his throat and turned away. He didn't want kind. He didn't want curious. Not from the siblings he'd made a purposeful effort to avoid.

"And I recognize our other companions," he said in the most breezy tone he could manage. "The Duke and Duchess of Willowby, if I'm not mistaken. Friends of our only legitimate sibling, the great Duke of Roseford. I assume you're here on *his* behest?"

He couldn't keep the bitterness from his tone, and he noted how Willowby's eyes narrowed in protective annoyance. "I am a friend of Robert's," he admitted. "But I'm not here because of that connection. My wife and I are in the War Department, Mr. Fitzhugh. I'm here on behalf of king and country."

Imogen gasped, and again her hand fluttered like she wanted to touch him in this moment. "*You* are the agents?"

The Duchess of Willowby arched a brow at her husband. "You act as though you've heard of us."

"Only rumors of your existence," Imogen breathed. "And that you were titled. He really *is* a duke, Oscar."

"I am that," Willowby said with a shrug. "Amongst a great many other things. My title might be the least interesting thing about me."

Oscar glared at him. He supposed that was this man's attempt to offer some kind of comfort when it came to this situation. That somehow he was better than the others who might hold his title. Well, he would believe that when he saw it. Which meant they should get down to business.

"And now that we've participated in Mrs. Huntington's required *pleasantries*," Oscar said with a quick glance for Selina, who glared at him in return, "perhaps we can get down to what we're all here for."

"Imogen, where have you been? What happened?" Aurora said, grasping her friend's hands and drawing her to a settee in the middle of the room. The rest took places around them.

Imogen shifted and her cheeks darkened. Oscar could feel her discomfort from across the room, and a wild and protective instinct rose up in him. Like he could just sweep her up and carry her away and never make her face this terrible thing ever again.

A patently foolish idea considering this room was full of people who might actually be able to leverage their connections to save her.

"I didn't expect to be telling this story for an audience," she whispered.

Lady Lovell squeezed her hand. "They're friends. I promise that. They can all be trusted."

Oscar shook his head and poured a splash of madeira into a glass. Imogen liked madeira in the afternoon if she had a drink. Sherry was for before supper. He knew that like he knew a dozen things about her. Like that she was stronger than she believed. Like that she was better than perhaps he deserved.

He moved to the settee and handed the wine over to Imogen. She lifted her gaze to him, and again their eyes held. He tried with all his might to pour all his support into her, tried to show her that he would not walk away, nor let anyone hurt her in this room or any other.

"You have *nothing* to be ashamed of," he said softly. "And you owe *them* nothing. None of them were invited, so they can all get the fuck out of my club."

Imogen swallowed as she glanced around at the gathering of strangers. His family…but strangers. "Can you truly help me?"

The Duke of Willowby stepped forward. "I think we can, Mrs. Huxley. *If* we understand what is going on. But if you don't wish to tell the story to an audience, we can step out. Only my wife would stay to record your statement if that would make you more comfortable."

Oscar glanced at the duke again. It was a kind offer. One he hadn't expected and yet appreciated.

"But she'll repeat it to you all anyway," Imogen said, letting out her breath in a shaky sigh. "She would have to in order for you to under-stand." No one denied that, and Imogen glanced up at Oscar again. As if he somehow had the answers for her. How he wished he did. "It will be worth the humiliation," she said at last.

He clenched his teeth at the absolute defeat in her stare. The pain that she would have to tell this horrible story yet again to an audience of outsiders. He wanted to touch her so very badly in that moment. But she had already mentioned humiliation. If he touched her, he wouldn't be able to hide their connection. So he watched helplessly as Imogen took a gulp of wine and handed her glass back to him.

"I...I was in dire straits after my husband's death," she began. He listened as she told the story, the one he could have recited himself, he'd pondered it so often since she careened into him in that alleyway. Listened as her strength went on display for everyone in the room to see.

Speaking of the murder she'd been witness to was the only time her voice wavered. The only time she hesitated. He felt her pain, her guilt, her horror on behalf of that poor woman, her terror that she would end up the same way. Discarded like trash in the river.

He couldn't help it then. He pressed a hand to her shoulder, fingers curling there for support as she continued.

"I stumbled into Oscar—Mr. Fitzhugh—and he has been hiding me ever since, trying to help me prove what I know. What I saw. *Who* I saw. He saved my life," she finished.

He caught his breath as she lifted her gaze to him. That gaze that had become so important to every part of his life, his day, any moment he was in. This woman had wound her way into his soul since he met her. There was no denying the importance of that as he stared down into her eyes. At least not to himself.

But he couldn't let her see it. Certainly, he couldn't let this roomful of people he didn't trust be a part of it.

He released her reluctantly and backed a step away. "I didn't do much. But this situation goes deep. Much deeper than one murder."

Willowby nodded with a small glance toward his wife. "The War Department suspects as much. Between what we've gleaned and what help we've had from Mr. Barber and Mr. Huntington's sources, I think we're close to uncovering the mastermind behind this...ring of blackguards."

Oscar tensed. Uncovering. That meant they didn't know about Roddenbury and his involvement.

Imogen seemed to have the same idea as she sent him a look and got to her feet. "If I could help I would—"

Before she could finish the sentence, there was an explosion of glass from the huge window behind them, followed by a series of shots that ricocheted around the room.

Oscar didn't think, he didn't plan—he just dove over the back of the settee and prayed he could protect Imogen. Because Imogen was all that mattered.

CHAPTER 20

I mogen screamed, but it was cut off as Oscar's heavy weight hit her, knocking the air from her lungs and dragging her to the floor. He covered her, his arms around her as they had been around her so many times in the past few weeks.

After what felt like a lifetime, the explosive shooting stopped and the room fell eerily silent.

Oscar rolled away so he no longer fully covered her body, but he said nothing as he smoothed his hands over her. Under any other circumstances, the touch would have been erotic, but right now he just looked terrified.

"Were you hit?" he whispered, and she wasn't even certain that he was asking her as much as asking the universe. "Please tell me you weren't hit."

"I-I don't think so," she said, and caught his arms. "Oscar." He tried to shake her off and continued looking for any injury. "Oscar!" she repeated, this time sharper. "I'm not hit."

He cupped her chin, and then he leaned down and kissed her. Hard. Heavy. Swiftly over, but powerfully felt.

She dropped her hands away from his arms and was about to ask him if he was hit when she noticed the wetness on her palm. Blood.

JESS MICHAELS

"Oscar," she said, sitting up. "You're injured."

He glanced down at the hole in his jacket. Blood seeped from the wound beneath. The others were calling out now, indicating they were unharmed, and she grabbed his arm with both hands, putting pressure on the wound as they rose from behind the couch.

"He's cut," she said.

"That's not a cut," Mr. Huntington replied as he moved forward. He was unwinding his cravat as he went. "You've been shot."

Imogen could scarcely hear over the rush of blood to her ears. The rush of terror as Oscar looked down at his arm with a shrug. "It seems I have."

"Oscar!" Imogen cried out.

He ignored her as he removed the jacket and he and Huntington examined the wound together. The Duchess of Willowby came to Huntington's elbow and also looked closely. Imogen swallowed at the sight of the horrible hole there in his upper arm, closer to his left shoulder than to his elbow.

"It went through," Oscar said. She saw him flinch slightly, but that was the only indication he gave that there was pain. "Wrap it, if you will, and I'll have it looked at later."

Imogen stared at him. How could he be so dismissive of the fact that he'd been *shot*? Because of her. The others seemed equally taken aback, but Huntington shook his head and wrapped the arm with his discarded cravat as he had been asked. Oscar hardly reacted as he did so, but instead looked around the room.

Imogen followed his gaze, and her heart sank. This beautiful room in the club he had spent so much of his life building was destroyed. The window was shattered, there were bullet holes in furniture, the decorations had been shredded by broken glass.

"Bloody hell," he muttered.

Imogen bent her head, guilt ravaging her the same way the attack had ravaged all he'd built. "I'm sorry."

His brow wrinkled, but the look of annoyance on his face didn't seem to change as he said, "Don't."

She could hardly breathe as he turned his gaze away from hers. He'd been so passionately worried for her, but now he put the wall up again. She was fine, but he had lost so much because of her. There was no wonder he might wish to be as far from her as possible.

Willowby had moved to the window and was carefully peering out from around the edge of the broken glass to the street below. "I don't see anyone. There must have been more than one assailant for all this carnage. Diana, Barber, we should go down and question witnesses on the street. Huntington, does that wound need more attention?"

Huntington finished tying off the cravat. "It's fine for now, though he'll need a doctor later."

Huntington kept talking. They were all making arrangements now to interview witnesses to the attack. To check on Oscar's servants in the back of the club. To send for more men to search for the culprits.

Imogen ignored it all. She could do nothing else but just stare at Oscar, his wound still seeping through the tight bandage. She watched him talk, watched him move as he took command of these strangers in his space.

He had been hurt because of her. He could have died because of her. And in that moment, she knew she loved him. She had fallen in love with him, and there was no changing that even if it was foolish and could only end in heartbreak.

He was still talking, completely oblivious to what she now knew was true. "...right now, though, I need to take Imogen away."

She blinked, drawn away from the startling truth of her heart and back to the room. He would take her away? Even after all the trouble she'd caused, he still wanted to protect her? Didn't that mean something?

Aurora had been standing in Nicholas Gillingham's arms, and now she staggered closer. "No, wait! Is that for the best?"

The others exchanged a look, and then Willowby, Barber and Huntington left the room. That left only the Duchess of Willowby, Aurora and Gillingham, for it seemed Mrs. Huntington had also gone out to check on the servants, as Imogen was coming to her realization about her feelings.

The duchess approached Oscar. She was a pretty woman, petite and curvaceous, with a kind face. An observant face, however, and Imogen realized she was trying to read the man standing before her. She almost snorted at the idea. Oscar took time to know. To understand. This woman wouldn't do it after only knowing him five minutes. "Mr. Fitzhugh, obviously this event has been upsetting."

Oscar tensed and glared at her. "Upsetting, Your Grace? You think this is *upsetting?*"

The duchess might not have been able to understand him, but Imogen did. She saw that he was at his boiling point. That the day's events had dragged him to the edge of his vast control.

"Oscar," Imogen said softly as she took his hand. He turned his head, his jaw clenching, but he didn't blow up. Imogen looked at the duchess. "Your Grace, he has protected me well in the last few weeks. Perhaps it would be better for me to go with him. I've endangered enough people as it is."

Of course, she had endangered Oscar, too.

"Imogen," Aurora whispered.

Imogen faced her dearest friend with a shaky smile. "You could have died because of me today. Please, just let me protect you."

Aurora flinched, but sent a glance toward Nicholas Gillingham. Imogen watched him too. She knew about the man. Aurora had often spoken of him during their friendship. He was her first and only great love. Only he'd left her suddenly when they were very young, went off to the army where he'd been so badly injured. It seemed he had returned, and Aurora looked so calm, so at peace as she looked to him for comfort.

At least Imogen knew *she* would be protected. Loved.

"We are all under a great deal of strain," the duchess said, and brought Imogen's attention back to her. "But the duke and I *are* part of the War Department, Mr. Fitzhugh."

"Yes, I know," Oscar said. He sounded so tired. Almost defeated. "I've heard of you before, though not by name. I heard a rumor the government was involved in investigating in some way. We clearly have a great deal to discuss."

The duchess nodded. "We do. Another reason not to hide yourselves where we cannot find you. We have the weight of the entire government to bring to bear onto this case. I do think Imogen needs to be hidden, I agree with you. The fact that someone shot at all of us the moment she was brought out of hiding means *someone* is desperate to silence her."

"We know who," Imogen said. The duchess's eyebrows lifted with interest. Although Oscar had worried titled would protect titled, Imogen got a very different impression now. The duke and duchess seemed genuinely concerned and willing to help. But it was possible Oscar couldn't see it. He was so blinded by his past with his father. So thrown off kilter by seeing two of his siblings. She needed to help him. "Oscar, please, they can help us. Stop fighting it."

He frowned but didn't argue, and Imogen knew that was a good thing.

"Let *us* provide the safe hiding place," Diana said. "Protected by armed guards, hidden from plain sight. Someplace where no one will find her, but where we will have access to what she knows about the people trying to hurt her."

Oscar paced off. When he lifted a hand to the place where Huntington had bandaged his wound, she felt an ache in her chest.

"Bloody fucking hell," he snapped at last. "Fine. But I'm going with her."

Imogen's mouth dropped open. She hadn't imagined he would let this situation go if she went with the Willowbys, but nor had she pictured he would compromise his life further and come with her. "Oscar, no! You protected me so well, but I can't ask you to—"

"I'm going with you," he interrupted. "That's final. Let me just make some arrangements."

He gave her one quick glance, but said nothing else. He strode from the room, leaving her alone with the duchess, Aurora and Mr. Gillingham. The duchess glanced at Gillingham, and her meaning was clear. They stepped away to speak to each other, and Imogen was left with Aurora.

"Imogen," her friend whispered, wrapping her arms around her. It was so comforting to feel that embrace. "*How* could this happen?"

"I was just in the wrong place at the wrong time," Imogen sighed. How true that was and how much it had changed her life. His life. She glanced to where Oscar had departed and her heart ached. "Can I trust your friends?"

"Yes." There was no hesitation in Aurora's voice, and relief cascaded through Imogen.

Which allowed her a moment to let go of her own troubles. She looked over her shoulder at where Nicholas Gillingham stood with the duchess. "That's the one you were in love with as a child, isn't it? The one who left you for the army?"

Aurora's face lit up instantly. She was so beautiful and so obviously in love that Imogen felt a tug of jealousy at it. "Turns out it's more complicated than that, but yes."

Gillingham was watching Aurora from the corner of his eye from time to time. And his emotions were as clear as hers. Their future, it seemed, was set. And it made Imogen's seem all the more desperate. She loved Oscar with the same intensity that Aurora and this man loved each other.

But there were no guarantees for her. No promises, in fact just the opposite.

"He seems to love you," she breathed.

"Yes," Aurora whispered.

"Then hold on to that," Imogen said, grasping her hands. "Hold onto it and to each other. Because others are...they're not so lucky."

Aurora tilted her head. "Are you talking about Mr. Fitzhugh? Because there is no denying your connection."

Heat flooded Imogen's cheeks. She was so easy to read, it seemed.

So obvious and foolish that the world would know. Oscar would know. It would only push him further away.

"Connection is one thing. Protection is another," she mused. Then she shook her head. "But he has made it clear that he *cannot* love me. So...I just would like one of us to be happy. When this is all over, I want you to be happy."

As she said the last, Oscar re-entered the room. There was the command on his expression again. Stern and certain. Her body reacted to that, as it always had. As she feared it always would.

"Arrangements have been made," he said. "An unmarked carriage is around the back, ready to ferry us away to whatever location you see fit, Your Grace."

"Good," the duchess said. "Then I'll accompany you. Mr. Gillingham, will you tell the duke of my plans? I'll meet with him back at home. And I would suggest you and Lady Lovell also take your leave. There is nothing else you can do here. The professionals will handle this and keep your friend safe."

Aurora seemed to sag at that suggestion and pivoted back to hug Imogen tight again. "I wanted to...to save you today. To bring you home."

Imogen clung to her all the tighter. "I'm so much closer to home now."

It was true, of course. Up until half an hour ago, she was certain she would have to take a new name and leave London, perhaps even England, entirely. Now there was hope...at least for how this matter with Roddenbury and the Cat's Companion would be resolved.

That was the gift her dearest friend had given, so she pulled back and kissed her cheek. "I adore you." Then she glanced past her toward Gillingham. "Mr. Gillingham, I wish I had more time to get to the know the man who has held my friend's heart for her entire life."

He drew back, but there was a flicker of a smile that crossed his face. It was very much like the way Oscar did his half-smiles. That made her like this man all the more. As did his genuine tone when he said, "And I wish I had more time to get to know the friend she loves as a sister. But we *will* have that time in the future."

"Yes," Imogen said with a shaky smile. "I know we will."

She was going to cry. She felt the burning in her chest and the pressure behind her eyes. She didn't want Aurora to see that, to worry more than she already was. She pivoted toward Oscar and he held her stare, the beacon for her the darkness. She needed him now, more than she needed anyone else in the world. Even the best friend she loved so deeply.

He offered his uninjured arm to her and she took it, holding tightly as he guided her from the room with the Duchess of Willowby trailing behind them. Imogen moved with him through the halls toward the back of the club.

The butler who had greeted them earlier was waiting for them there. His expression was grim as he nodded to his master. "The arrangements have been made, Mr. Fitzhugh."

"Very good," Oscar's voice was low and rough. "Reach out to Will as soon as I am gone. And tell him I'll contact him as soon as possible, myself."

"I shall. Be well, Mr. Fitzhugh. And to you, as well, Mrs. Huxley."

Imogen hadn't been expecting the kind words, nor the gentle nod in her direction. The tears that swelled threatened to fall even more immediately, and she bent her head. "Thank you. Goodbye."

They stepped into the afternoon sunshine. So bright that it was almost offensive considering the day's dark events. Oscar glanced over his shoulder. "You'll give my man directions to your preferred location?"

The duchess eyed the driver. "He can be trusted?"

"He can," Oscar said without hesitation as he handed Imogen up into the carriage and then slung himself in, as well. He said nothing as he took a place beside her on the bench and put his good arm around her. She said nothing either. What was there to be said? He had been forced to deal with the family he had cut himself away from. She was in more danger than ever, it seemed, and had placed so many people in it with her.

There would be time enough to digest all of that later. The duchess was helped into the carriage by a footman and the door closed behind her. Imogen sank her head onto Oscar's uninjured shoulder as they began to drive toward the blurry future. For her. For them.

CHAPTER 21

O scar wasn't sure what he expected from the safe house the Duchess of Willowby had briefly described on their way here, but as they stepped into a small but perfectly appointed parlor, he knew it wasn't this. It was a lovely townhouse in one of the quiet, middle-class neighborhoods in London. Many a sophisticated merchant lived on the tidy lane, some of whom were members of his own club.

Certainly it wasn't the expected place for spies to hole up, waiting for danger to pass. He supposed that made it perfect for the job, as long as they weren't recognized.

He pivoted to look at Imogen and could see her reading the room the same way he had as she crossed away from him. She smiled at him, a little distant, almost shy. But then, he'd felt that same hesitance the entire carriage ride here. He didn't like it. He wanted it to stop.

"Imogen—" he began.

Before he could finish, the duchess entered the room, carrying a kit of some kind under her arm. She smiled at them both. "I hope the house will suit you."

"It's—it's lovely," Imogen said. "It seems very comfortable."

"Excellent. Everything is prepared," the duchess explained as she bustled around the room, checking the sideboard for its selection of drinks and the fire for how high it burned. "Our staff is carefully vetted and trained. They're trustworthy and can protect you if it comes to that."

"Physically?" Oscar said in disbelief.

The duchess nodded. "Indeed. And they're always at the ready for unexpected situations, so the rooms are made up. There is a maid who can help you with preparations, my dear. And I'll arrange for a gown or two to be sent to you in the morning, as well."

"Thank you. You are very kind, Your Grace," Imogen said softly, her gaze casting down to her gown. Only then did Oscar realized there were a few small streaks of blood on the fabric. His blood. A testament to how close he'd come to losing it all, and he didn't mean his life.

The duchess smiled. "I think we're all going to know each other well enough by the time this is over to forego the formality in private. You may call me Diana."

"Is that some spy's trick meant to put her at ease?" Oscar ground out, almost wanting to put himself between the duchess and Imogen as a shield, because as kind as she was, he didn't fully trust her.

Diana turned and her gaze flitted over him. She didn't reveal what she thought, but she did move toward him, fearless and seemingly without guile.

"I hope she *is* at ease," she said. "I can only imagine the terror she has endured these past few weeks, seeing what she did, running as she had to. I can imagine you didn't fare much better, Mr. Fitzhugh. It is difficult to see someone we've come to care about...hurt. To want to help them and know we aren't fully equipped."

He shifted beneath the careful words, meant to have an effect—and succeeding. "I've kept her alive."

Diana nodded. "You have, and I'm glad of it. But now you are not alone in that goal. In the desire to save Imogen's life and perhaps even put a stop to the horrific acts committed by the people responsible for the threats against her. We're on the same side, Fitzhugh."

"I hope that is true," he said softly, and this time it was he who meant to have an effect. "I have watched *many* a titled person of power only protect the others who share his...or *her* status."

Diana shook her head. "Then you have not dealt with me, nor with my husband. That is not who we are, not as people, not as spies. You don't have to believe that, for we'll prove it to you, and hopefully sooner rather than later." She smiled and then stepped closer, setting her kit on the table beside him and opening it. He could see all matter of tools and wraps and potions inside. "Now let me look at that wound, will you?"

He wrinkled his brow. "Look at the wound?"

"Yes. Mr. Huntington did an admirable job with field dressing." Diana motioned him to sit and remove his jacket as she spoke. "I would assume he had some experience due to his time in the army. But I'm a trained healer, and I want to get a closer look now that we're not being actively shot at."

Oscar glanced at Imogen, who had come closer, as well. The color had left her cheeks as he pulled his jacket away and then untied his cravat. He unbuttoned his shirt and pulled it over his head, trying not to react to the sharp pain of the bullet wound he had been ignoring as much as possible.

While he sat down in the chair before her, Diana looked back at Imogen with a knowing smile. "Bring the candle a bit closer if you would, my dear."

She did so, and when Diana unwrapped the field dressing, Imogen winced. "Oh, Oscar. It looks terrible. You must be in so much pain."

He glanced down. There was a decidedly ugly hole that went in one side of his arm and out the other. He moved it slightly and a slash of pain rushed through him, but not the kind that indicated broken bones. He was lucky at that.

"It's not comfortable," he admitted as dismissively as he could manage so as not to worry Imogen even more. "But I've felt worse."

Diana fussed with the wound a moment, using the light as she cleaned it with a fluid that made the injury sting. She looked up at him. "This isn't going to be comfortable."

"It hasn't been so far," Oscar grumbled.

She laughed as a response. "My husband will like you. He groused when I took care of him a long time ago, as well. You can compare notes later about what a dreadful fiend I am."

"Judging from the way the man looked at you after the gunfire, I would assume he doesn't think that of you at all," Oscar said.

She smiled as she brought out a needle and heavy thread and swiftly stitched the wound on either side of his arm. Then she placed a soothing salve on both and carefully rewrapped it, this time with a bandage rather than the bloody cravat she tossed into her kit to be destroyed.

"I'll leave some materials here," Diana said as she tied off the wound with an expert flair. "Along with written instructions. Imogen, you'll need to apply more of that salve and rewrap it tomorrow morning. Then I'll look at it again tomorrow when Lucas...er, Willowby... and I return to speak to you tomorrow afternoon."

"Tomorrow afternoon?" Imogen repeated. "Oh, Your Grace—"

"Diana," Diana interrupted gently.

"*Diana*, surely you must have something to tell us later tonight. Or tomorrow morning."

Diana stepped away from him and reached out, grasping both of Imogen's hands gently. Oscar watched as Imogen's shoulders relaxed a little. The duchess was a balm herself. A healer in spirit, as well as body.

"Imogen, I know you've had a very long day. A long few weeks. And you're anxious for an answer. But you must allow Lucas and me to have time to pursue everything we've discovered today." Diana glanced back at Oscar. "Speaking of which, you said you knew who attacked us at your club. Would you mind sharing that information? It will very likely fill in some blanks in our knowledge."

Imogen stepped away from her and moved a little closer to Oscar.

He held out a hand and she took it, her fingers lacing through his and seeking comfort.

"You may not believe me," she whispered. "But it was the Earl of Roddenbury who was with the body I saw. He admitted he killed that poor girl, whoever she was. And it didn't sound like it was the first time he'd...he'd hurt someone."

Diana's eyes squeezed shut. "Roddenbury. Of course. We'd had some suspicions about him, but...well, this confirms it." She let out her breath slowly. "He has a great deal of power—it will be complicated. But I'll pass this information on to Lucas. We'll all talk about it tomorrow, once he and I have had a chance to discuss this update with each other and with Mr. Barber and Mr. Huntington. They've been invaluable resources since they began their search for you and our purposes crossed paths."

There was something in her tone, in her face, that made Oscar's worries about her fade, at least a little. "We have no choice," he said, but with no heat to his tone. "I suppose we must trust you."

"You must," Diana agreed with another of those warming smiles. "And now I'll go and join my husband so we may eventually prove to you that trust is well placed. Tonight try to relax, try to enjoy the very good food the cook here will provide." She moved forward and smiled at them both. "Try to take care of one another. Today was a terrifying experience for both of you. Don't discount its effect."

"Thank you again, for your help," Imogen said.

"Yes. Thank you," Oscar said, a little reluctantly but certainly less so than a few moments earlier. There was something about this woman that couldn't help but put a person at ease.

"Of course. Now please don't get up. I'll show myself out and see you tomorrow."

She slipped away, leaving them alone together. Oscar glanced at Imogen as he grabbed his bloody shirt and put one arm through. He struggled with his injured arm, and she stepped up, helping him slide it up the sleeve. He left it unbuttoned for a moment and looked up at her from his seated position. When her gaze darted away, he wrapped an arm around her waist and drew her closer.

She settled down into his lap and sighed as she smoothed her fingers over his face. In that moment there was only her in the whole world. He didn't want or need anything else but those amber eyes holding his, those slender fingers touching him, the feel of her backside in his lap.

He knew that shouldn't be all he needed. But it was.

"Do you want to tell me why you've struggled to look at me since the club?" he asked.

She stiffened a little, but didn't pull away. Her eyes filled with tears, but she blinked them away. "I ruined everything," she said softly.

His brow wrinkled. "And how did you do that? Were you the one shooting from below? If so, that is a wicked feat, because I seem to recall dragging you under me."

She rolled her eyes at him. "You're being glib, but we both know the role I've played in this. I've brought down hell on you, Oscar, since the moment you met me."

"Imogen—"

She shook her head and continued, "For weeks I've invaded your house and thrown off your schedule. You've been very kind and never mentioned it to me, but I know I've been an unwelcome burden."

"Not unwelcome," he insisted.

"And today," she continued, not even acknowledging what he'd said. "Today your club was ruined because of me. The physical damage and the fact that it was...shot up in public. I know that will hurt you."

He ducked his head because there was no arguing that. Certainly there might be repercussions if his members decided they didn't want to be linked to such notoriety. And he'd spent a lifetime building the reputation of the place. Yet he couldn't manage to care about it in this moment.

"Plus, there is the bonus horror that because of me you were forced to come in contact with two of your siblings." She sighed. "I know you didn't want that. But I swear to you, I didn't know. I didn't know."

He pressed a finger to her lips, stopping her from talking for a moment. "First off, I realize you didn't know. In that initial moment when I turned and saw Nicholas and Selina standing there in my parlor, I..."

He trailed off as he thought of that startling moment. He'd been angry to see them, even if neither of them had ever done anything to him directly. He'd been thrilled to see them, too. He might have banned them all from his life, but he'd still followed them. He still... cared in some way, even if he didn't want to do that.

A weakness, surely.

"They were both very kind," she said softly. "And Aurora has loved Nicholas her whole life. I knew that, though I didn't know his connection to Roseford."

"He looked happy with her," Oscar mused. "And he has suffered greatly, so I cannot be anything but happy for him. But *this* is a change of the subject. You said that you destroyed everything, but do you know what I thought when those bullets started to fly?"

"I don't know," she said.

He cupped her neck, letting his thumb trace the fluttering line of her pulse. "All I thought about was protecting you. And when I got up and looked at the carnage, all I could think was how lucky I was that you weren't injured."

"But *you* were," she said, pointing at the bloody shirt and the bandaged arm beneath it. "All because of me."

"Not because of you," he insisted. "Great God, Imogen. This is because of Roddenbury and this Maggie woman. This is because of *their* horrible plan. None of this is your fault. I don't blame you. I couldn't blame you because I—"

He stopped himself. Staring up at her, seeing her lower lip tremble, her gaze hold his, feeling her whole and safe in his arms, it had forced a thought into his mind. One he had very nearly spoken without deliberation into the consequences.

He loved her.

Looking up at her, that fact was perfectly clear. Not even surprising, despite all his attempts to keep himself from surrendering to such a dangerous emotion. Despite all his attempts to distance himself from her in any way beyond the physical. She had never allowed that, finding her way over and under and through all the barriers he'd erected. Wedging herself firmly in his heart.

He had never let himself love someone like this. And now it terrified him. He wanted to push it away. But not her away.

"You what?" she whispered.

He leaned up, drawing her down at the same time, and kissed her. She shifted in his lap, and he groaned at the way that little wiggle woke up a body that should have been happily sleeping after the trying events of the day. But she did that to him. Regularly.

"I want you," he said, pulling his lips away just far enough that he could talk. It wasn't a lie, even if it wasn't the thought that had filled his mind. "I need you."

She nodded, brushing her nose along the side of his as she did so. "You need me? I need you. You were shot, you could have died and—" Her breath hitched and she kissed him again, deeper this time, her fingers pressing against his jawline. "I need you."

They stood together and he grasped her hand, leading her from the room to find one of the bedchambers. But as they walked up the stairs together, fingers laced, he fought against the desire in his chest. Not just to make love to her. But to allow himself to love her for all the rest of his days.

He would have to restrain himself if he didn't want to lose control of this entire situation.

CHAPTER 22

There were two bedchambers upstairs, both made up for guests. The first was smaller than the other, and Imogen had frowned at the narrow bed. But the second…well, it was obviously the master, made for exactly every fantasy she wished to play out with this man she loved and had nearly lost.

The big bed faced a large window. Its curtain was drawn back and late afternoon sunlight filtered in, casting a golden glow on the turned-back sheets on the bed.

He closed the door behind them after they entered and turned the key to lock it. He leaned back, his shirt still fluttered open to give her a peek-a-boo glimpse at his chest, and her heart throbbed with love and desire in a potent mix.

For a moment, she saw the emotion in his eyes, on his face. His own fear at what they had gone through, at what they had nearly lost. But he shook them away. He hardened his expression, his face darkened to that look of pure desire, command, control. She shivered, for she knew what it would bring to her body and soul when he touched her in this state. She knew he would take her pleasure, demand even more until she was weak and mewling his name.

Only now she saw that act for what it was. Not just a way to pleasure, but to distance. He didn't want to feel the pang of fear or loss. He didn't want to experience any connection they'd built or mourn the lack of connection he had to his siblings.

He was using desire and dominance to keep all that at bay.

He came across the room toward her, stripping his shirt away with every step. His arms wrapped around her, hard and heavy and his mouth claimed hers. She lifted into him, her body craving him even as her heart screamed out for more. More than pleasure. More than orgasms and lust. More than protection given out of a sense of obligation.

She wanted his heart.

His tongue drove into her, and for a moment that deeper yearning faded. He would take her and it would soften the edges of the fear today. She could surrender to his demands and both of them could remain in the comfort zone of sexual connection.

He pressed her back against the edge of the bed and then caught her hips, spinning her so her back was to him, so she was bent partly over. He stripped her dress open with one hand, tracing the path of the parted buttons with his lips and searing a heated path through her thin chemise beneath. When he tugged and brought both down to flutter at her feet, she gripped the coverlet tighter and found herself spreading her legs, offering him exactly what he wished to take.

He made a little growl behind her, possessive, animalistic. She peeked over her shoulder at him and watched as he shucked his trousers away. The hard curve of his cock told her how much he wanted her. But the brief expression of desperation that crossed his face when he looked at her reminded her he also wanted something else. He wanted to build a wall, even if it was with pleasure.

But she loved him, so she couldn't let him. She wouldn't. When he curled his body around hers, she slowly turned beneath him, facing him and meeting his eyes evenly. He had the same stern, focused, heated expression as he'd ever had when he looked at her. The one that turned her knees to jelly and made her hands shake with desire.

But she saw something different now. In those dark eyes she saw pain. He was having a harder and harder time hiding it from her. She reached up to touch his face as she saw it, smoothing her fingers along his harsh jawline, hands tickled by his beard.

"Don't," he growled, and his mouth found hers. He pushed her hands away, inching her back on the bed, flattening her wrists against the mattress.

She didn't seek escape. In fact, the heavy weight of him holding her down, stealing her control, was arousing in ways she couldn't have put into words. This man was built for pleasure, certainly. Built to give her pleasure, even as he never asked for anything in return.

She wanted to give it. But he wasn't allowing that as he held her down, so instead she tilted her head. Their lips were inches apart as he pushed her legs open and positioned himself at her entrance. He drove into her in one long thrust and she caught his mouth at the same time. He took and she gentled her kiss in return. She sucked on his tongue, she explored as he plundered.

And just as she'd hoped, her tenderness changed him. Slowly, he eased his drive, softened above her. His grip on her wrists loosened, his fingers came into her hair instead and he let out a low, quiet moan. Of pleasure or pain, of all of it mixed, she couldn't be certain. All she could do was swallow it down, as if she could dissolve it as he passed it to her.

He pulled back, staring down at her in the quiet of the room. He was fighting. Fighting the hardness, fighting the way he'd trained himself never to let someone close again. She knew why. But it didn't matter. That was the past.

"No," he whispered, that desperation lacing his tone just as it had relaxed his expression.

She ignored him and lifted against him from beneath. Gentle, pulsing movements that made her pleasure mount but also set a pace much different than any other time he'd made love to her.

"Imogen," he whispered, her name a plea and a demand all at once. He thrust hard again, and she gasped as she lifted to meet him. Then she cupped his backside with both hands and ground him against her in a smooth, gentle circle.

She came from the friction of his pelvis against hers. He watched her as she jolted beneath him, fingers smoothing over his back as she whimpered his name again and again.

"Please," she murmured as the ripples of undeniable pleasure faded.

He caught her mouth and kissed her again, deeper, longer, softer. He caught her hips and they moved together, rising and falling in a patient, gentle rhythm. There was no more fight, no more dominance, there was nothing left but her and him and everything between them that remained unsaid.

If he had been good at commanding her experience, at drawing her passion from her, he was even better at just...loving her. He lifted her all the way onto the bed, rolling to his back, guiding her thrusts with a hand on her hips as the other one cupped her head and angled her for a kiss that seemed to merge their souls.

They weren't two bodies warring for release. They were one person in that moment, and when she jerked against him this time, he pushed her on her back and ground her through the crisis. And then he pulled away and the heat of him splashed against her stomach as he moaned her name into the quiet of the room.

He rolled onto his side, back to her when it was over. She followed tucking herself around him as she smoothed her hands over him, across his chest, through his hair. She traced the area of his arm around his bandage and kissed his shoulder, tasting the salt of him on her lips.

His breath shuddered out, so soft and so painful that her heart broke for him. He pivoted to look at her, their faces inches apart. His brow furrowed low as he let a finger drag across her jawline, her lips, around the shape of her ear. She shivered at the intimacy of that.

But then he frowned, and she knew he would take it all away despite her fight to make him give it.

"I can't," he said.

She shut her eyes. She didn't need an explanation of what he meant by *can't*. They both knew what he meant.

"Why?" she whispered.

"I *can't* love you, Imogen," he declared as he pushed away from her. He sat on the edge of the bed, his shoulders rolled forward in defeat. "If I can love you, I can lose you. And I'm not doing that again."

He got up and gathered his clothing from the floor, piling it in his arms without putting any of it on. As she watched him, she shook her head and sat up. She'd been drawn in by this man, intrigued by him, connected to him, felt guilty for what she'd cost him. But in the weeks they had spent together she had never felt *angry* with him. Until that moment.

"You coward," she whispered.

He jerked his head up and glared at her. "What did you call me?"

"A coward," she repeated. "Today I almost *lost* you, Oscar. So what does that mean? Can you say it? Can you face it?"

He stared at her, unblinking for what felt like a lifetime. Then he shook his head. "This was sex, Imogen. Don't confuse it or we both risk...we risk something I'm not willing to risk."

He didn't wait for her response, he just stepped out of the room, completely naked, and shut the door behind himself, leaving her alone with the realization that this man already loved her.

And that he might never allow himself to nurture that, or her. That broke her more than almost anything else she'd faced in the last lonely year of her life.

She threw a pillow at the door with a grunt and then flopped back on the bed, letting her arm come over her eyes. She'd hoped that after today, she might have some answers about what to do next.

But there were only more questions than ever.

∼

Oscar was on his third drink when there was a knock at the small chamber's door. He glanced up at it, his heart jumping almost out of his chest.

"Imogen?" he said as he moved to the door, but when he opened it, only the butler for the safe house stood there.

"I apologize for the interruption, sir, but you have a visitor."

"A visitor?" Oscar said, blinking at the man as he tried to clear his foggy head. "Who would know we're here?"

"There is no danger, I assure you," the butler said. "She comes with a password from the Duke of Willowby, himself, or she would not have been allowed in. I only didn't know if you'd like to see someone in your current...er..." He glanced down, and Oscar tightened his dressing gown at his waist. "Your current state."

"Who is it?" he asked.

"Miss Joanna Fitzhugh," he said.

"My mother," Oscar said, and shook his head. "And have you also knocked on Mrs. Huxley's door?" He winced at that thought. He wasn't sure he had the strength to face Imogen after what he'd said and done.

"The maid who assisted her earlier said that she was asleep, so I didn't think it wise. But I can rouse her if you'd like," the butler said.

"No. Let her sleep. She's earned that," Oscar said softly. "And yes, I'll see my mother. Give me a moment and I'll meet her downstairs."

"Very good." The butler bowed away and left him.

Oscar sighed. He had been in hiding for all of a handful of hours, but of course his mother would find him straight away. Through Will, no doubt, since he would have come in contact with the Duke of Willowby when he arrived to survey the damage to the club, as he had been called to do.

And now Oscar would have to face her, with all her ability to read him. With all her pointed questions and looks. While he was slightly drunk, no less, and reeling from how he had treated Imogen after they made love.

He opened the drawers in the room and found a few items there that would fit him. As he dressed himself, slowly thanks to his drunken state and his injured arm, he thought about Imogen.

Of course he hadn't stopped thinking about her the entire time he'd been drinking to make himself do just that. When he'd recognized that he loved her, it had been the most terrifying moment of his life. Oh, he'd been in danger before, both during the time he'd been watching her and before. But that was physical threat. Loving her? That was a threat to his very core.

That was a threat to his heart and his mind and his soul.

And what had he done? Followed his instinct, of course, and tried to fuck his way out of those feelings. Tried to put up walls to her and to his own heart. Tried to make himself forget that he loved her, which meant he was vulnerable to every single thing in this world that could rip her away from him.

And Imogen, in her strength and her warmth and her sunshine, which changed his whole world...had defied him. Forcing him to sink into her instead of pull away. Forcing him to love her more, even if he'd told her that he couldn't or wouldn't.

Seeing the hurt in her stare when he said those words, knowing she was right when she called him a coward...he would never forget that moment until he took his dying breath.

He tucked his shirt into his trousers and sighed. He couldn't think about any of that when he faced Joanna. He had to wipe it all away, challenging as that had somehow become.

He made his way back to the parlor where the Duchess of Willowby had tended his wound earlier in the night, and drew a long breath before he entered. His mother was standing at the sideboard, a drink in hand as she glared at the door, awaiting his arrival.

The moment he entered, she set her glass aside and crossed to him. Her arms came around him and she hugged him tightly. "My love."

"I'm fine, Mama," he said. Lied. He lied. "I assume Will was the one who told you what happened."

"Yes. And he knew I would insist on coming to see you, so he got the information and password from this duke." She laughed, but it was a raw sound. "The trouble you get yourself in, son."

"I'm trying to get myself out," he said as he paced away. "And her."

He felt his mother watching him as he moved to the fireplace and stared into the dancing flames. "Are you *drunk?*" she asked, her tone incredulous.

He pivoted back to her and shrugged, wincing when he tweaked his injury. "I am," he admitted.

Her face pinched, and she crossed to him and touched his arm, feeling the bandage beneath gently. "I don't think I've seen you drunk in ten years. Is it to numb the pain?"

He almost laughed. Numb the pain? Oh yes, it was for that. But not the physical pain. "It will heal," he said.

"Will it now?" she asked, and he realized she wasn't talking about his arm either.

He pulled away. "I'm fine."

She was quiet for a moment before she said, "And what about Imogen?"

"She wasn't hurt—" He cut himself off, because that wasn't true. "She wasn't shot this afternoon," he said. "She's resting in her chamber."

He could almost hear her voice right now. Saying he was a coward. The word rang in his ears, and he shook his head. He turned back to his mother and stared at her. She looked worried, of course. But she also looked...peaceful somehow. Calm.

"Has Will taken on the role as your protector again?" he asked.

She snorted out a surprised laugh. "*That* is a change of subject."

"If you get to grill me on my life, I suppose I feel I am owed the chance to do the same," he said. "And perhaps the drink has loosened my tongue a little. Is he?"

"Who told you that?" she asked.

He ran a hand through his hair. "Imogen said something about the connection she saw. And then it was all I could see when you two were together."

"He's not my protector," Joanna said softly.

He bent his head, a little bit of disappointment rushing through him. The time when Will had been Joanna's protector was one of the happiest of Oscar's life. He trusted the man, as he had never trusted anyone else she'd let into her bed.

"He—" The way her voice wavered when she cut herself off made Oscar glance back up at her. She worried her lip a little. "He's the love of my life, Oscar."

He swallowed. His mother so rarely called him by his given name. That made her declaration feel all the more...serious. "I see," he said, and sank down into the closest chair because his wobbly legs felt even less certain.

She took the chair opposite him and grasped one of his hands between her own. "Do you know why we ended it all those years ago?"

He shook his head.

"Because I was afraid of my feelings," she admitted, and in that moment all the walls Joanna expertly erected were gone. She was entirely vulnerable and more beautiful than ever. "When I started to see myself fall, I thought of...I thought of your father."

He flinched. "I'm sorry."

"It's not your fault." She squeezed his hand gently. "I'm not sorry about my experiences, including that one. But the younger me was still afraid. I didn't trust myself, so I couldn't trust Will, even when I knew he was decent, caring. Even when he told me he loved me."

His mouth dropped open. "He told you that?"

"The last night we were together," she said, and shook her head. "And I refused him...quite flippantly, even though in my heart I felt anything but. It broke us apart. And yet somehow that lovely man still wanted to call me a friend." She laughed. "And so we were. But in the last year that's changed. Shifted. Bloomed back into something more like it once was. When he told me he loved me this time, I knew what it was like to have that and lose it. I knew the cost. So I took the chance. He wants to marry me, Oscar."

The joy that declaration brought made Oscar smile. It felt so rusty to make the expression, though far less so after weeks with Imogen bringing light to his once-dark existence. "I'm glad, Mama. I'm happy for you and for Will. If you need my blessing, you have it."

"I'll take it." She gave a long sigh. "But I look at you, my love, and I see...me."

"It's not the same," he insisted, though he felt the lie as clearly as she could see it.

"Yes, it is," she said, her tone brooking no refusal. "I'm afraid you are on your way to losing love twice."

He blinked. "Twice," he repeated. "Are you...are you talking about Louisa?" She nodded, and he got up on those shaky legs, pulling his hand from hers. "I was not in love with Louisa."

"Weren't you?" she asked. "Or was it that your feelings terrified you? Did you not trust yourself because of your father? Because of other men who traipsed through your life thanks to my profession?"

"Mama—"

She ignored the interruption. "Did you push her away because you feared losing yourself? Losing the control you have always wielded as a shield? And now you're doing it all over again with Imogen. It will be worse this time."

"Why?" he asked, drawn in by all those questions that he secretly knew the answer to. That he despised her for asking, and yet...

"Because I've seen you two together. I see how you are with Imogen. I see what she makes you."

"What does she make me?" His voice trembled.

"Whole," she said softly.

He dropped his chin and squeezed his eyes shut, but blocking his mother from his line of vision didn't block how true that one word felt as it tore through him as surely as the bullet had earlier in the day.

"Perhaps," he admitted without even meaning to say that word out loud.

"That you can say perhaps gives me hope," she said. She got up and moved to him to place a kiss on his cheek. "I adore you, you know."

"I know you do, just as I adore you," he grumbled.

"Then listen to me." She smiled at him. "Put away the bottle tonight and don't hide from what is in your heart. Think about what you want, what you really want, and what you might lose if you aren't careful. If you don't stop running from a past that you can't change." She moved toward the door, and there she stopped. "Oh, and be careful."

He nodded. "I will," he said, and they both knew he was agreeing to more than just her last admonishment.

"Goodnight, love. Send word when you can, and know that Will and I are protecting your interests until this is over."

She slipped away as he called out, "Goodnight."

And when she was gone, when he was alone in the big parlor, he moved to the fire and stood there, mesmerized once again by the flames. The very thoughts his mother had encouraged him to pursue rose up in him, overtaking him. The same thoughts he'd been avoiding since he first met Imogen.

Since before he met her.

It was going to be a long night.

CHAPTER 23

Imogen entered the breakfast room the next morning and expected she would be alone. It was early, after all. She'd hoped too early for Oscar, since she had heard from the maid assigned to her by the Willowbys that he hadn't slept much last night.

And yet there he was at the head of the table. He pushed to his feet as she entered, and she caught her breath. He was entirely pulled together. Dressed impeccably, not a hair out of place, his beard neatly trimmed. His brow furrowed and his dark gaze held on her as she walked to the place at his right. If he hadn't slept last night, it did nothing to reduce the command he had of this room or any other.

"Good morning," he said, his voice rough.

She nodded as politely as she could while she took her seat. "Good morning, Oscar."

He sat back down and she let her gaze flit over him again. He was wearing a coat, waistcoat and shirt she hadn't seen before. Certainly not the ones that had been torn and made bloody by the carnage yesterday. "They had clothing brought for you, as well, it seems."

He glanced at himself. "There were items in the wardrobe in my room. These fit. I might nick the waistcoat, if I'm honest."

She smiled at the way he puffed up his chest so she could see the intricate brocading in the fabric better. "It does suit you. Do you need your wound cleaned?"

He shook his head. "No. I asked the valet this morning and he obliged."

"Ah."

She glanced up at the footman who had brought her a plate laden with food. It was good he had interrupted when he did. She hated to show Oscar her disappointment in his response. It was foolish, after all. Having the valet do the duty was a perfectly reasonable idea. Only she felt a little jealous. According to Diana, Imogen had been meant to help him. It seemed he was finding any way he could not to allow it.

The chasm that had opened between them after they made love seemed to be widening with every passing moment. Their time together was almost over, and it felt like Oscar was preparing himself...preparing *her*...for when it would be at its close.

"*You* look beautiful," he said.

She glanced down at herself. The gowns the Duchess of Willowby had sent over fit Imogen perfectly. Better than Louisa's old dresses. This one was a gray-blue with a lace overlay that cascaded across the skirt.

Honestly, she was pleased to be out of Louisa's hand-me-downs. They were always a reminder that Oscar found a way to put up walls, to escape furthering his connection. He'd done it to his previous lover. He was doing it now to her.

"Thank you."

An awkward silence fell over them for a moment as he stared at her. Then he opened his mouth. "Imogen...I wanted to talk to you about...about last night." He stopped and shook his head. "No. It's about more than last night. It's about so many nights since I met you."

"Oh?" she whispered, her hands shaking as she set her fork down and looked at him. He looked truly troubled, and her heart leapt. "What is it?"

He ran a hand through his hair and was about to speak again when the butler appeared in the doorway. "I'm sorry to disturb your breakfast, Mr. Fitzhugh, Mrs. Huxley, but the Duke and Duchess of Willowby are here."

Imogen's eyes went wide as she looked at Oscar. "They said they wouldn't call until this afternoon. Something must have happened."

He pursed his lips at the interruption, but tossed his napkin aside. "I suppose we should find out what."

He offered her an arm, and she got up and took it. Even with so much unsaid and undone between them, having him at her side as they went across the hall to the parlor was a comfort. Perhaps she shouldn't have allowed it to be when she knew he wanted to separate them, but it still was.

She loved him. His demand that she stop, his reminder that he couldn't or wouldn't return the emotion, wasn't enough to change her heart.

In the parlor, the Duke and Duchess of Willowby were standing by the window. Along with them were Derrick Huntington and his partner, Edward Barber. After the pleasantries were exchanged, Oscar tilted his head. "I'm shocked Selina didn't join you. And the rest of my family. I honestly expected the great Duke of Roseford to descend upon my head himself."

Imogen heard the strain in his voice and clung to his arm a little tighter. If he offered her strength, she wanted to do the same if she could.

Willowby pursed his lips. Imogen knew he was friends with Oscar's estranged brother. It was clear he didn't like the attitude Oscar held toward him. "I know he would like to come, but I asked that the family limit their involvement in this. There are already a great many high emotions as it is. They can only serve to confuse matters and endanger all of us."

"I practically had to tie Selina down to get her to obey that order, if it helps," Huntington said with a shake of his head. Oscar released Imogen as he said it and took a step away, his shoulders tightening with every word. "She's off doing some research to fill her anxious mind."

"We expected you later in the day," Imogen said, changing the subject for Oscar's sake as much as her own. "Not that I'm complaining, but has something happened?"

"Not exactly," Diana said as she came forward. "We weren't clear on how much research Mr. Barber here had put in on the Earl of Roddenbury already until I told everyone the connection. So it was much easier to compile our resources and come to you as soon as possible."

Barber nodded. "You see, I was brought into the realm of this case when the granddaughter of a Russian nobleman, visiting friends here, was kidnapped. It was a delicate matter and not one those involved wanted to be made public. In that way I discovered the potential involvement of Roddenbury in the selection and trade of these young women."

"I see," Imogen said with a shiver, and leaned into Oscar's hand when he placed it on the small of her back gently.

"In the past few weeks," Barber continued, "Roddenbury has been putting out feelers, looking for a specific young lady. He wants it known he only wishes to talk to her, that she won't be in any danger."

Imogen's lips parted. "Me."

"Yes," Willowby said. "You see, when the Duchess of Roseford reached out on Aurora's behalf to look for her friend—you, Mrs. Huxley—we knew it had to be connected to this case and the disappearance and deaths of several young women. When we linked our information with Mr. Barber's...well, it became clear Roddenbury has been looking for *you*."

"We can use this," Diana said gently. "Both his desire to find you and his lie that he won't hurt you. By using you, we can draw him out and get the final evidence we need against him."

Oscar stepped forward, placing her behind him like he could shield her from the suggestion. "You want her as bait."

Willowby's eyebrows lifted. "An indelicate way to put it...but not invalid. If I could hear Roddenbury admit that he was trafficking in young women, my testimony would be enough to move the case forward."

"Because you're a bloody duke," Oscar growled.

Willowby looked at him impassively. "You don't like that the titles give us power. I don't love it either. But I am trying to use it for the betterment of those I can protect."

"Including the young woman in my case who was taken," Barber said. "We believe she's still alive. We think we can save her if we can interrogate some of the players in Roddenbury's scheme. Once he's taken care of, underlings like the woman running this brothel, Maggie, will likely be more willing to discuss what they know. Especially if some leniency is put on the table for them in trade for the truth."

Imogen swallowed hard. She'd been taking all this information in as they spoke. And it terrified her. The whole idea of facing off with Roddenbury, of putting herself in a room with him where her friends would surely be too far away to protect her, even if they were listening…it was horrifying.

But she could see it was the only way. Not just for her, but for all the women who had been injured or killed by the man they sought to stop. To those who could still be saved. Those who hadn't yet encountered him but would be his next victims. How could she say no to the opportunity to do all that?

"I'll do it," she said softly.

She expected a reaction to that statement, especially from Oscar. What she didn't expect was how he pivoted toward her with a look on his face unlike anything she'd ever seen before. All the control he had always mastered over his reactions, his actions, his emotions, was gone in that moment. What was left was fear on her behalf, desperation and something even more potent than all of that. Something she almost couldn't believe was real.

"No!" he cried out. "You cannot mean that."

"Oscar—" she began.

He caught her upper arms and tugged her closer, his wild expression burning down into hers.

"No," he repeated. "I *love* you, don't you see that?" Her ears began to ring and she opened her mouth and shut it in pure shock. "I *love* you and cannot bear the thought of you endangering yourself like that."

~

Oscar was aware of the others in the room slowly backing out, of Willowby closing the door behind them all and leaving him alone with Imogen. But he never looked away from her and neither did she. She stared up at him, amber eyes wide with shock and, he thought, disbelief. Not that he could blame her. He had been insisting he would never say this to her for so long she didn't believe it. He'd earned it.

This wasn't how he had intended to tell her he loved her. He hadn't exactly worked out *how* he did mean to do it. But not like this, as an argument against her helping anyone but herself.

All he knew was that his long night looking into the darkest depths of his soul had only proven two things: that he needed this woman like he needed breath. And that he would regret letting her go if he were so foolish as to do so. And when he had been able to feel that, as powerfully as he felt his love for her...

It was like someone had set him free.

"Last night," she whispered, her voice cracking with both words.

He shook his head. "I know. I know what I said, what I did. But last night I was panicking. I was *exactly* the coward you so astutely accused me of being. But then again, I should have expected you might call me out on the truth because you're patently incapable of lying."

He smiled as he said it, and her breath caught, just as it had every time she'd seen that expression on his face. That was why he did it, because his smile belonged to her. She had inspired more of it in less than a month than he'd probably allowed himself to show in the last ten years.

"Imogen," he whispered as he caught her hand and drew her closer to him. "I *love* you. That terrifies me because love has rarely ended well for me. But when I look at you, I can't deny it any longer. I can't lose you. Please don't accept this plan—you would be in such danger."

She placed each hand on his chest and leaned into him, lifting her face, brushing his lips with hers. He wrapped his arms around her, drowning in her, surrendering fully, loving her with all his heart. He was rewarded with such joy, such pleasure, such warmth he had never felt.

She pulled away at last, gazing up into his face. "I love you, too," she said.

His breath shuddered out. If he'd thought the pleasure of loving her was amazing, this was even better. He'd hoped, he'd prayed into the night, offering trades of everything he had if she might feel even a fraction of what he did. And here they were. She asked for nothing, but offered everything.

She sighed softly and reached up to cup his cheek. "I love you," she repeated. "And *that* is why I need to fix this. Because if I don't, we can't have a real future together. You'll have to give up too much, I'll have to give up too much. We'll start with suffering, not joy, and I don't want any more of that than either of us has already experienced in our lives."

He pulled away a fraction and ran a hand through his hair. "Imo-gen...I hear what you're saying. But surely there must be another way than to throw yourself into the path of an evil villain."

She nodded. "There might be. Perhaps in six months or a year or ten years we could find a way to manage Roddenbury that doesn't involve a direct confrontation to end it all. But that isn't what I want. I want to start my next chapter with you tomorrow, not when it's too late to enjoy it."

He frowned, thinking of his mother and Will. They could have had a lifetime of love if she'd allowed it. Instead it had been diverted, put off. That wasn't sad, exactly...but it had been avoidable.

He set his jaw. "I worry."

"But you'll be there," she whispered. "We'll demand it. Because we're doing this together. I trust you. And you...you trust me, don't you?"

"I do," he insisted.

"This is the only way. The best way to not only save me, but anyone else in this man's path. The only way I'll be able to sleep at night knowing I tried all I could to stop him." She took his hands and lifted one to her lips, kissing it gently. "Will you be at my side?"

"Yes," he said.

She smiled. "Then let's call in the others and make the next step to the rest of our lives."

She moved as if to go to the door, but he held her steady. He cupped her cheeks, looking down into her eyes and memorizing every beautiful line of her face. He brushed his lips to hers, gently, carefully, before he fully claimed her mouth once more. She lifted into him, opening to him, merging them together until they were one being, one heart.

When he pulled away, he didn't feel excited by this decision. But he also had faith that they could survive it. They had to. There was no longer another choice. He just hoped neither of them would come to regret whatever happened next.

CHAPTER 24

I mogen paced her small parlor back at her home, straightening items on the table, as if somehow that could bring order to her fluttering heart. She hadn't been in her house for weeks and it felt like a foreign land. Even more so because her own servants had not been brought back from the paid holidays Oscar had bankrolled weeks ago.

Instead, her staff was replaced by agents, some of the same ones who had staffed the safe house. Even in this moment, Molly, the maid who had helped Imogen the last two days, was smiling at her.

"You needn't worry, Mrs. Huxley," she soothed. "The others are positioned all over the house. The Duke and Duchess, as well as Mr. Fitzhugh, can hear us through the holes we drilled for just that purpose. And Mr. Huntington and Mr. Barber are at the ready in the yard. They'll take positions near the windows, ready to come in if there's trouble."

"Yes, and I know you are armed." Imogen forced a shaky smile as Molly patted the holster hidden in her boot for easy access. "And so is Tidwell."

"I am, Mrs. Huxley," the butler called out from the hall. "But I see a carriage coming into your drive, so you must ready yourself."

Molly nodded toward her and then stepped from the room,

leaving Imogen to pace across the floor and peek out the window. She watched as Roddenbury exited the carriage. And at his side was Maggie, the woman who ran the Cat's Companion.

Imogen's heart leapt. No one had expected her to be here.

"Roddenbury has Maggie Monroe with him," she said so the others could hear.

"Steady, love," Oscar's voice was muffled through the wall, but it soothed her. "Steady."

Tidwell came to the door and met her eyes, his stare kind but firm. "The Earl of Roddenbury, Mrs. Huxley, and Miss Maggie Monroe."

"I will see them," Imogen said, wishing she didn't sound so breathless. Not that it mattered. Roddenbury would expect her to be nervous, afraid. She had to guess he'd love it.

The earl entered the room, followed by Maggie, and glared at the butler. "That will be all."

As Tidwell stepped out, Roddenbury shut the door and looked across the room toward Imogen. "G-Good afternoon, my lord," she stammered. "And Miss Monroe, I wasn't expecting you."

Maggie flashed a smile. "I bet you weren't. Little Miss Snit. But lookin' 'round this place, I don't think you have such a reason to be so high and mighty."

"Hush, Maggie," Roddenbury said, never taking his eyes off Imogen. He smiled at her, but it didn't put her at ease. "You are a hard woman to find, Imogen."

She flinched at his use of her first name. "I-I was afraid," she admitted. At least that didn't have to be a lie. "After what I...what I saw, I was afraid of you both and what you would do."

Roddenbury moved into the room and took a seat on her settee without asking her leave. He waved Maggie to the sideboard, and she obediently walked there and began preparing a cup of tea for him. Imogen edged to the seat across from his, but he shook his head. "No, no. Why don't you come sit next to me? We're friends, aren't we? Wouldn't you rather have me as a friend?"

Imogen swallowed, but went to the settee beside him. Oscar had to be going mad in the other room, watching all this through the peep-hole. But what could she do? She needed Roddenbury's trust. "I would very much rather have you as a friend," she said. "I haven't liked being enemies."

"Neither have I," he cooed as he set a hand on her knee. Through her dress, she felt his fingers burn. "So let us talk about how we could repair our relationship and do good for each other."

"Yes," she gasped out.

"You saw me, with that poor girl's dead body," he said.

She stiffened. This was what the Willowbys needed, after all. Only admitting he was with a dead body wasn't the same as admitting he had been the cause of her death.

"I saw you with her, yes," she said. "And I heard Maggie say that you had k-killed her."

Roddenbury's eyes darted to Maggie, and she bent her head, her fear palpable, as she brought him his tea. "I see. So you believe *I* killed her."

"Didn't you?" Imogen pressed.

He arched a brow. "Why don't we talk about something else?" he suggested.

Her heart skipped. If he didn't admit he had murdered that poor woman, it was going to make everything so much harder. "But—"

"How can we resolve this so that no one else has to be...hurt?" he insisted, and the hand on her knee grew tighter. His fingers pressed into her skin, and she tried to pull away, but he kept her where she was.

"I-I don't know. I ran because I was frightened, like I said. But now I don't have anywhere to go."

Roddenbury's eyes lit up. "Does that mean Oscar Fitzhugh has grown tired of you?"

She tensed. "You guaranteed that when you had his club shot to pieces. He blamed me. Kicked me out of his bed and his house."

Roddenbury smiled. "Then the plan worked."

"How—how did you know about him?"

"I guessed after he threatened me." Roddenbury shook his head. "I thought he'd be harder to get rid of, after the look in his eyes when he stepped up to me. He was your knight gallant, I thought."

"Not so very gallant. He gave up quickly enough when I caused him trouble. But I heard you were looking for me. That you wanted to talk. So what can I do to get myself out of this?"

"Your situation is dire," Roddenbury said. "But you were at the Cat's Companion looking for a protector. Plus you let Fitzhugh bed you for weeks in trade for what he could provide. It's clear you are willing to offer your body, if need be. Miss Monroe and I have a... business of sorts where we offer women to those who want their company."

"Something like the brothel, you mean," she said.

He shook his head. "No, on a more permanent basis. I could take you to where we keep the women during the transition. And then you'll be sent someplace where you can live out your days in...comfort."

Maggie snorted at that, and in an instant, Roddenbury was on his feet. He backhanded her so hard she careened to the floor, her bottom bouncing across the carpet as she stared up at him in utter terror.

Imogen lurched from the settee and stepped away from him, her heart throbbing at the violence. "No," she whispered. "I don't want to go with you. I don't want the life you're describing. You are a monster. That cannot be the only way out."

"It's not," Roddenbury sneered, and he moved toward her, trapping her against the wall. He put a hand out and traced her cheek with his fingers. "I could kill you like I killed that screaming bitch at the Cat's Companion. Or like I've killed plenty of others. That's the other way out, Imogen. So what do you prefer? Because one way I can do right now and I will enjoy it immensely."

He smiled, something ugly and terrifying. A threat, but before he could go further, the door floor open and Oscar, the Willowbys, Huntington, Barber and the agents burst into the room, guns drawn.

"That's enough, Roddenbury," Willowby said. "You are under arrest by edict of the Crown. Unhand that woman and come with us."

Roddenbury looked at him, his expression stunned. He had truly not anticipated this turn of events. Imogen might have enjoyed that realization more had he not grabbed her, thrown her in front of himself like a shield and pressed a pistol into her side.

~

O scar couldn't breathe as Roddenbury's gun jabbed into Imogen's side. If he fired, she would die. There was nothing else to it.

"You can't escape," Willowby said, remarkably calm. But then again, it wasn't the love of his life with a gun in her side.

"It's over," Diana added. "Just let the woman go. It might inspire mercy in the judges you'll face for your crimes."

"Mercy?" Roddenbury said with a laugh. "Mercy is for the weak. No, what I'm going to do is walk out of this room with Mrs. Huxley as my leverage. And you're going to let me go because if you do I might...I might not kill her before I leave this country." He looked past the Willowbys at Oscar. "That's what is going to happen, isn't it, Fitzhugh?"

Oscar knew what he was demanding. Diana and Willowby couldn't allow for an escape. They were here to protect the Crown and they might trade that for Imogen's life. But he had a different purpose. Crown be damned, he wasn't going to let her die in front of him.

"You—you promise you'll release her?" he choked.

Roddenbury smiled. "The chance of me cutting her down in front of you is one hundred percent. It's much lower if I'm allowed to depart this house."

Oscar had pulled his gun the moment they'd heard Roddenbury's admission in the other room, and now he slowly trained it off of the earl and onto Willowby. "Let him go."

Diana's eyes went wide as she looked at him. "No, Fitzhugh. This isn't the way. If he takes her to another location, the chance of her dying is much higher. And he'll escape anyway."

"Please don't do this," Imogen whispered.

He shook his head. "I have to."

Her eyes filled with tears that ripped him apart. Willowby lowered his pistol slowly, as did Diana, and let out a curse as he said, "Then go."

Roddenbury smiled and urged Imogen forward. As she passed him, Oscar locked eyes with her, praying she would understand the message he was sending. Praying she would take it with her until they could be together and safe again. Her eyes went wide, and he thought she did know.

They were almost past him when Oscar shot out a leg and hit Roddenbury squarely in the knee. The earl yelped in surprise and tipped forward on all fours. Imogen dove to the side as the Willowbys raised their weapons toward Roddenbury. He growled in anger and pivoted the gun in his hand on Oscar.

But before he could fire, Imogen let out a scream and kicked him squarely in the face. His gun fired as Oscar dove to the left, and Diana and Lucas both shot at the same time.

And then it was quiet. Eerily quiet in the aftermath.

"Oscar!" Imogen screamed as she ran to him. He straightened and opened his arms to her.

"I'm fine. I'm not hit. Your clock can't say the same." He motioned to the clock on the mantel behind his shoulder, which was shattered from the bullet.

"Is everyone unharmed?" Derrick Huntington asked as he and Barber hurried into the room.

"We're unharmed," Imogen said.

Then Imogen and Oscar turned their attention to Roddenbury, motionless on the floor as Diana felt his neck for a sign of life. She glanced up. "He's dead."

From the opposite side of the room, Maggie let out a moan of pain and began to cry. Lucas motioned one of the agents toward her, who bound her hands before taking her out.

Willowby looked at Oscar. "You never intended to let him go."

"No," Oscar admitted as she held Imogen closer. "I wouldn't have shot you either. I hope you know that."

"I think I do," Willowby said. "And your quick thinking saved the day."

Oscar got up and pulled Imogen to her feet as he did so. He looked at the still form of the once Earl of Roddenbury with a shake of his head. "Will this end the threat to Imogen?"

"Roddenbury had lackeys, not partners," Barber said with a frown. "It shouldn't be too hard to break them up and bring whomever is left to justice."

Willowby nodded. "I agree. And since you can't name any of them, Imogen, there would be no reason for them to pursue you. You are safe."

She pivoted into Oscar's chest with a great cry of relief that warmed him to his very toes. She had always had such a good attitude, despite all that had happened, but when her fear bled away, her expression was even brighter and more beautiful than it had ever been.

"And the women?" she asked. "The ones he talked about?"

Diana cocked her head. "He said there was a place they were kept before they were sent off to their next destination in the chain. If you listen closely, you can hear Miss Monroe screeching as she's put in a carriage for transport. I believe she's confessing everything. We'll send agents to wherever those women are as soon as possible. I promise you we'll help them and determine the fates of any others."

"Louisa," Oscar whispered, and it was like a dagger to his heart. "There was a woman named Louisa Tucker. She's...dead...I've heard she's dead. But I need to know the rest. I need to know what happened and when. If there is a body that can be recovered for a proper burial."

He thought of her, the woman who had loved him. Who he had

loved but refused to admit he could. If he had been able to give her what he was giving Imogen now...he might have saved her life. But now, at least, he could honor it.

Imogen took his hand in both of hers and he looked down into her upturned face. There was no jealousy there, no hesitation. Only her loving support. Only her understanding. Only everything he ever wanted for the rest of his days.

Willowby stepped forward and placed a hand on Oscar's forearm. He nodded. "I will make a special effort to determine her fate and recover whatever I can for you. We owe you that and much more. Both of you."

Oscar cleared his throat. "Thank you." He shifted. Perhaps one day this kind of vulnerability wouldn't make him hesitate, but one step at a time. "Then may we go?"

"You may," Diana said with a smile for Imogen. "We'll likely need to speak more and you may both need to present your stories to our superior, but for now you are free to go back to your lives."

"Then that's all," Imogen whispered.

"Not all," Oscar said, and gave a glance toward the others. "But the rest is between you and me. I'm taking you home."

They said their farewells, then Oscar took her hand and drew her from the room, out to his carriage and back toward the life he hoped to build, as long as he could manage to show her what that future looked like. And he found, despite knowing her love for him and pulsing with love for her, that he was nervous he would somehow destroy it all regardless of his good intentions.

CHAPTER 25

I mogen sank into the settee before the fire in Oscar's bedchamber, warming her cold hands at the flames as she kept an eye on the door. After their return to his home, he had sent her up here to wait while he took care of a few things. What those were, she didn't know.

Nor did she know what the future would look like now that the threat had passed.

Oscar loved her. She knew that was true and that it didn't hinge on some heightened emotion like the fear that had hung over them for weeks. But that didn't mean their future was without hurdles. He'd never spoken of what they would mean to each other tomorrow or in ten years or in fifty.

She knew better now than to make assumptions.

So her hands shook as he stepped into the room and looked at her with all that dark intent and bubbling passion and, yes, love. He crossed the room to her and his mouth was on hers, passionate and claiming. She lifted into him, never resisting as he swept her up and carried her to his bed. He laid her on the pillows, his weight pushing her down, his mouth tracing words of love on hers. She surrendered to the passion, clinging to him.

If this was what they had, she would take it for as long as he offered it.

But to her surprise, he didn't strip her clothing off or take her. Instead, he eventually rolled to his side and propped himself up on his elbow as he looked down in her face.

"My lovely, lovely Imogen," he whispered before he leaned down to kiss the tip of her nose. "What would you like to do for the rest of your life?"

She smiled at this lightness she'd never seen in him before. But then she shook her head. "I don't really...know. I've never had a protector before."

His brow wrinkled. "A protector? Is that what you think I want?"

She shrugged. "I know you love me, but we never talked about anything else."

He sat up straighter and stared down at her. "I want to marry you, Imogen."

When he said the words her heart soared and she gasped out his name into the quiet.

"I want to make you mine, I want to share my name and my life with you. If you'll have me."

She reached up to touch his face, loving the nervousness around his lips, the worry in his eyes. This meant something to him, just as it meant something to her.

"I would have you today and for the rest of my life," she said, and then pulled him into her arms. "Yes, I will marry you, Oscar."

He broke into a wide smile, the widest, brightest, most beautiful thing she'd ever seen. He kissed her and for a long while she just surrendered to him. He to her. But at last he broke away from her.

"Things will change now, you know," he said.

She sighed. "I suppose they will have to. We're no longer going to be living in our bubble. You'll have your business to repair, and I have a feeling your siblings will no longer accept the barriers you've put up between you."

He pinched his lips. "My business will recover, of that I'm sure. I don't worry about that. As for my family…" He trailed off.

"Yes?" she said, holding back her own opinions, at least for now, to allow him to process his own.

"I put up walls between myself and them," he said softly. "Built a life where I didn't have to acknowledge their existence. But in the last few days, since Aurora dragged them back into my life to help you, I have…appreciated their assistance. That they would do so much for you."

"Without Selina's husband or Nicholas's influence, I don't think we would have been able to resolve this so quickly," Imogen said carefully.

"No," he said. He rested his head back on the pillows, the moments ticking away on the clock. "Walls have not served me well, I don't think," he said at last. "If I've learned anything since you careened into my life, it is that. I learned to build them to protect myself, but all I did in the end was cut myself off from possibilities. I don't want to do that anymore."

She smiled. This remarkable man was so capable of seeing his own flaws. Of admitting them and finding a way to change. To be better. She hadn't known many people in her life so filled with such awareness.

No wonder she adored him.

And she wanted to help. Because they would be married and his happiness would be the joy of her life. "Then perhaps we can take some of those walls down together," she said. "Welcome in your family."

When he caught his breath, she grabbed for his hand. "Slowly," she said. "Perhaps even one at a time. Start with Nicholas, as he will be with Aurora, I'm certain of it."

"He's a good man," Oscar admitted. "And I would be proud to call him my—my brother."

He squeezed his eyes shut, and she saw how much that idea meant to him. He had been so alone through so much in his life, by chance and by choice. But now...now he was ready for more. For her. For them. For everything.

She touched his face and he opened his eyes and looked down at her. She traced his lips with her fingertips. "I will be at your side, your protector and your champion, every step of the way."

He nodded. "I will count on your to help me slay my dragons then, fair lady. And I'll slay yours."

"*That* is a bargain." She snuggled into his chest and he began to run a hand over her hair.

After a few moments he cleared his throat. "You know that wasn't what I meant when I said things would change."

She jerked her head up. "Then what did you mean if not us getting married and then living happily ever after, slaying dragons and perhaps expanding our family to include your siblings?"

He narrowed his gaze and the light there went dark. Dangerous. Her body twitched with response. There was the beast. He wasn't gone, and she welcomed him back as he tugged her a little tighter against her.

"I meant here...in our bedroom," he said, his voice suddenly low and rough.

She laughed despite the charged air around them. "I don't think I want what we do in the bedroom to change."

"Of course you do," he said, and his smile fluttered at the edge of his lips no matter how he tried to loom and intimidate and challenge. "You'd get bored if I simply made sweet love to you. All tender and gentle like the last time."

"I liked tender and gentle," she whispered.

He nodded. "So did I, despite fighting you every moment that it happened. And sometimes I *will* be very tender and gentle with you, Imogen. Sometimes I will just hold you and touch you and tell you I love you with every thrust until we wash away on it."

"But sometimes you won't," she urged as she slid a hand beneath his jacket and hissed at the body heat trapped beneath. She wanted that heat. Now.

"Sometimes I'll hold you down and force you to orgasm over and over until you're pleading with me to make the pleasure stop."

She wiggled against him. "That sounds fun."

He growled in response. "And sometimes…sometimes I'll spank that arse of yours raw for being such a very naughty girl and *then* I'll be gentle and loving."

She smiled even as her body responded to all his wicked promises. "Good," she whispered. "I'm here for all of it, Oscar. For all of you. For all of us. If I haven't made it perfectly clear, I'm here forever."

His eyes held her and she saw his faith in her, his love for her, his desire for her. Then he caught her hand and dragged her over his lap, flipping up her skirts and tugging down her drawers to reveal her bare backside. He rested a hand there, the caress before the sting.

"Good," he said. "Then let us begin."

EPILOGUE

Three weeks later

"And so you just...ran off to Gretna Green?" Aurora said with a laugh as Imogen stood beside her in the very fine parlor of the Duke of Roseford. Oscar's brother had insisted in arranging this family gathering the moment she and Oscar had returned from their extended and very passionate honeymoon.

She'd had to be just as passionate to convince her husband to accept the invitation. Bargains had been made, promises collected. But he'd come to the party, as agreed.

Now she looked across the room at Oscar. He stood with Selina, Nicholas and Roseford, along with their other brother, Morgan. Oscar didn't look entirely comfortable, but nor did he look upset. He was trying. So were they.

Imogen was completely certain one day they would all find their way. That one day this kind, if sometimes wild, group of siblings would one day be close as they should have been growing up. And it would be all the better for them all.

The only ones missing from the gathering were Joanna and Will, who had joined them in Gretna Green to witness their madcap

THE REDEMPTION OF A ROGUE

nuptials and surprised them by staying for their own. They were still locked away together in Scotland, and Oscar couldn't have been happier. The only father he'd ever had was now that in truth.

"Imogen?" Aurora said, squeezing her arm.

"I'm sorry. Once I start looking at him, I have a hard time focusing on anything else," she admitted with a blush.

Aurora sighed and followed her gaze to her Nicholas, who she would marry within days. "I know the feeling. I can't wait to be Nicholas's bride after all this time apart."

"Somehow we seem to have both found our happiness, despite a very bad beginning," Imogen said. "I'm so happy for you. For me."

Aurora wrapped an arm around her. "As am I. I would never wish on you what happened. But it created a path that led us both to love, and saved half a dozen women from Roddenbury's wicked schemes."

"Hearing how many were rescued and returned to their families or safe places to recover was satisfying. And retrieving records about the fate of the rest...at least it may some closure to their loved ones," Imogen agreed.

Oscar had found out the final fate of Louisa a few days before. Remains had been buried properly. She was mourned by them both, and she would be for many years to come. That didn't threaten Imogen's happiness with her husband—it only deepened her love for him.

Oscar had pulled away from his siblings and was moving toward her now. His dark eyes snagged hers, and she pushed the sadness away and shivered with delight that this man was hers. All hers. Forever.

He reached them with a nod for Aurora. "Might I steal the bride?"

"You already did," Aurora said with a giggle. "But I will forgive you as long as you keep that smile on her face."

"I intend to try," Oscar said as he took Imogen's arm, and guided her out of the parlor and onto the terrace.

It was early evening and the bright pinks and purples of sunset cascaded over them both. He caught her hands and smiled at her.

Her heart melted. "Oh yes, please I love to see that."

"See what?" he asked.

"That smile," she clarified. "I live for it."

He broke into a wider grin that could have split his cheeks. "Give me everything I want, my love—and that is you and always you—and I'll smile for you all day, every day."

"For the rest of our lives?" she asked.

He leaned down to kiss her.

"For the rest of our lives."

ENJOY AN EXCERPT OF MISMATCHED UNDER THE MISTLETOE

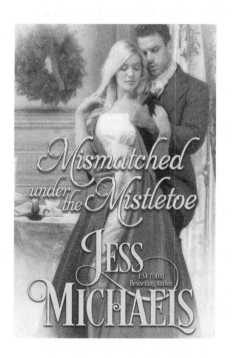

Available November 10, 2020

Lady Emily Rutledge took the hand her groom offered her and stepped down from her carriage on the walkway. She shook her head and looked up the stairway toward the front door. Outside, a footman swept the afternoon's dusting of snow away from the walkway and she paused.

"Good afternoon, Arthur!"

The footman looked up from his work and gave her a smile. "Good afternoon, my lady. Almost finished here."

She nodded. "I see that."

"And how was the shopping?"

Emily laughed as she lifted the two satchels in her hands and motioned to the carriage, which was being unloaded as they spoke. "Productive. Thank you."

"Mr. Cavendish is here," the young man said.

Emily pursed her lips. Cav was always late to every appointment except the ones he took with her. It was a joke between them now, but on days like today she wished he hadn't changed that bad habit for her. "Oh, I know. I'm so late. Good afternoon, Arthur!"

As she scurried up the freshly swept steps, she heard the footman laughing after her. "Good afternoon, my lady."

She burst into the foyer to find her butler, Cringle, already waiting for her. She smiled as she handed over her packages, then her gloves, scarf and coat in rapid succession.

"Should these go in the gift room, my lady?" he asked, indicated the bags.

"Yes, those two and the ones outside." She gave him a conspiratorial look. "How long has Cav been waiting?"

"Mr. Cavendish has been in the parlor for a bit over a half an hour, my lady." He tilted his head.

She smothered another laugh. "Oh, I shall be railed upon for sure. Thank you, Cringle."

He nodded as he moved away to the room upstairs that Emily had long ago set aside for gifts and wrapping. She kept it well-stocked with items all year round, but never was it so packed as the weeks leading up to Christmas, when Emily filled it to capacity with gifts for her relatives, friends and servants. Just the thought of it now filled her with giddy anticipation of the reactions of those she cared about when they opened her perfect gift for them.

She threw open the parlor door to find Cav sitting on a settee beside the roaring fire. In the fraction of a moment it took for him to rise to his feet in greeting, a wash of emotion hit Emily in the chest. It had been five years since her husband died of a sudden fever, followed by both her parents.

Five years of heartbreak and mourning and loneliness. She had only truly begun to feel herself again in the last twelve months. But seeing Cav always brought Andrew back to her mind. Cav had been his best friend, after all.

He had become hers, too. When loss had become a constant companion, so had Cav.

She shook those thoughts aside as Cav got to his feet. He was a handsome man. Tall, broad shouldered, with dark blond curls that always looked just a bit mussed. Like he'd run his hands through it. Like someone else had done the same. Certainly plenty of someone else's had. The man had a certain reputation with the ladies.

"Emily," he said with a teasing arch of his brow and a quick flick of his head toward the clock on the mantel.

She laughed, pushing her thoughts away as she rushed to him and took his outstretched hands. "I know, I know!" she gasped. "I'm sorry to have kept you."

His gaze flickered over her face. The smile remained but someone darker entered his eyes. She found herself glancing away from it. He often had that expression when he looked at her. Something a little... forlorn. She supposed she reminded him of Andrew, just as he reminded her.

"I am freezing," she said, releasing him and rushing to the sideboard to look at what had been brought for refreshments. "Did you pour yourself tea?"

He held up the cup on the table beside the settee. "And Cringle brought those cakes Mrs. Lisle makes this time of year. She must know I crave them."

"*Everyone* knows you crave them," she teased as she put sugar in her tea and then took a sip with a sigh of pleasure. "You make a very theatrical expression of it any time they are served."

"I know my audience," he said with a wink in her direction. "Mrs. Lisle loves my boisterous declarations, which allows me more cakes."

She shook her head. "You are hopeless. I don't even know why I invited you here."

He laughed, but he set his cup aside and took a long step toward her. The warmth of him hit her, the spicy scent that always accompanied his arrival a comfort.

"I'm not sure why you invited me either," he said. "But I'm sure I can ascertain the answer if you give me a moment to observe." He pressed a finger to his lips and looked her up and down. "You are happy."

She wrinkled her brow. "Don't sound so surprised by that fact. I'm a happy person, am I not?"

"You are, indeed. Practically bottled sunshine," he teased. "But today you are positively glowing. You are up to something."

"You do know me so well." Emily leaned closer. "Cav, I have had an idea. No, not just an idea, the *best* of ideas, and I need your help!"

Cav held her stare for a moment, then tilted his head back and laughed. The tendons in his neck flexed around his cravat as he did so. Emily blushed. She knew she was exuberant. She couldn't help it. Emotions were something she had never been able to hide. If she was joyful or excited, she showed it.

"All right, Emily. You have intrigued me. What is this idea?" he asked.

"Although we...lost Andrew five years ago," she began, and the smile on Cav's face fell slightly. He was truly the only one who felt the loss as keenly as she did. He had practically been Andrew's brother. She hastened to continue, "I have only returned to Society in the last eighteen months or so."

"Yes," he said, drawing out the word with a look of concern on his face. "And?"

"I've been doing something of a study of the gentleman and ladies of our acquaintance during that time," she said.

"I see," he said. "And what have you determined?"

"I have developed a few theories about matches that end up being successful to both partners." She smiled. "Not just financially or by linking important families, but by the happiness and affection the couple ultimately develops."

His mouth twitched. "Are you...in the market for happiness and affection in a match?"

She shook her head. "Gracious no. I had both, you know I did. I am not in a position where I must marry, thanks to the financial protections Andrew put in place for me. I do not think I would *ever* be tempted to wed again."

He turned away and paced to the sideboard, where he fiddled with the bottles of liquor lined up along the top. "Then why make a study?"

"For other people," she burst out.

He stared at her, his expression utterly blank. "I don't understand."

She huffed out her breath. "I'm saying that *I* could successfully match couples who might not have ever thought of each other, if only I could seclude them together in the proper circumstances."

Cav leaned back. "Play...matchmaker."

Emily nodded. "*Yes*. And this is the perfect time of year to do so. The Christmas holidays are just around the corner, and there is romance in every snowflake and cheery red ribbon."

Cav smiled at her in that indulgent way he sometimes did when she was going on like this. "You should write one of those novels you insist on reading out to me in the winter."

"Oh, you love them," she said with a playful scowl. "I intend to have a party out at my estate in Crossfox and invite six ladies—and their chaperones, of course—and six gentlemen. Then I shall see if I can end the party with six very happy couples."

His eyes went wide and for what felt like an eternity he just stared at her. "A whole party to matchmake these poor unsuspecting people."

Emily pursed her lips in mild annoyance. "I know you are a resigned bachelor, Cav, and an unrepentant rake, but you act as if I intend to do something horrible to them."

"No. Just force them into each other's arms," Cav muttered. "And when do you propose to do this thing?"

"We will start the day after Christmas. Crossfox is so close to London, it isn't a difficult journey for any of those I intend to invite. I plan twelve days of merriment."

"Twelve days," Cav said. "Like the poem."

"Exactly." She clapped her hands together. "I know it doesn't line up exactly with the *real* twelve days of Christmas."

"Yes, one whole day off the true timeline. What will the scholars think?"

She laughed. "They will have to forgive me and say it's close enough. I have so many plans for each day and the fun that can be had with the poem."

"Wait, you are proceeding with the *theme* of the Twelve Days of Christmas?"

She tilted her head. "Of course! What could be more festive?"

"There are a great many birds in that poem, Emily," he said. "So, so many birds."

She folded her arms. "And I will manage them all. It will be enchanting."

He chuckled again. "Of course it will be. With you in charge, how could it be anything but?"

ALSO BY JESS MICHAELS

≈

The Duke's By-Blows

The Love of a Libertine

The Heart of a Hellion

The Matter of a Marquess

The Shelley Sisters

A Reluctant Bride

A Reckless Runaway

A Counterfeit Courtesan

The Scandal Sheet

The Return of Lady Jane

Stealing the Duke

Lady No Says Yes

My Fair Viscount

Guarding the Countess

The House of Pleasure

The 1797 Club

The Daring Duke

Her Favorite Duke

The Broken Duke

The Silent Duke

The Duke of Nothing

The Undercover Duke

The Duke of Hearts

The Duke Who Lied

The Duke of Desire

The Last Duke

Seasons

An Affair in Winter

A Spring Deception

One Summer of Surrender

Adored in Autumn

The Wicked Woodleys

Forbidden

Deceived

Tempted

Ruined

Seduced

Fascinated

The Notorious Flynns

The Other Duke

The Scoundrel's Lover

The Widow Wager

No Gentleman for Georgina

A Marquis for Mary

To see a complete listing of Jess Michaels' titles, please visit:

http://www.authorjessmichaels.com/books

ABOUT THE AUTHOR

USA Today Bestselling author Jess Michaels likes geeky stuff, Vanilla Coke Zero, anything coconut, cheese, fluffy cats, smooth cats, any cats, many dogs and people who care about the welfare of their fellow humans. She is lucky enough to be married to her favorite person in the world and lives in the heart of Dallas, TX where she's trying to eat all the amazing food in the city.

When she's not obsessively checking her steps on Fitbit or trying out new flavors of Greek yogurt, she writes historical romances with smoking hot alpha males and sassy ladies who do anything but wait to get what they want. She has written for numerous publishers and is now fully indie and loving every moment of it (well, almost every moment).

Jess loves to hear from fans! So please feel free to contact her in any of the following ways (or carrier pigeon):

www.AuthorJessMichaels.com
Email: Jess@AuthorJessMichaels.com

Jess Michaels raffles a gift certificate EVERY month to members of her newsletter, so sign up on her website:
http://www.AuthorJessMichaels.com/

 facebook.com/JessMichaelsBks
 twitter.com/JessMichaelsBks
 instagram.com/JessMichaelsBks
 goodreads.com/JessMichaelsBks
 bookbub.com/authors/jess-michaels